He set the last seats on the floor and went back to the house. He got a bucket of water, some scouring powder and rags, and began cleaning up.

He looked at the clock on the mantel. It was just before eleven P.M. Perfect. It would take a while to clean up all the blood. Then he'd make his trip well after midnight. That way, the road would most likely be clear. He couldn't risk being pulled over; he didn't have a driver's license, or even a learner's permit. Carlyle Biggs was fourteen years old. . . .

By Judith Smith-Levin

DO NOT GO GENTLY
THE HOODOO MAN*

*Published by Ballantine Books

THE
HOODOO
MAN

JUDITH SMITH-LEVIN

BALLANTINE BOOKS • NEW YORK

A Ballantine Book
Published by The Ballantine Publishing Group
Copyright © 1998 by Judith Smith-Levin

http://www.randomhouse.com

Library of Congress Catalog Card Number: 97-95017

ISBN 0-345-42065-9

Manufactured in the United States of America

First Edition: May 1998

10   9   8   7   6   5   4   3   2   1

For Maureen O'Neal:
my editor,
my champion,
and my friend.
Without you, none of this would have been possible.
Star and the gang are very grateful, as am I.

Thanks to.   Marillyn Holmes,
             Mary Ann Johnson,
             Revé Mason,
             and
             John Thompson

             for their help in researching this novel

PROLOGUE

New York City
7:45 P.M.
December 25, 1991

Pain. Brilliant. Sharp. Excruciating.

Carlyle Biggs couldn't believe what he was feeling.

With each burst of fire from the muzzle of the weapon pointed at him, his body slid further and further into agony.

Two more shots.

Rapid.

His shoulders caught fire. His fingers curled. His arms jerked, then fell useless on the fat, round, thickly upholstered blue and white striped La-Z-Boy reclining chair. A loving Father's Day gift from his family three years before.

He tried to breathe, but pain snatched the breath. He heard his life whistling through the holes in his chest and throat.

The next bullet tore into his stomach, releasing a spatter of blood onto his Christmas-green knit T-shirt. His cop's mind, logical through the pain, knew that his back had a hole in it three sizes larger than the perfect round opening in his abdomen.

He'd bought the bullets.

The department-issued ammunition wouldn't stop a fly on a pile of shit. He was on the street every day, and he wouldn't allow himself to be outgunned by gangbangers.

He'd never thought about his own son.

Misery raced through his guts.

His eyes looked up, reflecting his agony.

His mouth gaped and blood poured down his chin, soaking his neatly trimmed goatee.

At the other end of the bursts of fire, holding the regulation Browning M1, his finger on the trigger, was his firstborn. His namesake.

Carlyle Biggs Jr. looked at his father. He smiled.

"Merry Christmas, Dad."

He raised the gun and put a bullet right between his father's tear-filled eyes.

Police Sergeant Carlyle Biggs Sr. struggled to breathe.

His son stood over him, calm and dispassionate.

He watched his father's bloodied chest rise and fall.

He heard his father struggle to get air into his collapsed lungs.

The son counted the breaths, his gaze on the slow rising and falling.

Up . . . down, up . . . down, up . . . down . . .

Still.

He leaned in, searching his father's eyes.

Carlyle Biggs Sr. could see his son.

The face, so like his own. The same smooth, caramel-colored skin, the Biggs eyes. Deep blue-gray, inherited from some long-dead French-blooded New Orleans plantation owner who had taken a yen to his great-grandmother.

His face. Only younger, without the worry lines and silver strands around the temples, with soft, golden, thick, wavy hair.

His face. Calm, curious, watching, as if it were observing a specimen in the biology lab.

No sorrow. No remorse.

The image stayed with him as darkness filled his eyes.

When his father's eyes dulled, Carlyle stepped back from the recliner and surveyed his work.

His younger brother, Christopher, looked surprised.

But then he hadn't expected the bullet that spiraled through his forehead and blasted out the back of his skull.

None of them had.

His baby brother, Cary, had been asleep on his back, on the floor in front of the television, a tiny Matchbox car in his hand.

When the first bullet crashed through his forehead, his eight-year-old body jerked, his eyes flew open, and the car slipped from his hand.

Carlyle quickly pumped slugs into his small throat, chest, stomach, and shoulders.

He didn't want his baby brother to suffer. He'd thought about sparing both his brothers. He loved them, but he knew he wouldn't be able to take care of them. They were better off.

He turned back to his father.

"Still think I'm a wimp, Dad?" he said softly.

His father said nothing.

"Guess not."

Carlyle set to work.

He put the gun down on the coffee table and hefted his

father over his shoulder. He moved him to the sofa, right next to his mother.

As he tossed the body down, his father made a noise that sounded like a belch.

"Too much turkey, Dad," Carlyle said. "You always overdo it."

His father had been the last to go.

His son had disabled him with a bullet to the throat and one to the chest, paralyzing him with pain and forcing him to watch his family die.

His mother, Charlotte, true to herself, was a doormat to the end. She never asked why, she just sat there, blubbering, watching her oldest child drill bullets into the heads of her younger ones.

Maybe if she'd said Stop, Don't, I love you, son . . . anything.

He looked at the sagging, sad corpse. Carlyle straightened her body.

"You never would fight for me, Mom . . . not ever."

He positioned them, leaning one against another on the sofa.

His dad, his mother, his two younger brothers, all staring at him with unseeing eyes.

He stepped back.

The work was good. His aim perfect.

He had killed his mother and brothers mercifully, with the first shot to the forehead, the second to the throat, the third to the center of the chest, and the fourth to the abdomen, all in a perfect, straight line, with the fifth and sixth in each shoulder.

Each body bore the perfect shape of a cross.

After all, it was Christmas.

His father's death had been different. Carlyle saved the killing shot for last. He wanted his father to see it all. Still, when the time came, his hand stayed steady and the shots were perfectly aligned. He'd never felt so in control.

"See, Dad, I *was* paying attention when you taught me. Aim and squeeze. Isn't that what you said? Slow . . ." He pointed his finger at his father's body. "Slow squeeze hits the target every time."

He stood there for a few minutes.

Maybe he should say something over them. But what? All he could feel was hungry. Dinner had been over by five and his stomach was talking to him again.

He went to the kitchen and made himself a sandwich, piling stuffing, cranberry sauce, and turkey on two pieces of wheat bread coated with mayonnaise. His mother hated that combination. But then, it didn't matter anymore what she thought.

He grabbed a can of Dr. Pepper from the fridge and went back to the family room. There, on the floor, in front of the television set, his back against the blood-soaked recliner, he ate his sandwich and watched his favorite Christmas cartoon.

"I guess I'm the Grinch now," he said out loud.

After he finished, he took his dishes to the sink, rinsed them, and put them in the dishwasher. He put the food away, wiped the counter, and went out to the garage.

Carlyle moved the lawn mower and tugged out the roll of plastic tarp that his father had bought a few weeks ago on sale at the hardware store. Carlyle Sr. had planned to do some painting in the spring.

He found his mother's old dressmaking scissors, which he jammed against his side between his belt and the rough fabric of his jeans. Then he dragged the heavy plastic roll into the house through the sliding glass doors off the patio and into the kitchen.

He put the scissors on the counter and mopped up the melting snow he'd trailed in.

In the laundry room, he found some old clothesline. After another Dr. Pepper, he went to work, laying out the plastic on the family room floor and cutting it.

By the time he'd finished making his bundles, he was hungry again, so he washed his hands and made himself another sandwich. He drank another Dr. Pepper and a cup of his mother's homemade eggnog. He'd have to go sparingly on the nog. He loved it, and there wouldn't be any more. Store-bought just wasn't the same.

He rinsed the dishes again and put them in the dishwasher. He waited until his neighbor's lights next door had gone out before he made another trip to the garage. This time he took the seats out of the family minivan. He needed all the room inside for his cargo.

Carlyle thought for a moment about the ceremony tomorrow night, at Desmond's church. His parents had never missed a service. In all the time that he could remember, the night after Christmas had been spent with the true believers in Desmond St. John's church. Well, he'd worry about that tomorrow.

He set the last seats on the floor, and went back to the house. He got a bucket of water, some scouring powder and rags, and began cleaning up.

He looked at the clock on the mantel. It was just before eleven P.M. It would take a while to clean up all the blood. He'd be making his trip well after midnight. Perfect. That way, the roads would most likely be clear. He couldn't risk being pulled over; he didn't have a driver's license, or even a learner's permit.

Carlyle Biggs was fourteen years old.

Brookport, Massachusetts
2:32 A.M.
December 25, present day

Annette Collins was dead tired. Her shift at the hospital had officially ended at midnight, but the emergency room was a madhouse. Two serious car accidents, a scalding, and a DOA from a Christmas family reunion turned drunken shootout, had made it impossible for her to leave on time.

She knew that Kenny, her oldest, had put his little sister to bed, so she'd be able to put the presents under the tree when she got home. Kenny was such a good kid. Since her husband died, he'd taken over, helping his mother and being both a big brother and a father figure to his seven-year-old sister.

The thought of Katie's face in the morning made her smile. Maybe next year she'd be able to take a vacation at Christmas, do something special, maybe take the kids skiing.

She stifled a yawn, and rubbed her eyes. She'd better take it easy. Her driving skills weren't the best in snow and ice, even though the highway was deserted. She'd only learned to drive in the past year, since George died. Her eighteen-year-old son had taught her. She had never gotten used to it. She didn't like the idea of hurtling down the highway in a machine that could be crushed like a paper cup.

At least the snow had stopped, but the roads remained icy. She slowed down, putting on her high beams, straining to see through the darkness.

Her exit was less than a mile ahead. As she moved to the right lane, toward the ramp, her headlights illuminated something on the side of the road.

She caught a glimpse of it out of the corner of her eye. A paper bag, nothing unusual, the logo of a local supermarket stamped on the outside.

She looked again. Her foot hit the brake. Her tires skidded a little on the ice. She stopped the car, and carefully backed up.

It couldn't be. She put on her emergency lights and got out. The soles of her boots slipped on the slick asphalt. She put out her hand and steadied herself on the trunk lid. She leaned forward, peering at the bag in the darkness.

She thought she saw a tiny hand sticking out of the top. "No," she said, as she carefully inched toward it. "No."

A gust of wind rattled the bag, just as she picked it up. The weight of the contents, coupled with the sudden force of the wind, caused the paper to tear. She instinctively put her hand beneath the bag, and through the leather of her glove, she felt the tiny, frozen bottom and legs.

Annette cradled the bag in her left arm and pulled the brown paper down. The face of a perfectly formed, black newborn emerged. The eyes were closed. A thin layer of ice frosted the face and head. Annette's eyes filled with tears at the sight of the little body, with its tiny, frozen fingers and frosted blue lips. She made it back to her car, opened the door, and laid the baby on the passenger seat. The overhead light flooded the car. She ripped away the bag.

It was then that she started to scream. The baby boy had been slit open from throat to testes. His body cavity had been filled with dried herbs, pieces of red fabric, and something that appeared to be skin of some type.

Annette Collins was still screaming when the first police car arrived.

Brookport, Massachusetts
2:32 A.M.
December 25, present day

Desmond St. John was in the middle of his third orgasm. The feeling was so powerful, he thought he would pass out. He gasped for breath, hearing the laughter over him.

He opened his eyes and smiled. The ganja he had smoked, and the rum he'd been drinking, combined with the glowing candlelight, made everything around him soft and fuzzy.

He was barely aware of his legs and arms being stretched out and bound with soft, silken ropes. He could hardly see the face leaning over him, but he knew it was grinning. That made him happy. The lips came down, kissing him, filling his mouth with tongue, nearly suffocating him. He gulped air as the mouth moved down his body.

"Not again," he moaned. The mouth pulled at him.

This was impossible. No man, no flesh-and-blood human, could do this again. But then, everybody knew he wasn't human. He was a god, a *Voudon*, a voodoo priest. His followers believed he was the human incarnation of one of the most powerful *loas* of all—Legba, the guardian of the gate between heaven and earth. The Great Intervener. He had the ears of the gods. He could personally take their prayers directly to the powerful *loas*, who controlled their fates.

At the urging of the hands sliding beneath him, Desmond raised his hips. His hard, thick maleness disappeared between ravenous, sucking lips. Then he felt it enter him. Hot, stiff, and painful. He moaned, the pain quickly turning to passion as it moved in and out of his body.

He cried out, a long, great, shuddering cry, as the eager mouth drained him.

Desmond St. John was in a hellish ecstasy, a place from which he never wanted to return . . . and didn't.

CHAPTER ONE

"Ho-Ho-Ho, Merry Christmas!" Detective Leo Darcy entered the squad room, shaking a wide, red leather belt covered with round, golden bells. "Ho-Ho-Ho!"

A chorus of "Bah humbug," "Get bent," and "Christmas this," rang out from the detectives.

Darcy pulled off his worn, dingy, red and white fur-trimmed Santa hat and tossed it and his jingle bells on his desk.

"You guys got no spirit. It's Christmas!"

Lieutenant Starletta Duvall eyed the ragged hat and the bells. Darcy never let her down. Her light, golden brown eyes sparkled, recalling the Christmas he'd dressed in a full Santa suit and visited the winos down by the waterfront, handing out sandwiches and coffee.

"Leo, you're truly a man for all seasons." She plucked a peppermint candy cane off the sad, artificial tree near her desk and took it to him. "Merry Christmas."

11

"Thanks, Star." Darcy grinned, his three chins dimpling. "I'm glad to see *somebody's* got the Christmas spirit."

"Hey, Star, if you're feeling Christmasy, I've got some mistletoe over here." Richardson waved a bag of something dried and green at her.

She turned. "Looks like dope to me."

"Nah! It's mistletoe, honest."

She smiled at him. "I wasn't talking about the stuff in the bag."

Everybody laughed.

"Merry Christmas, everybody." Detective Sergeant Dominic Paresi walked into the squad room, carrying a shiny, bright red shopping bag trimmed with decorated Christmas trees. The bag brimmed with wrapped presents.

Another chorus of seasonal displeasure rang out.

"You clowns are the worst." Paresi sat down.

"Morning, Paresi," Star said, going back to her desk. "Merry Christmas."

"Hey, Paresi, those for us?" Richardson called out.

Paresi put the bag on the floor near his desk and hung up his coat.

"They're for my sister's kids." He sat down. "None of you perverts touch it. This is stuff for little girls."

"Yeah? So's this." Rescovich grabbed his crotch.

Star shook her head disgustedly. "You think we could hang him from the ceiling and say he's a really big piece of tinsel?"

"Works for me." Paresi leaned back in his chair. "Did you have a good time last night?"

Star nodded. Her partner was dating her best friend and had joined in Vee's family's Christmas Eve the night before. Though she adored Paresi, he'd had lots of "doggy" moments since she'd known him. She'd initially had misgivings about his dating Vee. But in spite of her fears, it was going well. And she loved the light the good-looking Sicilian put in her friend's eyes.

"I was just going to say that," she said. "It was great. Everybody had fun. Thank you for the *Total Motown* CD set. I am one happy Mickey's Monkeyin', Shotgunnin', Hitchhikin' fool. You should have caught me in the shower this morning. I was Twinin' back." She rocked in her chair, snapping her fingers. "Hey."

Her partner grinned at her. "I thought you'd like it."

"Like it?" Star laughed. "I think if I go to the Function at the Junction one more time, my cat's gonna smother me in my sleep! It's a great present, Paresi. It has jams on it that even *I* forgot!"

"Good. Invite me over sometime to hear some."

"Anytime. In fact, Vee and I will teach you all the old dances that go with the songs."

"Cool," he said.

"Did you like your present?"

"Are you kidding? I didn't even know you knew I was into that kind of stuff."

"You'd think I'd have figured it out. We've only been partnered up five years. Vee told me you took her to Boston to see the Three Tenors at Symphony Hall. She said you were in heaven."

"I'm Italian, opera's in my blood," he said. "I had a great time last night."

"Me too," she agreed. "Vee and I have spent every Christmas Eve together since we were in diapers."

"She and the kids really made me feel like family," Paresi said.

"They really like you."

"Yeah." He smiled. "Go figger . . . me. You think the kids liked their presents?"

"Are you kidding?" Star grinned. "Rollerblades for Lena, and Super Nintendo for the boys. They think you are way cool."

"And I am!" Paresi laughed.

"The pad and helmet set for Lena was a nice touch too," Star said. "Everything's protected, her head, knees, and elbows." She leaned across her desk and smiled. "It was a very daddy thing to do."

"She's a great kid. I just wanted to be sure she'd be safe," he said.

"You're getting soft, Paresi." Star grinned.

"Not a chance." He shook his head, but couldn't hide his smile. "Think about it," he said. "I give Lena blades, she breaks something . . ." He leaned toward Star, his azure eyes filled with mischief. "There's no more snuggling with mama. Capeesh?"

"You're not fooling me. I watch you with that little girl. She's got you." Star held up her little finger and wiggled it. "Wrapped and tight."

Paresi laughed. "Shows, huh?"

Star leaned back in her chair. "It works both ways. She's nuts about you."

Paresi nodded. "I know. What can I say? All females love me."

"Gee, gorgeous and modest, too. Whatta guy!" Star said. They laughed.

"I'm glad she liked the blades," he said.

"Vee said yours was the first gift she opened. She was blading in the hallway at six this morning. She can't wait for the snow to clear so she can be Xena and save the world on her blades."

"If anybody can give the world some hope, she can." Paresi opened his desk. "So where was the good doctor last night?"

At the mention of Mitchell Grant, Star blushed.

Dr. Grant was the county's Chief Medical Examiner. A six-foot-seven-inch basketball-loving, Harvard-educated scion of old Boston money and a walking contradiction.

In his university days, Mitchell Grant had been a star center on Harvard's basketball team. He favored the New York Knicks, fine wine, gourmet food (which he cooked himself), and Italian designer suits. But he could still put away hot dogs and beer, toss off his Armani jacket, roll up his French-cuffed sleeves, and get down in the dirt with any cop or member of his forensic team.

With his cool demeanor and exquisite face, she'd been attracted to him since her days in the Academy. He had been married then, but word was that his wedding ring didn't even slow him down. After his divorce, the stories of the doctor's conquests reached legendary proportions.

Determined not to be a "notch on the bedpost," Star had kept her attraction in check. Through the years, they'd had a good professional relationship, but now it was changing.

Working together, side by side, nearly twenty-four hours a day, on her toughest case had shown her the man behind the locker room legend.

Yes, he'd had his and seemingly everybody else's share of women, but with her the dynamics were different, and they both knew it.

Their relationship was progressing, but she was still

dealing with her own issues of trust. Mitch was being patient, and she appreciated him for it.

"His daughter is in town. He's spending Christmas with her."

"That's good. Family should be together this time of year."

"Yeah," Star agreed. "So, I guess that's why we're both here."

Paresi looked at the assignment board.

"I hope this is a slow day."

"Don't count on it." Star sighed deeply. "You know what Christmas does to people. Graveyard's already pulled an infant John Doe this morning."

Paresi looked up. "A baby?"

"Uh-huh." She nodded. "Some nurse found him on the highway, in a paper bag, around three this morning. I don't know all the particulars, I didn't want to know. It's Lieutenant Speery's. He told me about it at shift change. His guys are handling it."

"Christ, what's wrong with people?"

"Don't get me started," she said.

The phone rang. Paresi picked it up. "Homicide, Paresi." He pulled a notepad from his desk drawer, cradled the receiver between his neck and shoulder, and began writing.

"Yeah, yeah, got it. We're on our way." He hung up.

"Where?" Star asked.

"Clarendon Square." Paresi put on his coat.

"Moneytown. What's happening?"

"Desmond St. John."

"The Hoodoo Man?" Star's eyebrows shot up.

"The used-to-be Hoodoo Man," Paresi said.

"Finished?"

"Totally. A few of his flock just went to pay a Christmas visit and found him."

Star reached for her coat. "Are they sure? Isn't he supposed to be immortal or something?"

Paresi buttoned his coat. "If he was, nobody told him."

The house in Clarendon Square was one of the most elegant in a neighborhood of million-dollar-plus homes. The squad cars, unmarked cruisers, and coroner's van looked as out of place on these streets as Snoop Doggy Dogg on stage at the Grand Ole Opry.

For all their old money and genteel ways, Desmond St. John's neighbors had been fearfully fascinated with him. He was a singularly exotic man.

His legendary prowess with both women and magic was whispered about at elegantly appointed dinner tables, and behind nearly every door. Some residents even began to view their black household help with a suspicious and frightened eye after the "Hoodoo Man" became a part of their community.

As with his life, they were curious about his death. The inquisitive watched from opulently decorated rooms, peeking through velvet drapes and snow-frosted leaded-glass windows.

Paresi stamped his feet on the monogrammed raffia straw doormat, shaking off the snow that clung to his shoes. Star walked ahead of him.

"Hey, Tommy." She smiled at the uniformed officer who stood just inside the door. "Merry Christmas. Where's the body?"

"Merry Christmas, Lieutenant. Upstairs." The officer pointed. "Down the hall, last room on the right."

Paresi and Star climbed the long, winding, cherry-wood staircase. She noted the paintings displayed on the pale yellow walls as they went up. Her eyes grew larger as they ascended.

"Don't look now, but I think all this art is the real deal." She pointed at one. "Including the Degas."

"So how much do you think they're worth?" Paresi asked.

"More than you, me, and your mama put together," she said. "I'll bet the insurance alone is more than we make in a decade."

Paresi smiled. "Think we're in the wrong business?"

"You must have been reading my mind." She looked at him. "I bet you'd look very hot in a loincloth, swinging a live chicken around."

"You'd be all over me," he said.

Their laughter preceded them to the top of the stairs, where a holiday arrangement of red and white poinsettias rested in a beribboned basket atop a mahogany game table.

"Chippendale," Star said, pointing. "Eighteenth-century, with what I suspect is the original brass."

"You know this stuff, huh?" Paresi asked.

"You bet. Vee, too. When we were in high school, she bought an old amber perfume bottle for fifty cents in a junk shop, just because she thought it was pretty. It turned out to be cabochon glass. One of our teachers saw it, told her what it was, and said it was worth about two hundred dollars. That started us studying antiques. Believe me," she went on as she pointed, "that table costs as much as my first car."

"How the other half lives . . . or used to," Paresi said.

They turned right and walked down the carpeted

hall. Another uniformed officer stood guard outside an open door.

"Merry Christmas, Billy," Star said, approaching with Paresi.

"Merry Christmas, Lieutenant." Billy Harris smiled, dimples flashing in his cocoa-colored skin. A slight gap showed between his prominent front teeth. "You too, Sarge."

Paresi nodded. "Yo, Bill."

It took a second for Star's brain to register the sight in front of her. The sparseness of the room hit her like cold water in the face. A shiver went through her body.

This room, in contrast to the rest of the house, was nearly empty. Still, it seemed alive, with a presence that passed through her suddenly cold flesh and made her want to run out of the door. Behind her, she heard Paresi's breath catch in his throat.

The two of them crossed the scuffed and neglected hardwood floor. The sound of their footsteps assaulted her ears, reinforcing her desire to flee, to run as fast as she could, out of the place. Somehow the sight of the forensics team videotaping, examining, and exploring the scene added to her fear.

From somewhere in the room, she heard the faint sound of Brenda Lee singing "Rockin' Around the Christmas Tree." She realized that someone had set a small radio on top of a camera case, in an effort to keep the holiday spirit. Instead, it just added another bizarre aspect to the scene.

The room was nearly bare of furniture and devoid of even basic warmth. The only hint of the opulence present in the rest of the house was a tall, ornate, black iron candelabra. It sat on the floor in a corner with twelve burned-out red candles in it.

A huge, specially made four-poster bed dominated the center of the room. Across from it, near a window, sat a rough-hewn, whitewashed wooden table, laden with a colorful array of bottles, jars, and more candles.

On the bed lay Desmond St. John, faceup, spread-eagled, wrists and ankles bound. His handsome ebony-skinned face was frozen in a grimace of what could have been great pain or ecstasy or both. His pale gray eyes were open, and fixed on the ceiling.

Star stood over him, finding him as fascinating in death as he had been in life. The fear that had been crawling over her skin since she entered the room was tightening. She pulled her coat around her. She leaned forward, looking at the neat round hole in Desmond's forehead and the splatter of blood and gray matter on the pillow, the headboard, and the wall behind him.

A shiver went through her body, and a shrill little sound escaped her lips. She jerked back, as if she had been burned.

"What?" Paresi said, as she bumped against him.

"I thought I saw his eyes move," she whispered.

"Don't do that," he said. "Not in here."

"You feel it too?"

Paresi nodded. "We're just stressing. It's Christmas, he's a voodoo guy, and we're freaking, that's all."

Star took a deep breath. "You're right. This case is no different than any other."

She stood back. "Check this out." She pointed at the braided black silk ropes that bound Desmond St. John's arms and legs to each of the four bedposts.

"Light bondage, or serious restraint?"

Paresi shrugged. "Not my thing. I'm not into pain."

"That's a relief," Star said. She took a pair of latex gloves from her pocket and pulled them on. "Talk about your straight shooting."

A pattern of bullet holes continued in a perfectly ordered line down Desmond's body. One to the throat, one to the center of the chest, one to the abdomen, and one in each shoulder.

In life, Desmond St. John had been a giant. He stood seven feet two inches tall, with the lean, muscular body of an NBA all-star. Now, he was just so much dead meat, naked, hips slightly raised, as if he had died mid-thrust.

Paresi whistled. "Here's a guy who lived up to the hype."

Star punched him on the arm.

"Ow!" Paresi rubbed his bicep. "I'm just making an observation here."

Everybody laughed.

He stood back, still rubbing his arm, looking at the body. "Great shooting, though. A perfect cross."

Star circled the bed, walking slowly around it twice, trying not to feel that the dead man was somehow watching her.

"What've you got?" Paresi asked.

"Nothing, I just wonder about this line." She pointed down. "See it?"

Paresi looked down.

"No."

"Right here. It's faint, but it's there." Star pointed again.

Paresi leaned closer. "Talk about your hawk eyes—I'm practically on my knees, and I still can't see it."

She stooped, and traced the line with her finger.

"Right here."

"Oh yeah!" Paresi squatted, moving his finger over the faint line. "Man, you got some eyes."

The thin line circled the bed.

"I wonder what it's here for?" she said.

"We'll probably find out when the bed is moved," Paresi said. He pointed to the whitewashed table near the window. "What's that, some kind of shrine?"

Star walked over. "It's an altar."

Paresi followed. "What's all this stuff?"

"I don't know." Star pointed to a strange-looking bottle on the table. It was wrapped in vertical strips of red, black, and white silk sewn together with coarse black thread. There were two small pairs of open scissors tied to the neck of the bottle with red and yellow silk embroidery threads.

"That one is very funky, check out the mirrors." She indicated the small mirrors framed in red and green plastic and tied around the bottle's midsection with the same type of red and yellow thread.

"I guess you can watch yourself getting ripped," Paresi said.

"Right, and if you cut yourself on the open scissors, then you've had enough," Star said.

"We need somebody over here." She turned and called out to one of the photographers. "Hey, Ted, can I get some Polaroids of this?"

Ted Hayes looked up. "Right away, Lieutenant." He walked over to the altar, and aimed his camera.

The medical examiner walked in.

Star was surprised to see Mitchell Grant. She felt his eyes on her. She tightened her lips to keep from smiling. Gossip about the two of them had been flying for several months now, and she didn't want to add fuel to the fire. Still, the doctor's appearance visibly lessened the feeling of dread that had attached to her since she'd arrived.

He wore a jet-black, calf-length Armani cashmere coat. She noted the glistening flakes of snow in his thick, blond hair.

"Happy holidays, people." He nodded toward the officers and coroner's crew in the room. "What've we got?" He removed his coat, and handed it to an aide who had appeared at his side.

"Hi, Mitchell," Star said. "It's Christmas, what are you doing here?"

His green eyes sparkled mischievously. "I'd never pass up a chance to see you, Lieutenant."

Star looked down at the floor. He was the only man on earth who could make her blush.

"It's the Hoodoo Man, doc," Paresi said. "In the cold, yet eternally well-endowed, flesh."

The officers laughed.

Mitch pulled a pair of latex gloves from the inside breast pocket of his black suit and put them on.

Star took in the custom cut of his suit over his long, lean frame. The thought that the doctor and the deceased shared a taste for finely tailored Italian suits crossed her mind.

Mitch stepped back, taking a long look at the body. "Nice touch," he said. "The cross." He moved in the opposite direction, looking at the body. "A fine comment on the spirit of the season." He stopped at the foot of the bed. "Tape and pictures done?"

"Yes sir, Dr. Grant." Paul Rodriguez from the Bureau of Criminal Identification packed away his video camera. "We're finished with him."

Mitch gestured to Paresi. "Let's untie him."

Paresi pulled on a pair of latex gloves.

Mitch touched Desmond's extended arm, applying pressure. "He's just about in full rigor," Mitch said. "Be careful."

They removed the silken cords. Desmond St. John's body remained stiff.

"There's something underneath him," Mitch said, leaning down and looking at the corpse's raised pelvis.

"I hope it's not his girlfriend," Paresi said.

Everyone laughed.

Mitch straightened up. "I don't want to break his arms. Let's roll him easy."

The two men turned the body on its side.

Star's hand flew to her chest, as if something had just struck her.

"Ouch!" Paresi shook his head. "That had to hurt."

Protruding from the corpse's anus was about seven inches of a black hard rubber dildo.

Mitch stood back. "Not necessarily. Maybe he was used to it."

"You certainly have some interesting ideas, Dr. Grant," Star said.

Laughter drowned out the rockabilly sound of Elvis belting out "Blue Christmas" from the radio.

Paresi grimaced. "How much is up there?"

"I'd guess about half of it," Mitch said. "These are buddy toys. They're designed for two, so that everybody has a good time."

The doctor carefully tilted the exposed end of the dildo. "Got a little blood here. I guess the other rider was out of practice, or a newcomer."

"Enough to type?" Paresi asked.

Grant nodded. "Jason," he called out.

Jason Williams, Mitch's favorite assistant, hurried over. He was nearly as tall as his boss. A lean, handsome, golden brown, hazel-eyed young man.

He seriously wanted a career in forensic pathology, but with his nearly waist-length, copper-colored, dread-locked hair, he looked more like a rock star.

Still, Mitch saw his promise, and had become his mentor.

"Yes, Doctor?"

Mitch pointed to the bloody tip. "I need a sample."

"I got it." The young man opened his bag and pulled out the kit needed to pick up the blood.

The cops and the doctor stepped back.

Star watched the rusty brown liquid seep into the testing strip in Jason's gloved hand. "Merry Christmas," she said.

CHAPTER TWO

When the officers returned to the squad room, Star heard her phone ringing. She picked it up.

"Homicide, Lieutenant Duvall." She wiggled out of her coat, letting it fall onto her chair. "Hello, Captain. Merry Christmas."

Across from her, Paresi mouthed, "Lewis?"

Star nodded. "Yes sir, it's true . . . this morning, as near as we can figure. Dr. Grant came in to supervise."

She made a face. "Yes sir, yes, I understand, we will, sir, yes, thank you, Captain, and Merry Christmas." She hung up.

Paresi folded his arms and leaned on his desk. "So Christmas doesn't exempt you from an ass-chewing."

"You got that right. He's heard about our present."

"I thought he was going to retire before the end of the year," Paresi said.

She picked up her coat and hung it up. "Guess again."

In spite of her partner's enthusiasm for a retirement party, she was glad Captain Lewis had decided to hang in.

He'd come through the Academy with her father, Sergeant Leonard Duvall. They'd been partners up until her father was killed. Lewis was her first sergeant when she came on the job. He was a tough guy, no doubt about it, but she respected and admired him. He'd always been in her corner, and he'd never let her down.

"I can see his point," she said, sitting down, facing Paresi.

"When the crap rolls, he gets the first faceful. He's afraid of what's going to happen when the news gets out about Desmond. And frankly, I don't blame him. You know how powerful Desmond was in the black community. The captain thinks there might be retaliation, especially against the police."

"Why? We didn't kill him," Paresi said.

"I know, but sometimes people think cops can be negligent, especially when it comes to black folks. Lewis knows this is going to go down hard and he wants us on top of it. He wants the people to know that we're not blowing it off, that we're on the case."

"So what does he want us to do? Get a bullhorn and travel the west side?"

"He's afraid of the media, what they'll do with this, how they'll spin it," Star said. "Some members of Desmond's church are already making noises."

Her phone rang again.

"Homicide, Lieutenant Duvall . . . You're kidding." She glanced at Paresi, a look of disbelief on her face. "Okay, all right, we're on the way." She hung up.

"What?"

"That was Mitchell. Some of St. John's followers have already descended on the morgue and they're insisting on performing some kind of ritual. They even tried to stop the body from being weighed and tagged. We've got to get over there."

Paresi looked at the bag of presents on the floor next to

his desk. "Think I should send a uniform over to my sister's house with these?" He pointed at the bag. "It's kind of a tradition for my nieces. You know, more presents to open later, after dinner."

"I think we can get this done and knock off in time for you to make it to dinner. If not, I'll handle it alone."

"No way." Paresi shook his head. "If you have to work through the night, so will I."

She smiled. "And everybody wonders why I love you."

CHAPTER THREE

When Paresi and Star arrived at the parking lot of the county medical examiner's building, a wave of reporters rushed the car.

"What's the story?"

"Is it a murder?"

"Is it really Desmond St. John?"

"Is it true there's a secret ceremony going on in the morgue?"

The questions came from all sides. Microphones were shoved in their faces, flashbulbs popped, and video cameras blocked their way. The two detectives were dogged all the way to the building.

Star stopped on the steps of the squat gray structure and faced the group.

"We don't have anything to say right now," she said, looking over the crowd. "Our department is beginning an investigation into the matter. When we know more, you'll know more."

"He was executed by the po-leece."

Star turned in the direction of the voice.

A tall black man with dreadlocks and a fur-covered hat stepped from the crowd, his hands jammed into the pockets of his dark brown imitation-leather coat.

"That isn't true, and you know it," she said.

The man walked up the steps to face Star. Paresi moved alongside her.

"Call off your dog, officer," the man said, his voice hard.

"Take your hands out of your pockets," Paresi said. "*Now.*"

The man removed his hands and held them up.

"See? No weapon, man, other than the truth. Desmond was executed because the white man hated him, hated his power."

The flashbulbs went off, the video cameras rolled.

"It's a free country," Star said to the man. "Everybody is entitled to their opinion, no matter how stupid it is."

She turned her back and walked up the steps.

"So how much they payin' you to sell out, my sistuh!" the man yelled at her.

"Hey!" Paresi got in his face. "You got a problem with the way we do our job? Take it up with me."

The man shook his head disgustedly. "Yeah, you really wanna hear what *I* gotta say."

Paresi and the man glared at one another, as the cameras rolled. Paresi stepped closer, his blue eyes stormy.

"I'm listening."

The man curled his lip. "You ain't worth it."

He threw up his hands and walked away.

Paresi watched him for a few moments, then turned and followed Star.

Some of the reporters swarmed the man, while others trailed the detectives to the door, surrounding them. The security guard unlocked one of the double chrome and glass doors.

Paresi put his arm around Star's waist and pushed their

way inside. The guard locked the door after them. The reporters pressed against the glass, still shouting questions, taping, and taking pictures.

"Glad you didn't punch him out on camera," Star said.

"Consider it another Christmas present." Paresi unbuttoned his coat.

She pulled off her gloves and jammed them angrily in her pocket. "Desmond was important for a lot of people," she said, "and it burns my butt to see some crackpot come up and start stirring up the shit. It takes away from what's really happening. I mean, don't they get it? Can't they figure out it's Christmas Day and we're all here, not home with our families. Can't they see we're working on this?"

Paresi kneaded her shoulders. "Chill out, champ, I'm supposed to be the one with the temper." He turned to the guard. "Make sure those dinks are off the steps when we come out."

The man nodded. "Yes, sir." He pointed down the deserted hallway. "Dr. Grant's waiting for you in his office."

"Thanks," Star said.

They headed down the corridor. The Christmas decorations in the darkened and deserted building added a decidedly creepy touch.

Mitchell Grant's outer office door was open. He sat at his secretary's desk, leaning back in her chair. His long legs were stretched out. His feet, in handcrafted black calfskin Italian shoes, rested on the desktop.

"The holiday joy just keeps on coming," he said.

"Tell us about it," Paresi said. "It's crazy out there, the wackos are already circling."

"Don't I know it." Dr. Grant stood. "I apologize for the welcoming committee."

"The power of the press," Star said.

"Yeah. The people's right to know," Paresi said derisively.

"Yes. Well, two of the people have landed in my office." Mitch nodded toward the closed door.

"So you said over the phone." Star hung her coat and scarf on the wooden coat tree. "Are they reasonable?"

"Depends on your definition of the word." Mitch put his hands in his pockets and leaned forward, amusement twinkling in his eyes. "They tell me there's a voodoo ritual that must be performed, so that Desmond can rest."

A little smile played at the corners of his mouth. "Seems they have to release the *loa*."

"Release the *loa*?" Star's eyes widened.

"That's right." Mitch nodded. "I've got a Mr. Stevens and a Mr. Dulac in my office, and they mean business. It's up to you, Lieutenant, to explain to them why the body can't be touched or released. They don't seem to believe me."

"Swell."

"Hey, I'll tell 'em." Paresi tossed his coat on the couch.

Star put her hand on his arm. "Now *you* cool off, this dance is mine."

Mitch indicated the closed office door. "After you."

The two black men stood when Star, Grant, and Paresi entered the room.

"Hello, gentlemen," Star said, extending her hand to the smaller man. "I'm Detective Lieutenant Duvall. I'm in charge of this investigation."

The man shook her hand.

"Hello, Lieutenant." His voice had a strong singsong quality. "I'm François Dulac, and this is Eric Stevens." He indicated the tall, unsmiling man to his left.

"I'm very sorry for your loss, gentlemen," Star said, shaking hands with Eric Stevens.

Dulac spoke. "Thank you. I know you people have things you must do in cases of this kind, but surely you know that Desmond is special."

"Yes sir, I do." Star indicated the sofa. "Won't you gentlemen be seated? By the way, this is my partner, Detective Sergeant Paresi."

Paresi nodded at the men.

"We both understand the situation here, with Mr. St. John," she said. "But you must also understand that as special as he was, someone murdered him, and to allow you access to the body before the necessary procedures have been carried out could be detrimental to finding out who that killer is."

"We realize that." François Dulac spoke in a soft voice. "But you must recognize our predicament as well, Lieutenant. Desmond's is a very powerful spirit, and if we do not carry out the ritual to free the *loa* from his earthly prison, we will suffer the consequences."

"What do you mean, free the *loa*?" Paresi asked.

"The spirit that lives in Desmond. It is perhaps the most powerful *loa* of all. His anger will be visited upon us if we do not carry out the ceremony to free him."

Paresi shot a look at Star.

"I understand, gentlemen, and I sympathize," she said, "but I can't allow you to contaminate the body, and possibly any evidence that might be there. We have to autopsy the remains and do our testing to get to the bottom of his homicide."

A light of anger flashed in François Dulac's dull brown eyes, but his face remained calm. "It is not important."

"Not important?" Star said incredulously.

"Desmond's body is still, but *he* is not dead. Legba is immortal."

Paresi cleared his throat. Star aimed a look his way.

"Perhaps in your belief, Mr. Dulac," she said. "But for us, Desmond St. John, and anything that might be inside him, is most assuredly dead. And by the hand of another, which makes it homicide, which is where we come in." She shook her head. "I'm sorry, but we're going to follow procedure."

The two men looked at each other. Eric Stevens whispered something to François, who nodded in response and turned to Star.

"Perhaps we can compromise."

"Let's hear it," she said.

"Instead of the accustomed ceremony, we will capture only the *loa*, and after you have made your investigation, we will take possession of the body and conduct our rites as usual."

Star looked at Mitch. "Dr. Grant?"

"Just what is it that you do to capture the *loa*?" Mitch asked.

"As I said when we arrived, Doctor, I cannot explain our ways to an outsider," François said. "I'm sorry."

"So am I," Mitch said, turning away from them. "This meeting is over."

François's cool facade shattered. His face looked anguished. "Please, Doctor." He walked toward Mitch.

"Please. It is most imperative that this is done. I promise you Desmond's body will not be harmed."

"Providing I agree to this, where would the ceremony be performed?" Mitch asked.

"Here, if that is all right with you." François indicated his friend. "Eric and I are prepared. We will capture the *loa*, just the two of us."

"We'll have to be in the room," Star said.

François turned to her. "Your ways are not our ways, sister." He smiled softly. "You would not understand."

"That may be," Star said, "but we're going to watch everything you do, and if we don't like what we see, the ceremony is over. We can't allow you to compromise this investigation."

"I see." François looked to Mitch. "The lady's word has that much power in this office?"

"You bet," Mitch said. "That's the best we can do."

"François." Eric Stevens reached out to his friend. "We must agree."

"Very well." Dulac turned to Star. "As you will."

Star, Paresi, and Mitch sat on folding chairs in the autopsy room, watching François Dulac and Eric Stevens prepare the area for the releasing of the *loa*.

After turning off most of the overhead fluorescent lights, the two men opened their large black satchels. Dulac pulled four tall, pillarlike white candles from his, along with a large, lidded black jar and a small, rough-hewn red bowl. He set these pieces on the dissecting table, and withdrew into a corner of the room.

Eric Stevens completed the layout. He pulled several colorfully lidded plastic containers from his bag and laid them out on the table next to the bowl and the jar. He bowed his head for a moment and then began methodically opening each plastic tub.

With the removal of the tops, each container released its secrets. The aromas of baked plantains, yams, roasted corn, coconut, and chicken wrestled with the ever-present smell of disinfectant and death in the autopsy room.

Stevens reached into his bag and retrieved two more plastic containers, which he opened and placed on the steel table. One was filled with cooked rice and the other with dry cornmeal.

Paresi leaned close to Star and whispered, "So, what is this, some kind of picnic for a dead guy?"

Star faced him. "Do I look like a voodoo queen to you?"

Mitch chuckled softly.

Eric Stevens looked up at the sound. The three observers felt like schoolchildren caught making faces behind the teacher's back.

"We must have silence," Stevens said, his eyes cold.

Star nodded. "Sorry."

In his corner, François Dulac was now sitting cross-legged on the floor with his eyes closed. His thin, dark face was calm and peaceful, as if he were deep in meditation.

After the foods had been laid out, Stevens dipped into his bag and produced an ornate pair of gold-plated scissors and a matching golden spoon. He placed these alongside the jar. The last item in his bag, a large bottle of rum, was set down next to the glistening utensils. The white label glowed in the candlelight. Star read it: Barbancourt Dark Rum.

The table had the look of a bizarre buffet.

Having effectively quieted his observers, Stevens turned and faced them.

"Doctor, we are now ready to receive Desmond," he said.

"Right." Mitch stood and turned to Paresi.

"What?" Paresi looked up.

"I'll need some help," Mitch said.

"Oh yeah, sure." He stood and looked back at Star. "Hold my seat," he whispered.

"Oh, like somebody is *really* going to want it," she said.

"Please." Stevens held his hands up. "This is serious, and you are all making light. Don't . . . please."

"Sorry." Star leaned back in her chair and crossed her legs.

Mitch and Paresi went into the cold room to retrieve Desmond's body. Star could hear the sound of the crypt opening.

The stainless-steel door made a scraping, metallic sound. Behind it was the room in which the bodies were kept. Corpses, draped in white plastic sheets, were stacked on shelves like knickknacks in some ghastly curio cabinet.

Paresi and Mitch entered. It was like stepping into an arctic winter. The room was vast. The crypt had been designed to store up to two hundred bodies.

During their time in Homicide, both Star and Paresi had seen it packed to capacity and beyond. In fact, these days, thanks to drug dealing and gang warfare, it seemed permanently full. Sometimes it was so crowded that corpses were left on steel tables in the center of the cavernous room.

A few moments later, Star heard the door close, and the sound of the gurney wheels on the hard cement floor. The squeaking made her flesh crawl.

Eric Stevens stood next to the dissecting table, his eyes closed as if in prayer.

Star got up and opened the door. She stepped partially behind it, holding it close to the wall, allowing Mitch and Paresi to wheel the gurney past her. Desmond's rigor had passed. His arms were now down by his sides, his feet together. His long form was shrouded with two white plastic drapes.

She sat down and watched the men position the body in the center of the room. They returned to their seats, Mitch to her right and Paresi to her left.

Eric Stevens opened his eyes, and made the sign of the cross over his chest.

He then picked up the four white candles, and arranged them around the table. He placed one in each corner, forming an oblong frame for the food, utensils, and pottery. Solemnly he lit them, filling the room with a chilling glow. He stood, his hands again clasped in a prayerful position.

Suddenly, François Dulac moaned, a deep, sorrowful sound that echoed off the walls of the sterile room.

Paresi took Star's hand. She laced her fingers through his.

Mitch glanced down at their entwined hands. An unwelcome tightness filled his chest. He coughed softly into his closed fist and leaned forward in his chair, his green eyes staring resolutely at the two men.

Eric Stevens approached the body and lifted the drape.

"Only the face and head can be a part of this," Mitch said.

"As you wish, Doctor." Stevens folded the top drape across Desmond's shoulders, covering the bullet holes visible in each, allowing his face and head to be viewed. "We need access only to the head for now," he said.

Still seated on the floor, François Dulac had begun a rhythmic rocking in the corner of the room. Soft clicking sounds came from his barely open lips. His eyes were shut so tight, they seemed to disappear.

Star looked at Desmond's face. His eyes were open, and for a second she thought she saw a gleaming light coming from them.

She shuddered, and a soft gasp escaped her.

Paresi put his free hand over their clasped ones.

Star decided the flickering of the candle was playing tricks on her vision. She took a deep breath and looked again at the body.

Desmond's eyes now seemed dull and flat. The grimace that had been apparent when she first saw the body seemed to have disappeared. Star calmly told herself that the reason for the change was that the corpse had slipped out of rigor mortis, and was therefore more pliable.

But reason wasn't calming her nerves. The holes in the center of his forehead and throat were barely visible in the candlelight, and Star wrestled down the thought that the wounds seemed to be healing themselves. She tightened her grip on Paresi's hand.

Mitch saw the movement out of the corner of his eye, and rocked farther forward, nearly sitting on the edge of his seat.

François Dulac shook his head and shoulders like a man emerging from a long sleep. He approached the table and opened the bottle of rum. The snap of the top as it tore loose from its plastic anchor was like a sharp fingernail down Star's spine.

Dulac tipped the bottle to his mouth, and drank.

Paresi nudged Star. "What about us?" he whispered.

Stevens glared at him.

Dulac put the bottle down and approached the dead man on the gurney. He stood at Desmond's feet and bowed to the corpse. A low, deep moan rose from his throat, as he made the sign of the cross in the air before him.

Stevens, still scowling, removed an object wrapped in white tissue from the bag and carried it to the sink in the corner of the room.

They watched him unwrap the paper, revealing an exquisite crystal pitcher. He filled it with water and took it to the dissecting table, where he put it down next to the displayed foods.

Dulac joined him, chanting something in French which the detectives didn't understand. Mitch, however, seemed to comprehend every word.

Star glanced at him. His eyes were riveted on François Dulac.

Eric Stevens picked up the red bowl and stood alongside the small man.

François, still chanting in French, picked up the golden spoon and dipped it into the plastic container of cooked rice. One by one, he put a spoonful of food from each of the dishes into the bowl held by Stevens. He continued the chant as they moved from food to food. When a sampling of all the foods had been put into the bowl, Stevens handed Dulac the crystal pitcher filled with water.

François poured some of the liquid into the bowl and stirred the mixture.

Star's blood turned to ice.

The men then went to the body and Stevens raised the bowl high in the air, while Dulac chanted unceasingly in French.

The only words Star understood from her high-school French were *homme*, which meant "man," *après,* which meant "after," and *frère*, which meant "brother."

Before any of them could blink, Dulac leapt up on the gurney and straddled the corpse. With both hands, he pulled Desmond's body to a sitting position.

Star and Paresi grabbed one another and Mitch was out of his seat like a shot.

"That's it, this thing is over."

"No, Doctor, no, please let us finish," Eric Stevens begged Mitch.

The drape had slipped to the dead man's waist. Unlike the wounds in his head and throat, the bloody bullet holes down his body and in his shoulders were clearly visible, even in the candlelight. François's tiny body was spread-eagled atop Desmond. He held the corpse's shoulders with both hands, his mouth inches from Desmond's dead face, chanting in singsong French. He seemed oblivious to the commotion around him.

"Please, Doctor, we are nearly finished," Stevens pleaded.

Star disentangled herself from Paresi and took Mitch by the arm. "Mitchell, please . . . Let them finish, please."

Dr. Grant looked down at her. She saw something in his eyes that frightened her nearly as much as the ceremony.

"C'mon." She led him back to his seat, feeling the

tension in his body as she guided him. They sat down, and she held his hand, and reached out for Paresi with her other one.

The three of them connected, their clasped hands forming a conduit. Star felt a sense of safety and protection passing between them.

François Dulac gently lay Desmond back on the table, and climbed down from the gurney.

"We love you, Desmond," he said in English. "Go in peace, and know that your family will always love and honor you."

Eric Stevens picked up the jar with the lid and the golden scissors that lay next to the food. He handed the scissors to Dulac.

Star could feel Mitch struggling with himself not to interrupt again. Next to her, Paresi softly whispered Hail Marys.

Dulac raised his hands.

"*Legba!*" he shouted in a clear, strong voice. "*Legba! Legba! Legba!*"

The sound bounced back from the blue tile walls, making Star's heart thump wildly in her chest.

Both men tightened their grips on her hands.

François Dulac solemnly walked around the gurney to Desmond's head. Stevens moved beside him and opened the black jar. Dulac quickly clipped a section from one of the dead man's long dreadlocks. He put the hair into the vessel and Stevens jammed the top down on the jar with a twisting motion. The high-pitched screech of porcelain against porcelain made Star wince.

Both men faced the corpse and made the sign of the cross. Stevens lifted the jar over his head. Dulac bowed toward it and spoke.

"Papa Legba, give rest to the earthly body of Desmond St. John. Show his soul across the water to peace. He who has carried and protected you on this journey of life, bless him, and bless us, your servants, who pray for your love and protection." He bowed again.

Stevens handed him the jar, and covered Desmond's face. He then stood at the head of the body, while Dulac remained at the feet.

"Desmond St. John," François said. "Good-bye, my beloved friend. Do not forget us, as we shall never forget you." He bowed again to the corpse, then turned toward the three people sitting across the room.

"Thank you, Doctor, officers. We have captured Legba, and our ceremony is over."

Star sat up in the center of her bed, spooning Häagen-Dazs ice cream into her mouth and talking to Vee on the telephone.

"So tell me about Desmond St. John," her best friend said. It was all over the six o'clock news.

"I can't talk about it."

"I know you can't give details, but you can tell me if he was really murdered, right?"

Star swallowed a spoonful of ice cream. "Yes, it's murder, that's for sure."

"Wow," Vee said. "I can't believe that. Seems to me, with all the power he had, anybody with any sense would be scared to even talk to him, let alone *off* the brother!" She sighed. "Murder for sure, huh?"

"He didn't kill himself," Star said.

"The news said some of his followers went down to the morgue to do some kind of secret ceremony. Is that true?" Vee asked.

"Now you know I can't give out information like that."

Vee sighed. "Girl, puh-leese! I know what color drawers you're wearing. You might as well just go on and tell me. You know you want to. Besides, the news already said some kind of voodoo ritual went on at the morgue."

"It's a ceremony." Star sighed. "They had to release the *loa*, the spirit that lived in Desmond."

"Girl, stop." Vee laughed. "You talking about a spirit, like a ghost, living in Desmond?"

"His followers believe Desmond was really the incarnation of the voodoo god, Legba."

Vee's laugh filled Star's ear.

"Don't laugh!" Star grinned, trying to hold in her own laughter. "It's not funny."

"Uh-huh, and that's why you sound like you're about to fall out. I can hear it in your voice," Vee said.

"All right. I admit I had a little trouble when they first told us." She took a deep breath. "But believe me, it ain't funny. I saw the ceremony."

"Tell me," Vee said, excitedly. "What did they do? Did they sacrifice something, you know, a goat or a chicken? Did they use snakes?"

"Chickens and goats and snakes?" Star laughed. "You been watching those devil-running-loose movies again? No. It was nothing like that." She talked around the mound of ice cream in her mouth.

"Will you please stop smacking in my ear?" Vee said. "What in the world are you eating?"

"Häagen-Dazs." Star licked her lips. "Midnight Cookies and Cream."

"Double chocolate. I should have guessed. Whatever you saw must have scared you simple . . . You ate the whole pint, right?"

"No," Star lied. Her spoon scraped along the bottom of the carton.

"I hear it," Vee said. "I know you. Tell me."

"I can't talk about it." Star set the empty container, with the cleanly licked spoon inside, on the night table next to her bed. "At least not now . . . Give me a little time, okay?"

"Okay," Vee said. "But when you tell me, I want to hear it all."

"Paresi was there, he'll tell you."

"He's worse than you are, he thinks I'm gonna faint if he talks to me about the job."

"He likes you," Star said. "He just doesn't want to scare you off. It's hard for cops to relate to civilians; they don't understand."

"I'm not a civilian. I've been on the job as long as you have."

Star leaned back against the pillows. "By osmosis, that's true, but I don't always tell you the details. Paresi was really freaked out by this. I doubt he'll even talk to me about it. The boy said so many Hail Marys, I thought Desmond was going to sit up and tell him to shut up!"

They laughed.

Star's cat stood on the edge of the bed, sniffing toward the night table and the smell of ice cream.

"No, Jake, it's got chocolate in it, you can't have it." She pulled the cat alongside her.

"Are you giving that fat thing ice cream?" Vee said through the receiver.

"He always gets the carton unless it's chocolate. That's not good for cats," Star said, licking her fingers.

"Girl, we have got to get you some kids."

"Get me a man first," Star said.

"You got one, you're just too stupid to realize it!"

"Don't start." Star hugged the cat to her body.

"Was he there while all this hoodoo stuff was going on?" Vee asked.

"Yep."

"And . . . ?"

"And what?" Star shrugged her shoulders. "He did a lot better with it than me and Paresi."

"Did he say anything afterwards?" Vee said.

"No, not really. It was hard to watch, and to tell the truth, I'm sure Mitchell was as rattled inside as we were. He's just better at being cool." She scratched the purring cat's ears. "He was cooler than Desmond! The man was totally together. But me and Paresi? Chile, we was like Willie Best and Mantan Moreland in those old movies. I *know* our eyes was bigger than our heads!"

Vee laughed. "I wish I could have seen that!"

"No you don't," Star said. "Believe me." She ran her free hand through her hair. "Honey, it was 'feets do yo' stuff' time for both of us. The only reason we stayed in our seats is that we were too scared to move!"

She laughed with Vee.

"If anything had happened, I'm sure Dr. Grant would have protected you," Vee said. "He's crazy about you. You better stop holding him off. Give him a chance."

"We're moving along, be patient. Just because you and Paresi act like there's no tomorrow, don't mean I have to."

"What you talkin' about?" Vee said. "Dominic ain't getting nothing off me."

"Your nose is growing," Star said.

Vee laughed out loud. "Well, he ain't got it all . . . yet. Just a little taste . . . you know, keep him interested. I'm making him work for it."

"Um-hmmm. That's not the way I hear it," Star said slyly.

Vee laughed. "You love trouble, don't you?"

Star smiled. "Paresi's a good guy. He'll stick with you as long as you keep everything honest, and I know you will. I'm happy for you guys."

"I'll bet the doctor will stick with you, if you just give him a chance."

"Maybe," Star said, softly.

"Stop listening to them jealous folks that don't want to see you and him together," Vee said. "He's crazy for you. I know. I watch him when he's looking at you."

"You watch him 'cause you like looking at him!"

"You ain't never lied!" Vee laughed. "But for real, he's crazy about you."

"We'll see."

"Trust him."

"Why?" Star said.

"Because people change. Dr. Grant used to be free with his zipper, but he's not like that now, because he wants you."

Star was silent.

"I know, you don't wanna hear it. You are the most stubborn fool I know."

"Thanks."

"Go on, ignore me as usual, because you'd rather stay home with that fat cat, and your head in a pint of Häagen-Dazs. You got to learn to open up. Give him a chance, that's all I'm saying."

Star shifted, and put the phone to her other ear.

"Finished? Let's talk about something else."

Vee sighed deeply.

"Did you know you were on the news tonight?" Vee asked, changing the subject.

"Yeah?" Star said.

"Uh-huh, six o'clock. You were facing down some guy on the steps of Dr. Grant's building."

"Oh, yeah, that was this afternoon. The media was there. I didn't even think about that."

"Well, you were impressive. Miss Gold Shield, with the stony eyes. Dominic standing with you, looking like Michael Corleone in a bad mood. Scared 'a y'all!" Vee said. "Y'all was fierce. When Dominic got in the brother's face, I had to sit down!"

"He pissed Paresi off, big time."

"I saw. Y'all was very large and in charge. The kids taped it."

"I'll have to check it out." Star looked at her bedside clock. "I guess I'd better get to bed, I've got to go in tomorrow."

"Okay, me too." Vee yawned. "But I got to say I'm sorry about Desmond. He was really a fine, good-looking brother, and it looks like the man was free of jungle fever."

"Yeah," Star agreed. "I give him credit for that. All the women I ever saw him with were unmistakably sisters. Not a light one in the bunch. He liked them big and black."

"Sho' did," Vee said. "He had to have them big, he was so tall himself."

"Yeah, he was that. A big, pretty black man."

"It's a shame," Vee said. "I know he was notorious, but he did a lot of good for the community."

Star stroked the now sleeping cat. "Yeah, he did. He put a lot of the money he made from those shops back into the neighborhood."

"That's right." Vee yawned again. "I wonder what's going to happen to his programs. You know that breakfast and lunch program is probably the only way some kids see food all day."

"I'm sure they'll find a way to keep things running." Star looked at the clock again. "I've got to go to bed. I'll call you tomorrow about New Year's Eve."

"Okay," Vee said. "You'll have to go shopping with me. The kids say it is totally uncool to be seen in the supermarket with your mama. They'll help me get the party together, but they won't shop."

"Well, duh! Don't you remember how we used to behave when we were kids?" Star said. "We would have rather walked down the street wearing our drawers on our heads than go to the market. That was just too square. I can relate."

"That's because you still act like you're twelve," Vee said. "I'll talk to you tomorrow, and we'll set a time. It has to be early, though. I want to get to the stuff before the crowd picks over the best of it."

"Yeszum." Star yawned. "Talk to you tomorrow."

"Good night," Vee said. "And Merry Christmas."

"Merry Christmas," she said, and hung up.

Star put the sleeping cat on the corner of her bed and pulled the covers up over herself. As she turned out the light, her mind flashed on Lieutenant Sperry telling her about the infant John Doe.

He'd started to give her details, but she stopped him. It was too painful to take in. Still, she knew she'd have to face it, and soon.

CHAPTER FOUR

Shoppers recovering from Christmas dinner crowded the supermarket, getting the goods for the all-important New Year's feast. The first meal of the year set the tone for the rest of it. Good food and good drink insured good luck.

Star pushed the cart while Vee piled groceries inside.

"All right." Vee picked up a box of cake mix. "Should I make chocolate, white, or yellow cake?"

Star looked at her. "You're going to make a cake from mix?"

Vee sighed. "Forgive me, I must have had a momentary lapse—no mix cakes."

"Right."

"For somebody who even burnt up her mud pies, you sure are picky."

"That's why you love me." Star grinned.

Vee put the cake mix back. "I'm rethinking that." She picked up a box of cake flour. "I guess I should get some cocoa, too."

Star didn't say anything. She just smiled.

"Look who I'm talking to. The Queen of Chocolate." Vee reached for the cocoa.

"Maybe you should get two." Star picked up another box. "You know, fudge icing."

Vee took it from her hand and put it back on the shelf. "One is enough. Trust me." She put her box in the cart. "Don't let me forget the butter."

"Check." Star wheeled the cart around a corner. "What's next?"

"Tomatoes." Vee pointed toward the produce section. "You get them while I talk to the butcher."

"You want me to choose the tomatoes?"

"Nothing to it," Vee said. "Just make sure they're red and they smell like tomatoes. You have to sniff them, though. The smell is important. Get a couple of bags and fill them up. The kids love tomatoes, they'll eat a whole bag in one sitting."

"Swell. The woman wants me to stand in the middle of a store, smelling tomatoes."

"Go on." Vee took the cart, and shooed her toward the produce department. She watched Star for a moment, then wheeled the cart toward the meat counter. Behind the glass window, she saw a young man arranging pork chops in a plastic tray. She pushed the service buzzer.

The young man looked up and smiled.

Vee's heart jumped into her mouth. Her blood froze.

The butcher wiped his hands on a disposable wet wipe, tossed it into a trash bin, and came through the chrome and glass double doors.

"Yes ma'am, can I help you?"

"Uh . . ." Vee's voice stuck in her throat. Her tongue felt thick. "Uh . . . I think I need to talk to my friend first. I was going to order a special cut, but I should ask her about it." She smiled at him. "I'll be back."

He returned her grin. "Yes, ma'am, I'll be here."

Vee wheeled the cart around, practically running over a woman in high-heeled red leather boots and a matching red leather coat. "Excuse me."

She caught up with Star. "Come with me."

"What?" Star held a bag full of tomatoes.

"Come with me." Vee pulled the plastic bag out of Star's hand and plopped it onto the mound of the displayed produce, dislodging a few tomatoes that fell to the floor.

"Wait." Star stooped to pick them up.

"Not now." Vee grabbed her by the arm. "Come with me." She propelled Star toward the meat counter, stopping a few feet short of the glass window. "Look. Look in there."

Star tilted her head. "What am I looking at?"

"The butcher, the guy inside."

"Yeah?" Star turned to Vee. "So?"

"Don't you recognize him?" Vee's voice was agitated.

"Should I?"

"Look again."

Star peered at the man behind the glass. "Sinbad?"

"Don't be funny." Vee's voice bordered on panic. "Take a real good look at him."

Star squinted her eyes. "I give. Who is he?"

"I can't believe you don't recognize him," Vee whispered through clenched teeth. "That's Carlyle Biggs!"

Star looked at her friend.

"What is a Carlyle Biggs?"

"Don't you remember? Christmas, about seven years ago in New York City? He killed his whole family!"

"Oh . . ." Star shook her head. "Right! I remember that. He was a kid, fourteen, fifteen or something."

"Fourteen. He shot them all, on Christmas night. Remember? I was so amazed because he's black. Black folks don't do things like that, kill their whole family."

"It's rare, I'll grant you that." Star stared at the young man. She turned back to Vee. "He's really changed. I never would have recognized him."

"He was a boy," Vee said. "He's a man now."

Star shook her head. "But there's no trace of the kid I remember. He was a scrawny-looking boy. Look at him. He's built like a wall. Even his face is different."

"Maybe that's what happens when you kill your whole family," Vee said. "He shot them all in a cross pattern, remember? One shot to the forehead, one to the neck, one to the chest, one to the stomach, and one in each shoulder."

Star's eyes lit up. "That's right . . . Vee, you're right. The Cross Killer. They were all shot in a perfect cross formation." She turned. "I've got to find the manager."

Vee waited by the pay phone while Star dialed Paresi.

"Hi," she said. "It's me. I'm at Brookport Farms market, shopping with Vee. Guess who's the new butcher here?" She leaned against the wall.

"No." She started laughing. "Captain Lewis is *not* moonlighting." She turned toward Vee. "Yeah, she's here, you can say hi later. This is official business."

"Go on, guess." She cradled the phone to her ear. "Does the name Carlyle Biggs ring a bell?"

"Uh-huh, exactly. Yeah . . . his whole family, about six years ago in New York City."

A wide smile crossed her face. "Give the man a cannoli—the Cross Killer, that's right . . . perfect formation, exactly like Desmond."

She dug in her pocket, and fished out a small piece of paper with the store logo on the top.

"There's a temp manager working for the holidays, so he wasn't much help, but I've got Biggs's address . . . Yeah, you're right, there's really nothing we can do yet." She looked at Vee.

"Okay, we'll talk later. Here, here she is." She handed Vee the phone and walked back into the main area of the store, to an aisle facing the butcher's counter. She watched Carlyle as he packaged more meat behind the plate-glass window.

He was a good-looking kid. Six feet and change. His eyes were startling. Mixed blue-gray. His wavy, golden hair set off his caramel-colored skin. She wondered if it was dyed. It was lighter than she remembered. He wore it cut short and close to his head. Star noted that his hands were long and graceful, as he wrapped the packages of meat on the tray in front of him. He looked like a college student working a job to pay his way through school, but she knew firsthand that looks could be deceiving.

Vee came out, pushing the grocery cart. "Dominic is so cute."

"Yeah, you could just swallow him whole," Star said absentmindedly.

"We can discuss that later," Vee said. "We've got to finish shopping. I've got to get a hog's head before they're all gone."

Star stopped. "Wait a minute. You're buying a pig's head?"

"It's tradition," Vee said. "You know you got to eat hog's head and black-eyed peas for your first meal right after midnight to bring good luck in the new year."

"Uh-huh, along with the stomach pump. How long have you known me?"

"Forever."

"And have you ever seen pig faces pass these lips?"

"That's why your luck is so bad. You need a change."

"I'd rather eat a fried baloney sandwich on Wonder Bread," Star said. "Besides, if you buy a pig's head, you're on the bus or walking, 'cause you ain't bringing it in my car."

"We'll see," Vee said. "Come on, we've got to go to Zannucci's."

"Another market?"

"I'm not going back to the meat counter here. Come on."

She grabbed Star's arm and pulled her toward the checkout.

CHAPTER FIVE

It was nearly ten P.M. on New Year's Eve, and Star sat at the 1930s art deco vanity she had splurged on at Discoveries Downstairs, Vee's favorite antique shop.

The ornate handcrafted piece was the first new furniture she'd bought last summer, when she began redecorating her house. She looked at the ivory, gold, and onyx antique clock on top of the vanity. Just two more hours of this terrible year, and it would be over. She couldn't wait to see it go.

She dabbed Shalimar perfume on her wrists and at the hollow of her neck. Last summer, she'd worn Boucheron. An expensive fragrance the department had paid for, as part of a sting. When it was over, she gave it to Vee—she couldn't stand to wear it.

She set the perfume bottle down. Its classic shape with the pointed gold cap fit perfectly with her antique vanity.

She stared at her face, looking into her own eyes. The thought of the infant John Doe found on Christmas Day looked back at her.

The baby's body was still unclaimed. She'd looked at Lieutenant Sperry's reports. In the back of her mind, the way the baby died, coupled with the death of Desmond St. John on the same day, gave her a very bad feeling.

57

The clock on the vanity chimed, jolting her back to the moment. "I'll think about it later."

She turned to the cat, who sat at the foot of the bed watching her.

"Tonight I'm gonna party out this lousy year, right, Jake?"

The cat tilted his head, his green eyes staring at her. He made a soft meowing sound.

"That's right," she said, standing. "Tonight I'm gonna have a good time ... Lord knows I deserve it." She checked her reflection in the nearly four-foot-wide round mirror. She turned, looking at the rhinestone seams in her black silk stockings, making sure they were perfectly straight. Her dress was long-sleeved, and black. The neckline dipped a little low, showing more cleavage than she was used to, but it was a find. Besides, it was time she became more daring. She was two years from forty, so if not now, when? She'd seen firsthand, every day, that life is short.

The doorbell rang. Jake looked up, yawned, stretched, and turned over on his side.

"I'm outta here, Jakey." She grabbed her evening bag, and rubbed the cat's head. He yawned again.

Star headed downstairs and opened the door. Mitchell Grant smiled.

"Wow!"

"Good or bad wow?" She grinned.

"Outstanding."

"Thanks. Come on in."

He walked into the hall, his dark blue Versace coat catching the light from the hall table.

"You're looking pretty fly yourself," Star said.

"Thank you."

She closed the door. They stared at one another for a moment.

"Can I get you something to drink?"

Mitch produced a bottle wrapped in silver foil from behind him. "For you."

Star took it. "Champagne?"

He smiled. "Am I getting predictable?"

"Never. Thank you."

"There's another one in the car for our hostess."

"She'll love that." She held up the bottle. "I hope you'll share this with me later."

Mitch grinned. "That sounds promising."

"Could be," she said. "Let me put this in the fridge and we're outta here."

When they arrived at Vee's, the party was in full swing. James Brown was on the box and everybody was on the floor. Star squeezed into the living room, Mitch at her side.

Vee and Paresi were dancing, bumping hips, gliding together, moving apart to the funky beat.

"Well I'll be dipped." Star laughed. "Paresi can dance!"

Mitch helped her off with her coat, and removed his own.

"He's very good," Mitch agreed.

"He always told me he could dance, but I didn't believe him." She clapped her hands, picking up the beat.

"Go Dom, Go Dom, Go Dom," she chanted. The partygoers took up the call.

"Living in America," propelled by James Brown's potent brand of funk, roared from the speakers.

Mitch watched her dancing in place, clapping her hands, shaking her shoulders, moving her hips.

He leaned down, his lips at her ear, so she could hear him above the music. "Go on."

She looked at him. "You don't mind?"

"No," he said. "Give me your coat."

"Okay." She handed over her coat and boogied her way into the center of the room, joining Vee and Paresi.

The chant and clapping picked up: "Go Star, Go Star, Go Star."

Vee's oldest son, Roland, jumped into the mix. Star took him as her partner. The hand clapping and foot stomping rocked the house.

When the music ended, the foursome collapsed on each other, laughing, slapping high fives, and acknowledging the applause.

James Brown gave way to War's "The Cisco Kid." Roland grabbed Star again.

"Come on, Auntie, let's show these hicks where it's at!" They danced off into the crowd.

Vee hung on to Paresi. "I am too old for this!" She laughed.

"Never." Paresi held her to him. He looked up and saw Mitchell Grant.

"Hey, Mitch, Happy New Year, man." He headed for the doctor, with Vee in tow.

"Happy New Year." The two men shook hands. Mitch took Vee's hand in his. He leaned down and kissed her on the cheek.

"Happy New Year, Vee."

"Happy New Year, Dr. Grant." Vee blushed.

"I'm sorry I'm so out of breath, I know I'm a mess!" She fanned herself with one hand.

"No such thing. You're beautiful. In fact, I was admiring you on the floor with my friend here. I had no idea he could dance like that."

"Hey, I come from a long line of street corner guys," Paresi said. "Getting down is in my blood. I can sing, too!"

"No argument here." Mitch smiled.

"Here, let me take these." Vee reached for the two coats he held.

"Thank you." He produced a bottle wrapped in gold foil from beneath the garments. "This is for you."

"Oh, thank you, Dr. Grant, this is very nice of you."

"You're welcome, and please, call me Mitch."

Vee smiled up at him. "Mitch. I'm sorry. You've only told me that a thousand times." She looked at Paresi. "I'll be back in a minute." She turned back to Mitch. "Make yourself at home. The buffet is set up in the dining room, right through there, and the drinks are over there, behind that crowd that's been hanging out at that table since they got here." Vee laughed.

Mitch laughed with her. From his position, he could see over the heads of most of the guests. He leaned forward and glimpsed the dining room table, with the roasted hog's head in the center.

"Maybe later. Thanks."

"You're welcome." Vee headed for her bedroom with the coats.

"You look like you're having a good time," Mitch said to Paresi.

"The best. After all the shit that's gone down this past year, I need to get loose."

"Liberate that wild man, huh?" Mitch said. The two of them laughed.

"You got that right." Paresi looked around the room. "Where's Star?"

"Over there." Mitch nodded.

Paresi turned to see Star and Roland high-stepping to Coolio's "Fantastic Voyage." "She's having a ball," he said. "God knows she needs it."

Mitch watched Paresi watching Star. She had kicked off her shoes, and her body moved in perfect synchronization with Vee's teenage son. The two of them appeared attached to the same string, as they strutted to Coolio's streetwise beat.

"That's some dress," Paresi said.

The tightness was back in Mitch's chest. "Oh yeah." He nodded.

A pretty, petite, cat-faced, inky black woman passed between them. Her close-cropped hair emphasized her big, slightly slanted brown eyes. She was wearing a spangly gold halter top, and a pale cream-colored miniskirt. She grinned up at Mitch.

"Hi."

"Hi," he said, smiling at her.

"I'm Gloria. Who are you?"

"Mitch," he said.

She turned to Paresi. "And you?"

"Dominic."

The woman moved back so that she could see the both of them.

"Very nice." She laughed, and headed toward the bar.

Paresi whistled, watching her walk away, her rear end swaying as she balanced on sparkling gold high heels. "Amazing, ain't it? Women by the yard, and I can only see one."

Mitch didn't say anything. He just looked at Paresi.

The music slowed down, Boyz II Men harmonized on "I'll Make Love to You." Star came back, carrying her black suede slingback pumps in her hand.

"Boy, that Roland can dance! The child would dance me to death if I'd let him." She put her shoes down on the floor, near the hall doorway.

"He's seventeen," Paresi said. "But this kind of music calls for a man with experience." He snaked an arm around Star's waist. "Let's do it."

She looked at Mitch. "The next one's yours."

Mitch nodded. "I'm counting on it."

Star moved onto the floor with Paresi. He put both arms around her and pulled her close. She wrapped both arms around his neck. He said something in her ear, she laughed, and rested her cheek against his.

Mitch watched them, his hands in his pockets. After an eternity, they came back to him.

Star looked around. "Where's our hostess?"

"Probably in her bedroom." Paresi pointed down the hall.

She looked at him with a raised eyebrow, then picked up her shoes and turned to Mitch. "I'll be right back."

Standing at her dresser, Vee was touching up her makeup.

"Hey." Star plopped down on the bed, and put her shoes on.

"Hey, girl." Vee finished reapplying her lipstick and stood back, looking at herself in the mirror.

"You look good, sweetie," Star said. "Red is definitely your color."

"Thanks." Vee patted her stomach. "I'm losing weight." She smiled.

"I don't want to ask why. But I gotta say Paresi looks

way too happy," Star said. "While we were dancing, he told me he's got big plans for you, with the emphasis on *big*."

"I told you, I'm making him work . . . but I think payday might be soon." Vee winked. "He looks so good tonight."

"All right, now." Star laughed. "Just don't kill him. He's got to work day after tomorrow."

"I'll leave enough for him to drag in." Vee laughed. She walked to the bed and picked up Mitch's coat. "I came in here to hang this up, but when I saw myself, I figured I needed a new paint job." She put the coat on a hanger. "I'll bet this is cashmere," she said, stroking the soft fabric.

"It is," Star said. "One hundred percent, count on it."

"Lord have mercy." Vee hung the coat in her closet. "It probably cost more than my whole wardrobe."

"Yours and mine together," Star said.

"Look." Vee picked up the champagne bottle from the dresser. She'd peeled off the gold paper. "It's the good stuff."

"Dom Perignon," Star said. "He's a class act."

"And of course when he came in, I was on the floor acting a fool. Lord, by the time I spotted him, I was sweating like a field hand."

"You look fine. He likes you. He was very happy that you invited him to the party."

"I'm glad. He classes up the joint." Vee touched the tip of her tongue to her finger and smoothed out her eyebrow. "I know I'm gonna be up and down the phone lines tomorrow for having him here, and those very women talking are going to be the ones I saw nearly faint when he walked through the door." She turned to Star. "Did you check out the faces when they spotted him?"

"Um-hmmmm." Star said. "Like feeding time at the zoo."

"You ain't never lied," Vee said. "Hell, even though you see him all the time, you got to say the man is fine!"

"Fine enough to make you slap your mama," Star said. The two of them high-fived each other and burst out laughing.

"Honey, that man will make you knock Mama out!" Vee said. She folded her arms and stared at Star. "He's perfect for you."

"Vee . . ."

"No, he's perfect. He's even taller than you. You still have to look up, even in those heels." She pointed to Star's shoes. "And that face . . . girl, and honey, the man smells like heaven."

"Xeryus," Star said.

"X who?"

"His scent. He wears Xeryus, by Givenchy," Star said softly.

Vee raised an eyebrow. "You know what kind of cologne he wears? Star, what are you waiting on? I don't know why you're hanging back. If you fool around and let some other woman snatch that, I'm gonna have to hurt you myself."

Star didn't answer. She raised her legs and stared down at her shoes, her face glum.

Vee took the hint and picked up the bottle of champagne. "I'm putting this in the fridge for us, after the other folks leave, so y'all stick around."

"You and Paresi can share it. He bought a bottle for us after the party, too," Star said.

"Uh-oh, sookie, sookie now! I like that!" She sat next to Star and took her hand. "Honey, let the old year go. And don't wander off at a minute to midnight. Make sure you're standing next to him."

Star looked at her friend. "I will." She nodded. "Promise."

Carlyle Biggs sat alone in his room, looking out of the window, watching the streetlights reflect on the snow. It was forty-five minutes past eleven. Fifteen minutes to the new year.

He opened a black leatherette-bound photograph album on the table in front of him. His mother, father, and two brothers smiled up at him, along with an image of himself that he almost didn't recognize. The picture had been taken when he was thirteen. One year before his life changed and theirs ended.

He got up and went to the small refrigerator in the corner. He grabbed a can of Dr. Pepper and the plastic-wrapped turkey sandwich on wheat bread that he'd gotten from the deli counter before he left the store.

He sat again at the table, looking outside. Ten minutes had passed. His fingers turned the pages of the family album.

At midnight, the noises started.

Carlyle Biggs finished his sandwich and soda, as he listened to the merriment and cheer from the street. He turned the album's pages, and stopped on a color photograph. As he looked at the picture, his eyes grew wet.

"Happy New Year," he whispered to the image.

Desmond St. John's handsome face smiled up at him.

* * *

The Four Tops' "Still Water" flowed from the stereo as the clock crept toward midnight. Star danced with Mitch. He held her tenderly, enjoying the feel of her body against his.

Vee and Paresi slow-danced on the other side of the room.

Her three children, Roland, Cole, and Lena gathered noisemakers and hats, which they passed out to the party guests.

"It's almost time, Mama," Cole said to Vee.

"I'll say," Paresi whispered in her ear.

She smiled lazily at him and moved away, turning to her fifteen-year-old. "Okay, baby."

She clapped her hands together. "Get ready, folks."

Cole turned off the stereo. Lena turned on the television, and went to her mother and Paresi. She wrapped her arms around Dominic, and leaned her head on his hip. Paresi picked her up.

In Times Square, the countdown had begun. Everyone in the room joined in. Mitch stood with his arm around Star's shoulders.

"Five, four, three, two, one . . . HAPPY NEW YEAR!"

Vee's living room exploded in noise. The combined sounds of "Auld Lang Syne" from the television and her guests filled the room. Everyone began kissing everyone else.

Paresi kissed Lena noisily on the cheek, making her laugh. "*Buon'anno, mia bella* Lena." He put her down and turned to her mother. Lena held on to both of them, still giggling.

Mitch leaned down and kissed Star gently on the lips.

She responded, and wrapped her arms around him. Their kiss deepened.

From across the room, Vee opened her eyes from Paresi's kiss. She remained in his arms, feeling her daughter hugging her hips. She looked over Paresi's shoulder, watching Star and Mitch.

We got this family working at last, she thought to herself. It's gonna be a fine year. She couldn't suppress her radiant smile. Thank you, Jesus. It's about time.

CHAPTER SIX

The first day of the new year found Carlyle Biggs walking the nearly deserted city streets. He volunteered to work at the market, since it was open, but the temp manager decided one worker in the meat department was enough.

He had been up at dawn, looking out of his window. During the night, snow had fallen on the city, and in the pristine whiteness, and with the newness of the year, Carlyle felt he might have a chance, a real chance.

He crossed Andover Street and headed east on Stanfield. He turned the corner. The sight of the shop made him catch his breath.

He stood there on the opposite side of the street, in front of the Walker Brothers Bakery, facing the building. A sign in the window read CLOSED. He knew it would be. The doors had been locked since Desmond died.

Taking a deep breath, he crossed the street. Icy air filled his lungs, numbing him. He stood before the red, hand-lettered sign on the window that read BOTANICA DE ST. ANTHONY. Thoughts and memories raced through his mind. The botanica. Desmond's shop, though very few called it that. Most of the customers named the shop after Desmond. They called it The Hoodoo Man.

He had heard the story of Desmond St. John and the American Dream for as long as he could remember. First from his parents and then from the man himself.

Desmond had arrived in the United States from Haiti, with no friends, no family, no prospects, and just five hundred hard-earned American dollars in his pocket. But the city, like most who came in contact with him, had been good to him from day one.

As he had wandered wide-eyed and awed through the streets of New York City, Desmond discovered that he loved the hot dogs sold from steaming carts on the streets. He also noticed that American women of all ages, colors, shapes, and sizes viewed his gray eyes, handsome ebony-skinned face, and lean and muscular seven-foot-two body as something special.

Frankie Mae Williams, a pretty, small-boned, café-au-lait–colored woman, was his first patron. She was from Clarksdale, Mississippi, but she'd lived in New York long enough to lose her accent and to know that a good man was hard to find.

Frankie Mae had drawn the long, lanky Haitian in her file of new processes at the immigration office. She processed Desmond into the country and into her bed. From her he learned the ways of the city, and in a short time he became a green-card–carrying, working man. He was a bouncer at a dance club in mid-Manhattan.

Desmond soon discovered that Frankie Mae wasn't the only lonely woman in New York City. He did his level best to cheer up as many as he could, and they in turn were extremely grateful *and* generous.

In almost no time he was earning serious money. He took his first real cash and, with Frankie Mae acting as a front, he purchased an old storefront building on Flatbush Avenue in Brooklyn. This became his first botanica.

The American blacks soon began calling him, and his shop, the "Hoodoo Man." Though the Haitians referred to him with reverence as "Papa Legba," he liked the nickname Hoodoo Man. It fit, because in his native Haiti, Desmond had been a *Hounon* of great power.

In his new country, he learned how to invest his money, and juggle his women. He worked his juju, with spells, magic powders, herbs, candles, and oils. Within eight years, Desmond St. John had become an American citizen, and a multimillionaire.

His shops catered to the superstitious and the true believers. His followers believed that his merchandise could bring them luck and love, that his potions and powders could drive evil from the door and curse enemies. They all knew Desmond possessed the gift, and a small bottle of oil or powder touched by his own hands was worth its weight in gold, which was what the people usually paid.

Desmond let it be known that he personally inspected all the juju in his stores. No one ever did the math to figure that if what he said was true, he'd have had no time to do anything else, for the rest of his life.

Desmond opened his first church in Brooklyn two years after his debut shop. From the beginning the church drew capacity crowds, all anxious to sit on the hard seats and breathe the same air as the Hoodoo Man himself.

Word spread of the miracles he performed. True believers and hopefuls came from all parts of the state, black, white, it didn't matter. Desmond was selling, and they were buying—especially the women.

The Biggs family had been among his first disciples, beginning with Carlyle's father.

Mrs. Newbelle Truetta Puckett, his grandmother's next-door neighbor in Metarie, Louisiana, had introduced Carlyle Biggs Sr. to the "old ways" when he was a boy. "Mama True" Puckett claimed to be descended from a long line of spirit-seeing, curse-throwing Dahomey queens. A rotund, blue-black woman, with snow white hair, she had ruled the neighborhood and the Biggs family by voodoo.

She took a liking to the light-skinned Carlyle, calling him her little "red nigger." From her he learned the secrets of luck oil, jinx-killer incense, and strong love oil. Even when he grew up and left Louisiana, Carlyle carried Mama True's teaching with him. He still believed in juju and conjure magic.

Even as a New York City police officer, Carlyle Sr. felt that no harm could come to him, because he wore a charm made of High John the Conqueror Root, Jerusalem Bean, Devil's Shoestring, Blood Root, and Snake Root. Desmond St. John himself had stuffed and sewn the little red flannel bag of protection. He blessed it and hung it around Carlyle's neck, declaring him forever under the protection of the tiger *loa*, Agasu.

Carlyle Jr. stared into the window. On display was a bottle of "Old Indian" clear water. His father had firmly believed that splashing the water on his face before going into court with an arrest assured him a win. He kept a bottle in his locker at the station. In his twelve years on the NYPD, Carlyle Sr. had a perfect record of convictions. He had never lost a case.

Right next to the water sat a jar filled with High John the Conqueror, a twisted, brown, human-shaped root said to grow from the sperm of a hanged man. Next to that, a bottle of van-van oil, an elixir of lemon juice and wood alcohol. A versatile mix, it could be scrubbed onto the floor, sprinkled on charms worn around the neck, or even, in his father's case, rubbed on the soles of the shoes. Any way that it's used, van-van is said to bring luck.

Too bad he had been barefoot and without gris-gris, his favorite protection, on that long-ago Christmas night, Carlyle said to himself.

Next to the oils and roots in neat display were several plaster statues of saints. Carlyle stared at the figure of St. Rita, the patron of children. A statue of the kind-faced saint had been in his and his brother's rooms for as long as he could remember. He closed his eyes, pressed his forehead against the cold glass, and whispered, "Why didn't you help me? Why didn't you help me?"

His parents believed in Desmond St. John. They worshipped at his church, prayed at his feet, and gave him their eldest son. They were totally caught up in the ceremony and the ritual—the part he hated the most.

Carlyle stepped back from the window, sweat suddenly breaking out on his forehead. His eyes moved to a painting displayed in the corner of the window. The same one had hung in his home when he was growing up. It depicted the *loa* Simbi Dleau, the god of spring and fresh water. In this incarnation, the *loa* was portrayed as a snake, said to bring good fortune. At least that's what Carlyle Sr. had believed.

"All his snake pictures, gris-gris, and charms didn't help him one bit. Not one little bit." Carlyle shook his head and looked away from the painting, taking in the rows of candles and bins and jars of powder and oils visible from the window. For a fleeting second, he saw

Desmond. His beautiful, full lips spread, revealing a white, gleaming smile. Carlyle stepped back, trembling, feeling the sensation starting in his spine. His eyes fixed on the spot and then closed, as a familiar, welcome, almost liquid warmth crawled through his body.

"New year, new life, Desmond," he whispered. "New life, new blood." Carlyle Biggs turned his back on the display and, shielding himself from a sudden gust of cold wind, pulled up his coat collar and walked away.

Star awoke to the sound of the telephone. She had been so zonked when she finally went to bed, she had forgotten to shut off the ringer.

"Hello," she mumbled into the receiver.

"Happy New Year."

"Mitchell." She struggled to sit up, dislodging Jake from his warm spot against her back. "Happy New Year."

"I had a great time last night."

She could hear the smile in his voice. She closed her eyes, remembering the champagne, his hands, and the kisses. "Me too," she said.

"I called to ask you if you'd like to have your first meal of the new year with me."

She looked at the clock on her nightstand. "Would that be lunch or dinner?"

"How about both?" Mitch said.

"That sounds wonderful." She sighed, settling back under the covers.

"Hey, wake up," he said.

"I'm awake, I was just thinking about last night."

"I'll bring more champagne, and we can have a repeat performance." She could hear him smiling again.

"Don't you have company? Your daughter is still with you, isn't she?"

Mitch sighed. "She's with her mother. The deal was Christmas with me, and New Year's with Carole Ann. I expect her back tomorrow night, though I doubt she'll show. I'm not high on her list of favorite people."

"How was Christmas, was it bad?"

"I was at Desmond's house," he said. "Remember?"

"You two will get it together, don't give up hope. I'd like to meet her."

"All right, but when you do, keep in mind she's been raised mainly by my ex and a slew of nannies."

"Meaning . . . ?"

"Princess of the realm."

"I see." Jake moved down on the bed and laid across her legs. "Does she know about me?"

"She knows I've got a friend whom I deeply admire," he said, his voice soft.

"That's a start," Star said. "Does she like champagne?"

"I'd like to think she's too young, but knowing her mother's influence and tastes, I'm sure she loves it."

"Maybe you'd better have some handy, when we meet."

"I see your point. I'll have a bottle accessible at all times," he said. "How about I pick you up in an hour?"

"An hour and a half." Star moved the cat off her legs. "I'll be ready."

"See you then."

New Year's Day celebrants crowded Sans Souci restaurant. Most of them sipped black coffee out of elegant navy blue cups trimmed in gold while they tried to recover from New Year's Eve. Mitch and Star sat at a table facing the window, with a view of the Brookport Art Museum and vast, snow-covered gardens. Star sipped a café mocha, looking out at the snowy scene.

He passed a few feet from the window, his collar high, his head down against the wind.

"Son of a gun!" she said, startled.

"What?" Mitch looked up from the menu.

"Carlyle Biggs. Suddenly he's everywhere." She pointed.

Mitch looked out the window, catching the back of the young man walking through the gardens.

"When did he get out?"

"You know him?"

"Know him? His case has fascinated me for years. I even arranged to get photos from the New York City medical examiner's office when it happened. I'd never seen wounds like that, until Desmond St. John."

"Do you still have the photos?" she asked.

"Yes."

"Good." She watched Carlyle until he disappeared in a swirl of wind and snow. "I'm glad you said that about the wounds. It lets me know I'm not crazy. I want to get a warrant and haul him in."

"That could be very dicey." Mitch put his menu down. "The details of his family's shooting were in every paper in the country. We could just have a copycat on our hands, but I'm planning to study the records of Biggs's family against St. John's."

"Want some company?" Star asked.

"Sure." He nodded.

"Today?"

"You know . . ." Mitch leaned close to her, his voice a soft, caressing whisper. "Last night I got the feeling this new year was bringing a fresh, unexplored level to our friendship." He gently glided one fingertip over the back of her hand. "I thought today we'd kind of relax . . ." He looked at her. "Enjoy the holiday . . . and each other."

He was making her shiver, and she couldn't control her eyebrows. They shot up.

Mitch laughed. "What's that look about?"

"Enjoy each other?" she asked, amused.

His smile made her press her thighs together beneath the white tablecloth.

"There's lots of ways to enjoy one another, Lieutenant."

"I know, Doctor," she said, savoring the game. "I'm just wondering if your definition of 'enjoying' is the same as mine."

"Could be," he said.

"Uh-huh." She nodded. "Does your definition include chocolate?"

"Most certainly," he said.

"I mean the kind you eat," she said.

"So do I." His green eyes sparkled mischievously.

Star looked down, feeling the warmth rising in her face.

"Let's start again," she said.

"Okay." He closed his menu, his eyes holding hers. "Today is the first day of the new year. We're both off, we've got an entire day *and* evening to enjoy ourselves, so let's relax and have fun. It's acceptable; in fact, it's encouraged."

"All right," she said. "I'm in your hands."

He stared at her. "That thought positively boggles my mind."

She couldn't meet his eyes. Her gaze shifted to the window. She looked out at the tracks left in the snow by Carlyle.

"It's a new year; I *should* put my priorities in a new order," she said.

"I'm in total agreement." Mitch raised her hand to his lips and kissed it.

She faced him.

Her eyes made him smile. He shook his head, resigned to his fate. "We're going to look at pictures, aren't we?"

"If you don't mind," she said.

He raised a finger. "On one condition."

"Name it."

"We eat something before we slog over to my office."

"Yeah." She grinned. "Sure."

"And . . ."

"And? You said *one* condition."

"Change that," he said. "Two conditions."

"Go on."

"You and I will spend no more than an hour in my office. Afterwards, we head for my place, a nice, cozy fire, some classic Motown, and another bottle or two of champagne, and we'll see what happens. Deal?"

"An hour?" She hesitated. "An hour and a half."

"No room for negotiation," he said. "Deal?" He extended his hand.

She took it.

"Deal."

CHAPTER SEVEN

Three days into the new year and Dominic Paresi sat in the squad room, leaning back in his chair, feet on the desk, studying postmortem color photographs of the Biggs family.

"This is nasty," he muttered.

"Yep." Star looked toward the pile of gruesome photos near her phone. "But the wounds are the same as the ones on St. John. I've done a little digging."

He looked up at her.

"I've also got a bad feeling about that baby."

"The little John Doe?"

"Yep. I took a look at Sperry's reports. It was so awful." She sighed deeply. "Sick."

"You think it's connected?" Paresi asked.

Star shrugged. "Maybe. I talked to Mitchell earlier. He's doing the autopsy today. If there's a link, he'll find it."

"Does he think it's connected?"

"To be honest, Paresi, I don't know."

"But you think it's hooked up some way to Desmond's killing?"

She shrugged. "All I know is that the wounds are horrible. I've never seen anything like it. I just want to be able to rule out a connection, or to prove one, if that's the case."

"Is Sperry okay with all this?"

"Yeah. I think he just wants to be able to close the file on it. It's such a terrible thing, he just wants it gone. Doesn't matter which shift ties it up. Meanwhile . . ." She slid the file she had been reading across their desks. Paresi picked up the manila folder.

"Desmond opened his first shop in Brooklyn over twelve years ago," Star said. "He was a big hit, and he expanded. New York City, Boston, Dorchester, Hartford . . . He covered a lot of the east coast."

"When did the church start?" Paresi looked at the papers in the folder.

"About ten years ago," Star said. "He also established his first church in Brooklyn. It was a monster. By the time he decided to come here, he was a genuine superstar."

"I remember when he arrived." Paresi looked up. "The media went nuts. You'da thought the pope had moved in."

Star nodded. "I'm sure those folks in Clarendon would have preferred that. When he moved in, he was on the news for a week! The neighbors went nuts. They didn't want some voodoo-practicing witch doctor living up the block."

Star swiveled in her chair. "Lord knows being black was scary enough, but a black man with an attitude *and* a bag of magic spells . . . Lord have mercy!"

Paresi put the papers down. "I thought it was pretty funny."

"What did they know?" Star shrugged. "Over seven feet tall, black as midnight. He would have been a really scary brother, if he hadn't been so fine."

"You thought he was good-looking?"

"You kidding? Both Vee and I had a thing for him. We even considered going to a church meeting, just to get a good look at him."

"Get outta town! You're shittin' me, right?"

"No. Not at all." She rocked in her chair, a cat-eating-the-canary grin on her face. "C'mon, Paresi, admit it, he was a compelling, charismatic, good-looking brother."

Paresi shrugged his shoulders. "I didn't see it."

"Well, the women in every town he hit saw it. He had a huge following, and not just blacks and Haitians. White ones dug him too. Everyone just fell in love with him. That's why he decided to settle in Brookport."

"Lucky us." Paresi picked up the pictures on his desk. "I think if this guy could've really seen the future, he'd have bought an island somewhere and gotten as far away from here as possible."

"His living here wasn't all bad," Star said. "He did a lot of good for the community."

"He made a lot of money," Paresi said.

"Yes, and he did the right thing. He put a lot of it back," Star countered.

"So he was great. Tell me about Carlyle Biggs."

She pointed. "Look at the pictures. The whole story's there."

"You think he's our guy?"

"I think he rates a good talking-to, but the D.A.'s office says we've got bumpkus to reel him in."

"For once, I agree with Sean Mallory," Paresi said. "The evidence is all circumstantial. This kid is fresh out of the joint, and, according to the state of New York, rehabilitated. Why would he mess all that up, especially to kill a public figure like St. John, somebody he supposedly worshipped at one time?"

"Just because his family was into Desmond's church, doesn't mean Carlyle bought the goods," Star said.

"Families usually stick together when it comes to religion."

Star shrugged. "Some. Did you know Carlyle's father was a cop? One of New York City's finest?"

"Really?"

"Yeah, and Carlyle dispatched the family with his father's gun."

"No shit?"

Star nodded. "Yep. His father's gun was the murder weapon, and you can see the results of his shooting skills." She pointed to the pictures on Paresi's desk. "Carlyle Biggs Jr., current solid citizen and role model, cutting meat at Brookport Farms Market."

"I shop at Zannucci's," Paresi said.

Mitch steeled himself in front of the tiny body on the table. He had avoided the autopsy for over a week, but he wouldn't assign it to any of his assistants. He'd known from the beginning that he would do it himself. Now that Star had asked him, he couldn't put it off any longer. He checked the body over and over, hoping for any clue that the infant had been stillborn.

Ordinarily he would have placed the child's lungs in a basin of water, and if the lungs floated, he would know that the child had breathed, at least once. But in this case, there were no lungs, or any other traces of viscera. The baby's body cavity had been rinsed clean and then coated with some kind of sweet-smelling oil. After the child's body thawed, the smell of lavender was overwhelming. The tiny body had been stuffed with herbs, bright red fabric, and as yet undetermined pieces of skin that appeared to be reptilian.

Mitch looked down at the tiny, pinched, newborn face. It brought up sad memories of one of his earliest cases. An eight-month-old girl whose drug-addicted father had poured a bottle of lemon furniture polish down her throat to stop her hungry cries. When he'd opened the child's abdomen, the autopsy room had flooded with the smell of lemon. Since then, Mitch had never allowed his cleaning people to use lemon oil or any other lemon-scented cleaner, either here in the building or at home.

In all of his years as a pathologist, he'd seen so much abuse of children that he thought he was immune.

Not a chance.

The morgue was at its busiest on holidays, especially Christmas and New Year's. Family holidays always brought out the worst in people. The morgue operated twenty-four hours a day, year in and year out. Even so, most of the workers tried to take off the week between Christmas and New Year's Day, as well as the week after. So, even though the holidays were officially over, the morgue was still operating, for all practical purposes, with a diminished crew. Still, he didn't want any company for this one. He had waited until the middle of a shift change, to assure privacy.

While workers departed and arrived, Mitch had removed the body from the crypt and found a remote autopsy room, a floor down from the main rooms. He laid the baby gently on the cool, stainless-steel table.

He worked over the small body, speaking into the tiny microphone attached to the V-neckline of his scrubs. The sound of the eternally whirring fans buzzed in his ears. As he spoke, documenting his findings, his voice grew husky with emotion. Mitch walked away from the table, stripped off his latex gloves, and shut off the microphone. He pressed his back against the cool, blue-tiled wall, and wiped the tears from his eyes.

Later that afternoon, as Desmond St. John was being buried, Star stood in front of the squad's fax machine. She'd phoned around and turned up still more information about Desmond, his church, and his followers. When the last page slid out, she took the papers and went upstairs to the lunchroom.

Elvis, the attendant, smiled as she walked in. "I know we're a few days into it, but Happy New Year, Lieutenant," he called out, his voice deep and tinged with a southern accent.

He reminded her of Melvin Franklin, the late original bass singer for the Temptations. He had the same kind of resonant voice that could make your bones vibrate. He also had big sad eyes. If only those eyes didn't wander off in different directions, Star thought, he would be a dead ringer for Melvin, that and the fact that he was white.

She sat down at a table, the papers in her hand. Elvis placed a hot cup of tea in front of her. She looked up. "Oh! Thanks, Elvis."

"I know your routine," he said shyly. "I thought I'd really like serving you your first cup of tea in the lunchroom for the new year."

"That's sweet." She smiled up at him. "Thank you very much." She looked at the cup. "It's even got milk in it."

"Too light?" he asked, concerned.

She sipped it. "Perfect."

"You want a pastry? They're fresh this morning. There's some double chocolate-chip muffins that are really good. I can open the machine."

"You really know me, don't you?"

Elvis blushed.

"Thanks," Star said. "But it's a new year, and I've resolved to cut back on the sweets, even the chocolate. It's beginning to show."

"Not on you," Elvis said, grinning. "You look good, real good."

"Thanks, but when I got on the scale the day after the holidays, I thought somebody was on there with me." She held up the cup. "Just the tea is fine, thank you."

"Okay, Lieutenant, but if you change your mind . . ." Elvis smiled and went back to cleaning the already immaculate table next to her.

"Thanks." Star sipped her tea and read the information on Desmond St. John. By the time she finished, she was convinced that she and Paresi should pay a visit to the Brookport Farms meat department.

The girl and her mother stood in front of the supermarket meat counter. The teenager had dry-looking, curly blond hair, and a puffy, flushed face. She chewed gum with her mouth open. Her mother was busily picking up each rolled roast and carefully scrutinizing it. The girl was giving the same amount of attention to the handsome young black man behind the plate glass window.

Feeling her gaze, Carlyle Biggs turned.

The girl smiled.

He didn't.

* * *

Mitchell Grant sat at his desk in the deserted office suite, still wearing his scrubs, finishing his report on the infant John Doe. He turned off the tape machine. The words wouldn't come.

He stood and walked to the window. It was dark out and beginning to snow again. He pulled up the blinds, unlatched the window, and opened it. A rush of cold air blasted him, making the golden hair on his bare arms stand. He leaned out, supporting his upper body with his hands on the sill, letting the snow fall on his up-turned face.

He couldn't say it. He had to, but he couldn't say it. He felt the soft, cold kisses of the snowflakes on his closed eyes, on his cheeks.

He had to say the word.

The ugly word.

Sacrifice.

CHAPTER EIGHT

It was after seven P.M., and Star and Paresi sat facing each other across their desks. They'd sat through the shift change, poring over the information on Carlyle Biggs and Desmond St. John.

The snow falling outside the window tumbled through the beam from the streetlight, and turned silvery against the night.

"Carlyle shot his family with a Browning M1," Paresi said. "The 935 Hi-Power."

"Right." She nodded. "His father's piece. Desmond was killed with a Desert Eagle .44."

"And, the only thing the two weapons have in common is that they are both weapons of choice for some departments," Paresi said.

Star nodded. "But there are differences. The Eagle is practical. It doesn't have to take special loads, it takes regular .44 rounds. It's economical. So if you were a recent parolee in a new job, a new city, trying to get your act together, wouldn't you opt for economy?"

Paresi laughed. "Makes sense. The Eagle clip holds seven rounds for the .44, and old Desmond just took six, so you'd even have a bonus round left over."

"Works for me," Star said. "Very economical. I say Carlyle didn't learn his lesson. I think he's at it again."

"The D.A.'s office doesn't agree with you," Paresi said. "Circumstantial, no hard evidence, not enough to annoy Carlyle with our pesky questions."

"What if we talk to him off the record," Star said. "You know, you and me, in a friendly manner."

"Are we taking him to dinner?" Paresi said.

The phone on her desk rang. "Homicide, Lieutenant Duvall." She smiled. "Hi, Mitchell, what's up?"

Paresi watched her face, as she listened to whatever the doctor was saying. He didn't like her eyes; something was wrong.

"What?" he said. "What's happened?"

Star held up her hand. "Are you all right? . . . Are you sure?"

"What?" Paresi leaned forward.

Star held the receiver tightly. "Okay . . . okay." She hung up. "I've never heard him like that. He's really upset."

"Why, what's going on?" Paresi asked.

"The baby."

"The Little John Doe?"

"Yeah."

"Tell me," Paresi said.

She looked at him. "Mitchell says the baby was sacrificed."

"Say what?"

Star's voice was strained. She was fighting to push down the emotion kicking in her stomach, rising in her throat. Her eyes teared. "The baby was a human sacrifice."

"Jesus, Mary, and Joseph." Paresi wiped his mouth

with his hand, as if he were tasting something horrible. "What kind of fuck could do this to a kid? A baby, for Christ's sake. Jesus!"

"Let's put Carlyle on the back burner for a minute," she said, her voice cold. "I say we pay a visit to Desmond's church."

"You think they're sacrificing kids?" Paresi's eyes were dark blue and stormy.

"I know they sacrifice animals," she said. "Chickens and goats mostly, and the law lets them do it, it's part of their religion."

"But babies?"

She looked at Paresi. "Let's go see François Dulac. He was the second-in-command, the Hoodoo Junior. He's the big man now. He should be able to come up with some answers."

"How do you feel about this stuff?" Paresi leaned back in his chair. "Do you believe in it? I know your dad's people came from New Orleans—did anybody in your family ever talk about this voodoo-hoodoo crap?"

Star nodded. "Yep. My Great-Granma Queen Esther."

"Queen Esther?" Paresi said. "Her name was Queen Esther?"

"Yeah, Queen Esther, but everybody pronounced it like one word, 'Queenesta.' She was named for the queen in the Bible. Queen Esther. When she was born, giving kids biblical names was the way to go. Her husband was Nabob."

"And I thought my family had the corner on stupid names," Paresi said.

"She was Pop's grandmother. She was really superstitious. She believed people could work spells on you. When I was little, she would braid my hair, then she'd burn any hair that came out in the comb and brush. She also cautioned me never to let anybody get ahold of my nail clippings. She believed anything that came from your body could be used to harm or even kill you. Whenever she clipped my toenails and fingernails, she'd burn the clippings too." Star shook her head. "I was twenty-three years old before I stopped doing my own manicures and pedicures."

"She ever give you any tips?"

"I remember some things she used to say. She had potions for everything. If you had a cold, or an upset stomach, Great-Granma Queen was on the case, with her herbs and stuff."

"What about working on other people?" Paresi asked.

"She showed me her spell books, you know, for making juju."

Paresi looked at her inquiringly. "So does that mean I should be searching your desk for a little wax man that looks like me?"

"Not to worry. I'm not into it. I just grew up hearing about it. Vee, too."

"Oh God," Paresi said. "Don't tell me that."

"What are you scared of, as long as she doesn't have any of your hair, nails, or . . ." she smiled wickedly at him, "body fluid."

"Christ."

He eased back in his chair. "Tell me more about Great-Granma Queen."

"Like I said, she had a potion for everything. Her house always smelled of this sweet incense. She was about a hundred when we were kids, and Vee was terrified of her. She was blind from cataracts, so her eyes were white. She always wore white and kept her hair tied up in a white scarf. When we were little, Vee was convinced she was a haint."

"A haint?"

"That's the way the old folks said 'haunt,' you know, a ghost," Star said.

"Was she?" Paresi asked.

"No." Star laughed. "She was a sweet old lady who loved her only grandson and his family. Pop used to say she couldn't see the present, but she surely could see the future."

"Did she teach you anything?"

"How to play 'Ain't Misbehavin' ' on the piano, that's about it. She was no voodoo queen, Paresi, just an old woman from New Orleans. But she did tell me once how to lay a charm to get my way."

Paresi's left eyebrow raised.

"She told me to smile at my daddy. It always worked." She picked up her coat. "C'mon, fearless, we're going to see François."

Paresi loosened his tie, and unbuttoned the top two buttons of his shirt. He pulled a gold cross on a chain from beneath his clothes and positioned it so that it was visible against his tie.

Star watched him button his shirt, tighten his tie, and carefully position the cross.

"Expecting vampires?" She grinned.

"You never know." Paresi fingered the gold cross, making sure it hung correctly. "Think of this as a condom for the soul."

CHAPTER NINE

François Dulac sat staring at the two detectives seated in his office. He noted with a grim, yet hidden amusement, that neither of them had touched the cups of tea he had poured for them.

"Surely, Lieutenant Duvall, you cannot be thinking that this church would have anything to do with something so vile as human sacrifice." His voice was cold.

"I'm not accusing you or your followers of anything—"

"Desmond's followers," François interrupted. "He is still the head of this church."

"Okay," Star said. "Desmond's followers. I understand."

"No, Lieutenant. No. You do not understand." Dulac stood. "You are insulting me and my people, as well as the memory of all that Desmond St. John stood for." His eyes blazed at Star.

She didn't flinch.

"We are not savages, dancing in the moonlight, no matter what the films or the books say. You *should* understand, but you don't. Your ignorance of your own people is appalling. We are practicing our religion. This country guarantees us the right to do just that."

"First of all, Mr. Dulac," Star said, her eyes just as

fiery, "I am *not* an ignorant person, and I take offense at your statement. I *know* who I am and where I came from. I'm not trying to malign you or your beliefs. I'm a police officer, conducting an investigation into a homicide and the slaughter of a child."

"We do not sacrifice babies," François Dulac said. "As a woman of color, you must know that we as a people value our children and love them unconditionally."

"Right now, Mr. Dulac, my only color is blue. I don't want to discuss African-American child rearing with you." She reached into her purse and pulled out the color photograph of the infant that she'd gotten from Lieutenant Sperry. "Whatever I believe is not the issue." She laid it on his desk. "This is."

François Dulac's dark skin actually blanched. He put his hand over his mouth.

"Dear God, who could do such a thing?" He looked incredulously at Star. "No one in this church could do this."

Star picked up the photo. "Thank you."

She and Paresi stood.

"Again, Mr. Dulac, I apologize if you're offended by this investigation, but you can see why we want to find whoever is responsible for this."

"Yes." François's hands shook. "Oh yes. I too apologize, Lieutenant. Perhaps all of our wounds are too new to warrant close inspection. Please forgive me. My people and I will help in any way we can. But . . ."

He raised a cautionary finger, and shook it close to her face. Star fought down the impulse to break it. "I will not allow our church to be held up to ridicule and stupid accusations."

She turned to Paresi. "Let's go."

"Gladly." He pulled on his scarf.

They walked to the door. Star turned and faced Dulac.

"Oh," Star said, turning to face Dulac. "Are you aware that Carlyle Biggs is now living in Brookport?"

"Should I know this individual?" François asked.

"He was a member of your church in New York," she said.

"Was he? New York is the site of one of Desmond's earliest churches. Brooklyn. He started there, you know, his first church *and* his first shop."

"I know," Star said, buttoning her coat. "This young man is from Manhattan. He and his entire family were members of that first church."

"Have they now moved here, to Brookport?" François asked.

"Only Carlyle." Star pulled on her gloves. "He's the only one left." She stared at the small man. "He killed the others."

François Dulac's face remained calm. "How unfortunate and terrible. When did this happen, may I ask?"

"About seven years ago," Star said. "He was a juvenile then, just fourteen. He did his time and he's been judged rehabilitated and released. For some reason he has chosen to live here in Brookport."

"Seven years ago, I was living in Port-au-Prince, Lieutenant," Dulac said calmly. "I've only been in America just about three years."

Star nodded. "Legally, I'm sure."

"Would you like to see my green card?"

"Not necessary. We'll be in touch."

The next morning, Captain Lewis was back at his desk, after a two-week vacation. He waved the detectives into his office as soon as they arrived.

"Have a seat, you two."

They sat.

"Did you enjoy your holiday, sir?" Star asked.

"Everything was fine until Christmas night. It went downhill from there."

"Sorry you had to interrupt your time off to call in, Cap'n," Paresi said dryly.

"A cop is a cop, Sergeant, even on the holidays."

"Yes, sir," Paresi said, enjoying the rise.

"What's going on with this case, Star?"

She opened her notebook. "So far, we haven't really been able to tie the baby's death with St. John's, but the connection appears obvious."

"Obvious can be deceiving, Lieutenant," Lewis said. "What else?"

"Nothing much. We've been sharing information with Sperry's crew, since the baby was originally their case."

"I see." Lewis sat back in his seat. "Baby killing is rough; you think you're up to this?" he said to Star.

If anybody else had asked her that, she'd have been pissed. But she knew Lewis's concern was real. Last summer, he'd seen her through her worst case, ever.

"I'm fine, Captain."

"Glad to hear it." He leaned forward in his chair. "Still, it never hurts to have another face at the table. I've got a detective, who has volunteered some assistance, coming in tomorrow from New York City."

"Any particular reason?" Star asked.

"Yes. A minister who sat on the parole board, and a New York City juvenile judge were murdered just before Thanksgiving last year. Both of them were shot in a cross pattern."

"Do you know what kind of weapon?" Paresi asked.

"A Glock .17," Lewis said. "In both cases."

"Another cop gun," Paresi said to Star.

"What?" Lewis said.

"A cop gun." Paresi leaned forward. "Carlyle Biggs's family was wiped out with a Browning M1-935, St. John with an Eagle .44, and now you're saying the two in New York bought it with a Glock .17. They're all cop guns."

"Good, Paresi. Very good." Lewis nearly smiled. "Have you two talked to Carlyle Biggs? I understand he's living here now."

"We haven't questioned him yet," Star said. "We don't have enough evidence to bring him in. If we try, he can scream harassment."

"Not that we'd ever harass such an upstanding citizen," Paresi said.

Lewis smiled in spite of himself. "I expect my officers to be fair." He opened his desk drawer. "I did some checking myself, over the holidays. I've got an old friend at One Police Plaza. He told me Carlyle booked out of New York for Brookport almost immediately after he was freed."

"We know that," Star said. "I think he came here because Desmond St. John had made Brookport his home. Carlyle was a lifelong disciple."

"Yeah, but he didn't go to the church here," Paresi said. "We've been in contact with the new head hoodoo."

"Dulac," Lewis said.

"Boy, Captain," Star said. "Did you have any holiday fun? Sounds like you spent a lot of time checking into this thing."

"There's no such thing as a furlough when one of the city's most prominent citizens gets popped, and your detectives are facing down civilians on the six o'clock news, Lieutenant."

Star blushed. "Yes, sir."

He slid the manila folder he'd taken from his desk drawer across to her.

"Carlyle?" she asked.

"The records show that he has been living here, practically since his release," Lewis said.

"Wait a minute," Star said. "These murders happened a *year* ago, November. Right?"

"Yes," Lewis said.

"Wasn't Biggs still locked up then?"

"For all intents and purposes, but because he'd shown such good behavior, he was released for the Thanksgiving holiday. In fact, Carlyle had dinner with the minister who was killed, and his family."

"So you're saying after dessert he just whacked the guy?" Paresi said. "What? Not enough whipped cream on his pumpkin pie?"

Lewis leaned forward in his chair. "According to the wife, dinner went well, no incidents. They had taken an interest in Carlyle, because they both felt he was a good boy inside."

"Just confused," Paresi muttered derisively.

"Right." Lewis nodded.

"After dinner, and a couple of games of Monopoly, the minister drove Carlyle back to the juvenile detention center. He never made it back home.

"The next day, when the cops showed up at his doorstep, his wife said he'd called the night before, shortly after he'd left the house with Carlyle. She said he told her he was meeting somebody and he'd be back. His body was discovered in the woods, about a mile from his house."

"Wasn't his wife worried, when he didn't come home?" Star asked.

"I guess she was used to his seeing parishioners and needy souls, and working all hours, so she went to bed. By the next morning, when the local cops woke her up, he'd been out in the snow all night. By the time they were able to thaw him out, it was impossible to pinpoint the time of death."

"Where was the solid citizen?" Paresi asked.

Lewis indicated the folder in Star's hand.

"In custody. Carlyle said the reverend took him to the detention center, signed him in, and left. The guards backed up his story. They said he was in the lockup at about eight o'clock, Thanksgiving night. The cops couldn't prove anything. Without an accurate TOD, they were spitting in the wind, and with witnesses backing Carlyle, they had zip."

"Was he questioned?" Star asked.

"Yes. As a matter of record, he was questioned, and so were his guards. The house captain said he did the room check at about 8:10, and another one at about eleven. He said he talked to Carlyle at the earlier check. Carlyle told him how much he'd enjoyed having Thanksgiving dinner with the reverend and his family. When the house captain checked him at eleven, he was sleeping."

He pointed to the folder. "The statements are all in there."

"So, what about the other one? You said the judge bought it too, right?" Paresi asked.

"Right." Lewis looked at Star. "That's another reason Carlyle was cleared. The judge was killed the same night.

He lived alone, so the body wasn't found for a few days. Everybody thought he'd gone out of town for the holidays. But he'd stayed home. There was no way Carlyle could have done both murders. He'd been seen by guards, and was in for the evening room checks."

"So the NYPD figured they had a copycat, right?" Star said.

"Right." Lewis nodded.

"The detective who's coming in from New York worked on Biggs's original case, and the shootings of the judge and the minister. We've set up a meeting tomorrow morning at eight sharp. Be here," Lewis said.

"No problem." Star looked at the file. "Is this our copy to work with?"

"Yes. Take it with you and go over the information tonight, so that we can hammer out a workable plan in the morning."

Lewis waved them out of his office.

"Okay, Captain, we'll get on it," Star said. She and Paresi headed for the door. She stopped and turned to Lewis. "Happy New Year, Captain."

"Let's hope so, Lieutenant, let's hope so."

CHAPTER TEN

The clock above Captain Lewis's head ticked loudly, filling the silence in his office with urgency.

Star looked up. 8:25 A.M. She looked at Paresi. He moved slightly, almost imperceptibly, studying Lewis. He looked back at his partner, laughter showing in his azure eyes.

The captain was very engrossed in stirring more cinnamon and nutmeg into his morning black coffee.

"The sergeant will be here any minute, Paresi," Lewis said without looking up.

"I didn't say anything, Cap'n," Paresi said.

"I still heard you, loud and clear." Lewis continued stirring his coffee. He had just taken his first sip when the long-awaited New York City detective walked in.

"Captain Lewis." The detective walked past Paresi and Star, without a glance.

"Sergeant Werner." Lewis stood, his hand extended.

"I'm so sorry I'm late." The detective shook his hand. "I don't know the city and I tried to get here on my own. Big mistake."

The detective smiled, a big, wide, toothy grin.

"Not a problem." Lewis smiled back, and indicated

Star and Paresi. They stood. "These are the two detectives working on the St. John case."

The sergeant turned to face them.

"Troops, this is Sergeant Lisel Werner, NYPD." Lewis looked like a proud papa showing off his firstborn.

Star's immediate impression was that this was the whitest white woman she'd ever seen.

Lisel Werner's hair was platinum blond and hung from beneath her black fedora in a straight blunt cut, resting on her shoulders. Her skin seemed nearly transparent in its whiteness. Star could tell the woman would have had no visible lashes or brows without the generous layers of brown mascara and eyebrow pencil.

Her pale blue eyes regarded the two of them with faintly disguised amusement. The only color in her face came from the bright crimson lipstick spread over her wide, generous lips.

She was about five foot seven and she wore high-heeled, black leather boots. Her leanness and the heel of the boot made her appear taller.

She nodded at Star. "You're Starletta Duvall."

"Yes," Star said. Her eyes never left Lisel's pale face.

"I've heard a lot about you." She aimed her smile at Star.

"All good, I'm sure," Star said unsmilingly.

"Absolutely." Lisel beamed. She walked a few steps toward Paresi. The smile became predatory. "Dominic Paresi."

"Yeah." He extended his hand.

Lisel shook it, holding it longer than necessary.

"You two are quite a team." She grinned. "I hear you know each other so well that words aren't always necessary for you to communicate."

"That's true," Paresi said.

"Like a couple that's been married for a long time," Lisel said. "The connection shows." She moved closer to Paresi, resting her hand on his chest. Her pale eyes sparkled. "I hope you and I can get that close."

Star rolled her eyes. Lewis caught the gesture. She stared at him defiantly.

"Lisel, let me take your things." Lewis moved from behind his desk. "Can I get you some coffee?"

"Oh yes, please." She removed her long black overcoat and hat. Her bangs were cut as straight and severely as the rest of her hair. "No sugar, light cream."

"Coming up." Lewis hung up her coat and hat and headed out into the squad room, toward the coffeemaker.

Star looked at Paresi. In her fifteen years on the job, she'd never seen Lewis get coffee for anyone. She leaned close to him and whispered, "Did he say Lisel or Lethal?"

Paresi coughed to cover his laugh.

Lisel settled into the vacant chair in front of Lewis's desk. She wore a tight-fitting black turtleneck sweater and a slim, short black wool skirt over opaque black stockings. Her boots reached to her knees.

She smiled at the two detectives as they sat down. Paresi returned the smile. Star didn't.

"So, Lieutenant Duvall," she said. "How do you like to be addressed? Starletta or Star?"

Lieutenant Duvall is fine, Star said to herself.

"Star," she said out loud.

"I guessed as much. The name suits you." Lisel shot her another phony smile. "And you?" She leaned toward Paresi. "Dominic, or do you have some colorful nickname?"

"Like Dominic the Destroyer," Star muttered.

Paresi swallowed a laugh. "Well, my sisters call me Nicky, but you can call me Dominic or Dom." He pointed to Star. "She calls me Paresi."

"And what do you call her?" Lisel said, teasingly.

"The boss," Star said.

Paresi laughed. Lisel smiled.

"Here you go, Detective." Lewis came back. He handed her a mug of coffee. "No sugar, light cream."

She sipped it. "Mmmmmm, perfect."

"Now, to business." Lewis sat down in his chair. "Why don't you bring my people up to speed on what you know about Carlyle Biggs."

Lisel held her coffee mug in her lap, with both hands wrapped around it, as if for warmth. Star noted that her nail polish matched her lipstick, and showed up the blue veins in her pale hands.

"Gladly." She turned to Star. "You might want to take a few notes."

Star said nothing.

Lisel swung her long, blond hair from her face. Star's teeth went on edge.

"I was a juvie officer, assigned to the Biggs case six years ago," Lisel said. "I worked extensively with Carlyle. It was very hard, not only because of the savagery involved in the killings, but because his father, Carlyle Senior, and I had been friends. Carl was one of a handful of men to give me support when I first joined the department." She looked at Star. "You understand how men can be when they feel threatened."

Star's face remained emotionless.

"At any rate," Lisel continued, "I was assigned this case. I fully expected to find Carlyle Junior a raving lunatic, out of his mind. Instead, he's actually a very sweet and charming kid. The murders came from his being unable to stand any more of the abuse that was being heaped on him."

"What kind of abuse?" Paresi asked.

"Physical and emotional. The investigation into the killings proved that Carlyle had suffered greatly. He had been unmercifully beaten and savaged by his father."

"Any particular reason the father took out his anger on Carlyle?" Star said.

Lisel took a sip of her coffee. "No one knows exactly why Carl hated the boy. He was ashamed of him, that much was known."

"Why?" Paresi asked.

"Because Carlyle was different, not at all like him. He was a quiet, bookish boy, the total opposite of his father."

"You knew his father; would you say he was a Neanderthal?" Star said.

Lisel turned toward her. "I adored Carl. He was a sweetheart to me." Her face warmed with the recollection. "He was my personal guardian angel during my early years on the job. That's why it was so difficult for me to relate to the image of the man that came out in the investigation."

"Was there tangible evidence that Carlyle had been brutalized?" Paresi asked.

"Yes." Lisel nodded, and sighed deeply. "It was the saddest thing. Relatives from both Carl's and Charlotte's families came forward. They told horror stories of the way he'd treated his son. I can have the transcripts sent to you, if you want to read them."

"No need," Star said. "We get the picture."

"It was awful," Lisel said. "Some of the things he did were brutal."

"What about the other boys?" Lewis leaned forward. "Does the record show abuse with them?"

"Yes," Lisel said. "But not as severe. They were young, and they didn't fight him. Carlyle fought, for his brothers as well as himself."

"What about the mother?" Paresi said.

"Charlotte was no help. She let Carl do whatever he wanted. I think she was as afraid as her children."

"So Carlyle finally hit the breaking point," Paresi said.

"Yes. His father had beaten him Christmas Eve, over some tiny infraction, and the taunts and anger had continued into Christmas Day. That night, the boy just snapped."

She sipped her coffee, leaving a red lipstick print on the rim of the cup. "Carlyle confessed. He had no choice. He was caught red-handed by the next-door neighbor while he was loading the bodies into the family van. The man had awakened after midnight and went to the kitchen for a snack. He saw the lights on in Carl's garage, and he went over to investigate."

She turned to Captain Lewis. "Carlyle didn't even try to hide, or fight. He just gave up. That's the kind of kid he is. He didn't really want trouble. He had just been pushed beyond his limits."

"What happened to him in juvie?" Star asked.

"For the first time in his life, he had a safe place. He was a model prisoner. He did a lot of work with the other boys, passing on his skills, teaching them to work with computers. In fact, Reverend Tilton, the minister with whom Carlyle had that fateful Thanksgiving dinner, was one of the boy's biggest supporters. He was so taken with Carlyle that he petitioned to have Carlyle move in with him and his family when he was released."

"Did this Tilton guy think that Carlyle had honestly been abused by his family?" Paresi said.

"Yes. Max was quite an advocate for Carlyle. He believed that the Biggs family had greatly contributed toward their eventual ends."

"In other words, they got what they deserved," Star said.

For the first time, she noted color in Lisel's face.

"Max himself came from a violent childhood background, Lieutenant, and so he was more than willing to stand on the side of the underdog."

"I can understand that, but it seems to me there must have been other options besides wiping out your whole family," Star said coldly.

"Maybe," Lisel said. "But for Carlyle, it was the only way."

There was an awkward silence.

"Why did he kill the rest of his family?" Paresi asked. "His beef was with his father, right?"

"It was Christmas, everybody was home," Star said.

"No, Lieutenant, it wasn't like that." Lisel's voice was hard-edged. "He killed his mother because he felt that she should have protected him. He was angry at her for never standing up to his father. His brothers died because he couldn't take care of them. He knew he'd either leave town or be caught and go to jail. He couldn't stand the idea of those two boys in foster care."

"Oh, I see. The cemetery is far superior," Star said.

"Whatever the reason, Biggs did what he did," Lewis said. "The question at hand is whether or not he's done it again."

Star sat back in her chair and turned away, looking out of the window.

"He snapped," Lisel said in Star's direction. "It's as simple as that. Carlyle was pushed to the breaking point and he broke. He went through extensive therapy and he's made a completely new person out of himself. That's why he was released."

"Swell," Star said.

Lisel sighed and turned her attention to Captain Lewis.

"Did you know that Carlyle was a member of Desmond St. John's church?"

"Yes," Lewis said. "My detectives are aware of his affiliation. In fact, yesterday they had a lengthy talk with François Dulac, the new head of the church."

Lisel turned to Star. "Did he have anything interesting to say?"

"We saw him on another matter. An infant John Doe, who appears to have been sacrificed around the same time that Desmond was murdered," Star said, still looking out of the window.

"A baby? Sacrificed? I didn't know about that," Lisel said.

Star opened the file folder she'd been holding on her lap. She handed Lisel the photo she'd shown François Dulac.

"Oh my God!" The sergeant's hand shot to her mouth. "My God. This is the most terrible, revolting thing I've ever seen." She looked at the detectives. "Who could do something like this?"

"That's what we're working to find out," Star said. "We're trying to see if any of this ties in with St. John's death. Our medical examiner, Dr. Grant, has ruled that the baby was a sacrifice." Star took the picture back and put it inside the folder.

"Grant? Mitchell Grant?" Lisel asked.

"Yes," Star said. "Do you know him?"

"By reputation, only. I'm so looking forward to meeting him. I've followed his career quite closely. He's something of a superstar when it comes to forensic pathology."

"Yeah," Star said.

"Does he feel that a connection of the two deaths is possible?" Lisel asked.

"He hasn't said it," Star answered. "But it seems that a sacrificed infant and the death of a so-called voodoo priest just might be hanging on the same string."

"We'll find out." Lisel turned to Lewis. "Do you think it would be possible for me to talk with Dr. Grant today?"

Lewis pointed at Star. "You'll be working with Lieutenant Duvall and Sergeant Paresi, so I don't think it will be a problem."

Star didn't say anything. She looked at Paresi, and her eyes spoke volumes.

He didn't like what he read.

"Excellent." Lisel beamed. "I can hardly wait."

"Welcome aboard," Lewis said, standing and walking around his desk. "Sergeant Werner is probably the only person who knows Biggs inside and out. She's going to be a lot of help in this investigation."

"Great," Star muttered.

Lisel stood. "I'm so anxious to get started." She shook Lewis's hand. "Thank you for bringing me here." She pulled him into an awkward embrace that reddened his face like a two-year-old's. It surprised and yet pleased him, a fact that was not lost on Star.

"We're grateful you came," he said softly.

Lisel turned beaming to the detectives, her words directed to Star. "Why don't we get me a desk, and get on the phone to Dr. Grant. Maybe he'll make time for me this morning."

"I'll get right on that," Star said, and walked out of the office.

"Talk to you later, Captain." Lisel took her coat and hat from the rack and hooked her arm through Paresi's.

"Looks like I'm in your hands, Dominic." She smiled at him, and ran her free hand over his bicep. "Don't hold back on me now, because I'm the new girl. I like to work hard, and I'm not afraid to sweat, so pile it on."

Paresi was glad Star was out of earshot.

CHAPTER ELEVEN

Mitchell Grant sat at his desk, listening to Lisel Werner enumerate case after case with which he had been involved.

"Honestly, Dr. Grant," she said, leaning toward him in her chair. "I know I sound like some kind of groupie, but I've been fascinated by your work over the years. Your skill, your expertise. You're exceptional, outstanding. I've learned so much from your published papers and case studies. I'm just thrilled to finally meet you at last."

"Thank you," Mitch said. "I appreciate your enthusiasm."

Don't we all, Star thought.

Lisel sat back in her chair for the first time since they'd entered Mitchell Grant's office.

Star caught the look in her eyes as the officer slowly let her pale blue gaze travel over Mitch, coming to rest on the shock of golden chest hair showing from the V-necked cut of his green scrubs.

Wait'll she catches him in civilian clothes, Star said to herself. I'll have to hose her down.

Lisel kept talking. "Excuse me for getting so carried away, I can't help myself. This work is so difficult and emotionally draining, and to see someone of your caliber consistently producing on such a high level is just inspiring."

She actually hunched her shoulders, like a schoolgirl facing her biggest crush. "I'm really excited." She beamed.

A smile flitted across Star's lips as she anticipated Mitch's secretary, Lorraine, returning from her Christmas vacation. She couldn't wait to see the fight, bimbo to bimbo.

"Thank you, Sergeant Werner, for such high praise. I appreciate it, and please, call me Mitch."

"Mitch." Lisel purred the name.

Oh, brother! Star said to herself. Puh-leese!

Mitch turned to her. "Anything new with St. John?"

"Nope." Star shook her head. "Sergeant Werner brought additional background information from New York, and news on the two men involved in the original Biggs case—the judge who tried the case, and a minister who counseled Carlyle. They were murdered a year ago, Thanksgiving."

"I know about that." Mitch turned to Lisel. "I read some reports back when it happened. Carlyle was still in custody at the time, as I recall."

"Yes," Lisel said. "He was questioned, of course, but there was no way he could have been involved."

"Hadn't he actually shared Thanksgiving dinner with the minister and his family?" Mitch asked.

"Yes." She nodded. "That's right. Reverend Tilden took Carlyle back to the facility and was killed later that night."

"Carlyle was eliminated as a suspect, wasn't he?"

Mitch said. "Although the method of killing was practically identical to the original murders, cross-pattern shots and all."

"The murders were written off as copycat," Lisel said. "No arrests?"

"No. No leads, no nothing." Lisel shook her head. "There hadn't been any more killings of that sort, until this Christmas, the killing of Desmond St. John." She looked at Paresi and Star. "I know that Brookport PD considers Carlyle their major suspect, but I don't agree. When I heard about this murder, I did some checking. Carlyle has led an exemplary life since being freed. He has a job, he's staying out of trouble, and to be honest, he never really was a problem. He's a nice kid, who was pushed too far. I personally believe he's atoned for his crimes, and is trying just to get on with his life."

"Copycat?" Mitch asked.

"I'd say so," Lisel said. "The details of the original murders were highly publicized. Still, this Desmond St. John case appears to put Carlyle back in the hot seat."

"I think we should haul him in for questioning." Paresi leaned back on the sofa, resting his feet on the coffee table. "We've danced around this guy long enough. It's time to move."

"Does the D.A. agree?" Mitch said.

"Nope, but since when do we care about that?"

Mitch and Star laughed.

Lisel looked shocked. "Are you saying you don't care about operating outside the system, Dominic?" she asked seriously.

"Paresi's respect level for most politically appointed decision makers isn't the highest," Mitch said.

"Except for you, Doc, you're my idol."

Everyone laughed, except Lisel.

"Idol or not," Mitch said, "I think we should do this one by the numbers. The courts are getting more lenient instead of the other way around. If Carlyle *is* involved and we miss dotting an *i*, or crossing a *t*, he'll travel."

"Probably in some bureaucrat's limo," Paresi said. "Okay, I'm with you, but I'm entitled to my opinion." He flexed his back and shoulders. "Mitch, you got any food around here? I'm starving."

"Paresi, you had three chocolate donuts and two coffees, not a half hour ago," Star said.

Mitch turned to Lisel. "Sergeant Paresi's appetite is legendary in this department."

"So's yours," Lisel said, her skin suddenly reddening.

Star's mouth dropped.

Mitch looked amused. He leveled his emerald gaze at Lisel. "Don't believe it." He turned back to Paresi. "Sorry, Dom, since Lorraine's out, I've been lax about the goodies. She'll be back on Wednesday."

"Well, I guess I'll have to hit Jessie Mae's for breakfast," Paresi said.

"Sounds good," Mitch agreed. "I have an autopsy scheduled for later this morning, but I think I'll go along." He looked at Lisel. "It'll give us a chance to get acquainted in a more relaxed atmosphere."

"What is Jessie Mae's?" Lisel asked.

"A soul kitchen, down on King Street, by the wharf. The best southern cooking in the city," Star said, standing.

"Soul food?" Lisel made a face. "Isn't that awfully heavy?"

"Nah." Paresi stood up. "It's good for you, puts hair on your chest."

"Why don't I get changed and meet you down there," Mitch said.

"Okay." Star pulled on her coat. "I think we could all use a good breakfast."

"Before we go," Lisel said, "I was hoping to see the baby Star told me about, if it's still here."

"The baby's downstairs," Mitch said. "He hasn't been claimed. We can go down after breakfast."

"You sure you want to do that?" Lisel looked at Mitch. "Won't that be disturbing?"

"To be honest, Sergeant Werner, there's no good time to see a slaughtered child. But I think after we've relaxed a little, it will be easier," he said.

"Eat light," Star advised her. "C'mon, Paresi, there's some cheese grits and eggs calling my name." She wrapped her scarf around her neck. "Coming, Sergeant Werner?"

"Yes, of course . . . unless Dr. Grant would like some company." She turned to Mitch. "I'd really like to ride with you, if that's all right."

"If you don't mind waiting until I've changed." He stood.

Lisel settled back down in her chair. "I'll wait."

Star looked at Paresi. "Suit yourself," she said. "We'll see you there." She and Paresi moved toward the door.

"Star?" Mitch called her.

"Yeah?" She turned.

"Tell Jessie to fire up the waffle iron. I'm in the mood for buttermilk waffles and hot sausages," he said.

Star nodded. "Done."

Lisel Werner watched Mitch's face. He waited until he could no longer see Star before he turned to her.

"Be ready in a minute." He headed for the dressing room off his office. "Make yourself comfortable."

Lisel crossed her legs and wondered just how well the doctor and Lieutenant Duvall knew each other.

Later, downstairs in the morgue, the easy style of breakfast disappeared. Jason Williams laid the tiny, cold body on the steel examining table. When he uncovered it, the officers gasped.

Under the bright, glaring lights, the baby's wounds were even more horrifying.

"This is ghastly." Lisel put her hand over her mouth.

"It's rough." Mitch, back in scrubs, pulled on his latex gloves. "I haven't been able to discern whether or not the wounds were postmortem. All the viscera were removed, and without it, I have no way to tell if this child ever breathed."

"My God." Lisel's face grew paler. "Where's the ladies room?" she gasped.

"Down the hall to the left," Star said.

Lisel ran from the room.

"There goes breakfast," Paresi said.

"Juvie ain't Homicide," Star said dryly, turning away. Her own heart was beating a rapid tattoo in her chest. She'd become almost accustomed to the horrific photo, but this, this was far worse than the picture.

Paresi moved closer to the little body on the table. "This *is* really bad, Doc. The pictures were terrible, but this . . ."

"Yes," Mitch agreed. "It's a horror show."

"I've got nieces, you know." Paresi's voice was husky. "I've taken care of them since they were . . ." His voice failed.

"I know what you mean," Mitch said. "I'm a father. I've changed my share of diapers, too."

"You okay with this?" Paresi turned to Star.

She looked toward the door. There was no sign of Lisel. She wiped her eyes. "No." She looked at the child. "What kind of person could do this . . . a baby . . ." She turned away.

Mitch signaled for a drape. Jason handed one to him. He gently covered the infant.

"I've been able to identify the cavity contents. That might give us something." He turned to his attendant. "You can put him back, Jason, thanks."

"Okay, Doc." The young morgue attendant tenderly folded the plastic drape around the tiny corpse.

"Is there a report?" Star said.

Mitch peeled off his latex gloves and tossed them into the waste container. "Yes, let's go to my office. We can talk about it there."

Lisel came back just as they reached the door.

"We're going upstairs," Mitch said.

She nodded, her face even paler.

In the office they sat in silence. Mitch pulled out the lab report file on the infant.

Lisel finally spoke. "I'm sorry. I saw the photos, but I wasn't prepared . . ."

"No problem, Sergeant," Mitch said. "We've all been at this a long time and this one has been hard for all of us."

"Still," she said, "I apologize for not behaving professionally."

"You didn't puke on his shoes," Paresi said. "That's professional."

His words broke the tension, everyone laughed.

"Consider yourself initiated," Mitch said, sitting down. He opened the file. "The lab says the infant's body cavity was swabbed down with a lavender-based oil."

Lisel interrupted. "Please forgive me, but I have to ask. What's going to happen to the baby?"

Mitch looked at her. "No one's come forward to claim him. More than likely, the arrangements will be handled by the Commonwealth."

"I'd like to pay for the funeral."

Lisel's words shocked them.

"What?" Star said.

"That poor baby deserves a proper burial," Lisel said. "He's suffered enough, the least I can do is make sure something is done right for him."

"That's very kind of you, Sergeant Werner," Mitch said, "but . . ."

"I can't stand to think of the pain he must have endured." Lisel shuddered. "He must have suffered terribly."

"So far, I haven't been able to prove the child was alive at the time of sacrifice, or if, indeed, he was ever alive," Mitch said.

"Of course he was alive." Lisel's voice rose. "Did you see his face? He was alive!"

Paresi and Star looked at one another.

Mitch closed the file. "The grimace doesn't mean anything," he said. "Muscles expand and contract after death. In all honesty, Sergeant Werner, newborns, still-born or alive, all have that slightly puckered look."

"Maybe. I wouldn't know," Lisel said. "I've never had a child. All I know is that the baby should have a decent burial, and I'll pay for it."

"When the investigation is over, I'll have the office contact you," Mitch said. He looked at Star. "I'll get you a copy of this report; maybe you'd like to look at it yourself, before you go any further."

"Thanks," Star said. "Good idea."

Mitch punched three buttons on his speakerphone.

"Medical examiner's office," a female voice answered.

"Lynda, hi. This is Dr. Grant. My secretary is out, and I need a copy of a report. Can you do that for me?"

The girl's voice was soft and flirtatious. "I'll be right there, Dr. Grant."

She must have run from the reception desk. Young, petite, and sable-haired, with dark eyes ringed in black liner. She wore silver rings on both her thumbs. She grinned at the officers.

"Hi, everybody." She looked at Mitch, pure lust in her young eyes. "I'll have this for you in a jiffy, Doctor."

She took the manila folder from his hand, caressing his fingers in the process. "Can I get you anything else, Dr. Grant?"

"No, that's it. Thanks, Lynda."

The girl smiled at him and left the room, closing the door behind her.

"We'll have the report in a few minutes," Mitch said. "Meanwhile," he turned to Lisel, "I think it's very kind of you to want to make arrangements for the baby."

Lisel's face was ashen. "It would make me feel better to do something for that child."

CHAPTER TWELVE

Two days before Valentine's Day, a new snowfall covered Brookport with nearly eight additional inches of fresh white powder. Carlyle Biggs shook this latest offering from his coat and entered the one-story, redbrick building on Stanfield Street.

The furnaces were working overtime, and the vast main room was sweltering. Long tables containing platters of chicken, fruit, hard-to-find white yams, dried fish, and colorfully iced and decorated cakes ringed the walls. Unopened bottles of whisky and rum sat on the altar, behind a statue of St. Anthony. Red candles burned on each of the tables, next to tall vases of red roses.

In the center of one table sat a large cake, iced in red, and covered with white and yellow sugar roses. Another offering in this ceremony to honor the *loa*, Legba, and Desmond St. John, his earthly host.

The crush of bodies made Carlyle feel as if a blanket of heat had been thrown over him. He found a seat in the corner, took off his coat, and settled in.

Around him, worshippers moved, preparing for the ceremony. Others sat in silent prayer, their bodies rocking rhythmically.

After so many years, it was strange, these sounds and smells, yet familiar. It all felt comforting and right.

The saints looked down on him from the walls. He closed his eyes and prayed. When he opened them, Desmond stood before him. Alive and beautiful, his white teeth displayed in a warm smile.

Carlyle reached out. Desmond's huge hand reached toward his. Their fingers were millimeters apart.

"Desmond," Carlyle whispered. "Desmond." The hand reached closer, Desmond's smile radiated. Carlyle could feel the warmth on his skin. He looked up, into the handsome, smiling, ebony face.

"Desmond."

Tears flooded Carlyle Biggs's eyes. He blinked.

Desmond St. John disappeared.

Kevin Lim, the manager of the Silver Street Brookport Farms Market, had been back from his long vacation for just two days. He was sitting in his office, drinking a cocoa-dusted café latte and looking at the two identical, huge, red and white rose-printed valentines he'd purchased with his store discount. He was rehearsing a way to tell his wife that he was in love with Carmen Ramirez, one of his cashiers, when they walked in.

"Mr. Lim?" Starletta Duvall smiled at him.

"Yes?" He looked up. "Yes, ma'am!" He stood and smiled at her. A very pretty woman—maybe Carmen and his wife would have to wait. "What can I do for you?"

Starletta took off her gloves and moved her long, black coat aside, letting him see the gold badge attached to her black leather belt.

"I'm Lieutenant Duvall, Homicide, and this is my partner, Sergeant Paresi."

Kevin Lim turned to see Paresi shouldering his way into the small office.

"We'd like to talk to one of your employees, Carlyle Biggs," Star continued.

Kevin Lim pointed to the two chairs squeezed in at his desk. "Please, sit down, both of you. What is this about?"

"Police business," Star said, taking the nearest chair. "We didn't want to just go in and drag Mr. Biggs off his job, but we need to speak with him."

"Is he in trouble?" Lim asked.

"No," Paresi said. "We just have a few questions."

Kevin Lim didn't know what to think. He reached for his phone and then stopped. "Is this something to do with his release? I mean, I know his history."

"No, sir," Star said. "We just have some questions."

"Will there be any trouble? I don't want any trouble." Lim picked up the receiver. "He's been doing a good job for us, but if there's a problem, I've got to notify somebody, right . . . ? The police or somebody?"

"We *are* the police, Mr. Lim," Star said. "He's not in any trouble. He's a free man. We just need to have a few words with him."

Lim pushed a button on his phone, and waited.

"Yes, Sammy, let me speak to Carlyle." He looked uneasily at Star and Paresi. "Carlyle, yes, can you come to my office? Yes, immediately. Yes, thank you."

He hung up the phone. "He's on the way up."

"Thank you." Star smiled at him. "Do you think we could use your office for our talk?"

"Sure . . . I guess." Kevin Lim stepped nimbly around his desk until he was near the door. As he opened it, Carlyle Biggs had just raised his fist to knock.

"Come in, Carlyle."

Biggs squeezed into the small office.

"These officers want to talk to you." The manager moved around the door, until he was on the threshold of the hallway.

"Am I in some kind of trouble?" Carlyle turned to Lim.

"No. No, you're not." Star stood up. "I'm Lieutenant Duvall, and this is Sergeant Paresi. We're from Homicide, and we just have a few questions, that's all."

"Homicide?" Carlyle looked as if he wanted to run.

"Yes," Star said. "Homicide."

Carlyle trembled visibly.

Star moved to the chair behind the manager's desk and indicated the one she'd vacated. "Have a seat, Carlyle, this won't take long."

Carlyle Biggs sat down. "I've got a special order I'm working on," he said timidly.

"I'll tell Sammy you're gonna be tied up for a while," Kevin Lim said. "Just go back to the department when you're through."

"Yes, sir, thank you, sir." Carlyle smiled weakly at his boss.

Lim closed the door behind him.

Carlyle turned to Star. "Am I in any kind of trouble?"

Star shook her head. It was the first time she'd seen him since shopping at the store with Vee. His demeanor didn't match his physical size. As much as she hated to think it, he seemed like a good kid.

"No, Carlyle, you're not in trouble," she said. "My partner and I just want to talk to you about Desmond St. John."

Carlyle hung his head but not before Star saw the tears forming in his eyes.

She looked at Paresi. He saw them too.

"Would you like something to drink, Carlyle?" she asked, indicating the cooler near her chair. "Can I get you some water?"

The young man looked down at his entwined fingers. "No, ma'am, I'd just like to get back to work."

"Okay." Star leaned back in Kevin Lim's chair. "As you know, Desmond St. John was found murdered in his home on Christmas morning."

"Yes." Carlyle's head remained down.

"Look at me, please," Star said.

He looked up. His eyes were moist.

"Are you crying because you were a friend of Mr. St. John's?"

"I knew him." Carlyle sniffed. "I liked him very much, and I'm sorry he's dead."

Paresi leaned toward the young man. "So you had nothing to do with his killing?"

"I know the cops think it's me, 'cause of the way it was done," Carlyle said.

"How was it done, Carlyle?" Star's voice was steady.

The young man looked at her. A tear ran down his face, his long fingers twisted in his lap. He looked down. A sigh escaped him.

"He was shot."

"Yes?" Star leaned forward.

"He was shot like my family."

"How was that, Carlyle?" Paresi said.

Carlyle looked up, his mouth twisted in grief, his tears running freely. "With a cross, okay? He was shot with the bullets forming a cross, just like those men in New York last year." He sobbed. "I didn't have nothing to do with that, and I didn't have nothing to do with killing Desmond, I . . ." He wept heavily.

"You what, Carlyle?" Star said, softly.

"I cared for him." He wiped tears with the palm of his hand, like a child. "I've known Desmond since I was little. He was always good to me. I would never have hurt him." He cried hard.

"You knew the two victims in New York City, too, didn't you?" Star said.

"They were my friends." Carlyle sobbed. "They were good to me."

"Seems to me that being your friend carries some risk, Carlyle," Paresi said.

The young man looked at him, his eyes red, his face wet. "I can't help it if people get hurt, I didn't do anything." His shoulders shook, more tears poured from his eyes.

"Reverend Max, and the judge, they always believed in me, when everybody else said I should die for what I did. Reverend Max stood beside me, he took up for me. He had me to dinner with his family the night he died." He looked at Star. "He didn't want me to be by myself on Thanksgiving. How could anybody think I could kill somebody who was so good to me?"

"You killed your family, Carlyle," Paresi said. "Weren't they good to you?"

He looked at the detective. His chest heaved up and down.

"No, sir. They wasn't good to me. They wasn't good to me at all."

Star looked at Paresi. He leaned back in his chair, his face serious.

"Carlyle," she said. "Listen. We're not here to arrest you, or pin anything on you, we just want to find out what you know about Desmond St. John's death."

The boy wiped his face again.

Star reached into her purse and handed him some tissues. He took them.

"Thank you, ma'am," he said, his voice choked and tearful. He wiped his eyes and blew his nose. "I don't know anything." He looked directly into Star's eyes. "I don't know anything, except he's gone." He sobbed.

Paresi shook his head at Star.

"Okay, Carlyle, thank you. You can go back to work now."

Carlyle Biggs stood up. "If I knew anything, I would tell you."

"I know," Star said. "Thank you for talking with us." She indicated Paresi. "The sergeant and I might want to see you again, okay?"

"Okay." He sniffed, and wiped his nose again. "I live at—"

"We know where you live, Carlyle," Star interrupted. "We know how to reach you."

Carlyle Biggs walked to the door. He looked back at the two detectives. "Bye," he said softly, and walked out.

"You know how much I hate to be wrong," Star said. "But I think maybe those shrinks in New York were on the money. This kid couldn't kill again."

"Maybe." Paresi's blue eyes were far away.

"What are you thinking?"

He looked at her. "I'm thinking that Carlyle is behaving more like a widow than a good friend."

"You saying . . . ?"

Paresi shrugged. "I spent a lot of time dealing with Howard Douglas last summer; I'm developing radar for this kind of thing. And let's not forget—"

Kevin Lim's knock interrupted him. Paresi opened the door.

"Is everything all right, officers?"

"Swell," Star said. She stood and walked around the desk. "You can have your office back. Thanks for cooperating."

Kevin Lim smiled at her. "Call on me anytime. I'll do anything for a pretty lady."

When they got back to the squad room, Lisel Werner was sitting at Star's desk.

"What happened to you two?" She stood. "When I got in this morning you and Dominic were gone."

"We went to see Carlyle Biggs." Star moved past her and tossed her coat on the now empty chair.

"Why didn't you tell me? I should have been with you."

"I don't think it would have been good for you to go along with us," Star said.

"I don't believe this." Lisel's voice grew shrill, her hands flew around her thin body. "I came here to work with you on this case, I shouldn't be left out. You can't just leave me hanging!"

Star faced Lisel, her hands on her hips.

"Uh-oh," Paresi muttered, sitting down.

"Sergeant Werner, I'm in charge of this investigation and I'm calling the shots. When I think it's all right for Biggs to know you're here, I'll bring you in. It's my call. Until then, I'd appreciate it if you wouldn't tell me how to handle my case."

Lisel's pale skin reddened. "I'm not trying to tell you what to do, Star," she said.

"Lieutenant Duvall," Star said coldly. "We need to define our boundaries."

Lisel glared at her.

Star put her hand on the receiver of her telephone. "Now, if you don't mind, I've got to talk to Dr. Grant."

"I've done that already, Lieutenant." Lisel's cold blue eyes flashed. "When I couldn't find you or your partner this morning, I went over to Dr. Grant's office. He was very helpful and forthcoming. He gave me a lot of what I need to work on this case."

"Good." Star picked up the receiver. "Sergeant Paresi will brief you on our visit with Carlyle."

"Right." Paresi stood up. "Let's go upstairs, Lisel."

Lisel Werner turned her back on Star. "Fine." She smiled at Paresi. "If you're hungry, *Dominic*, I'll be happy to buy you breakfast." Her voice rose. "I've already had mine. Dr. Grant was kind enough to take me."

Star didn't respond.

"I've already eaten too," Paresi said, "but the coffee's on me. Come on." He herded Lisel toward the double doors.

Rescovich was puffing his way upstairs as they entered the hallway.

"Morning, Dink," he said to Paresi, as his brown, salt-stained, leatherette shoes reached the top step. Dominic ignored him.

"How are you today, Ms. Werner?" He stood, out of breath, sweating, panting, and leaning against the banister.

Paresi wished it would give way and send his fat ass down a couple of flights to the basement.

The fleshy detective's watery eyes traveled hungrily over Lisel's short, deep purple wool dress and matching knee-high leather boots.

"Just fine, Detective." She smiled. "Just fine."

Paresi took her elbow and moved her along. He didn't have to turn around to know Rescovich was leering at her after they passed.

CHAPTER THIRTEEN

"So how's this new woman working out?" Vee said.

Star cradled the telephone receiver between her chin and her shoulder, and touched up her fingernail polish.

"I ain't got but one nerve left, and she's stomping on that." She blew on her nails. "Can you please tell me why you pay a small fortune for a manicure and your nails chip the very next day?"

"I'm not Madge," Vee said, "and it ain't the manicure that's pissing you off, so stop trying to change the subject. Bring it on, let me hear it. What did she do?"

"You mean besides make me want to plant my size tens in her narrow butt?" Star put the bottle of blackberry parfait nail polish on her night table and blew on her fingernails again. "She just irks me."

"Is it because there's another woman in the squad room with stripes? You know you've been the queen bee for years."

"Thanks a heap." Star sighed. "That's not it. Besides, I've got bars, that beats stripes."

"Is it Mitch?"

"No. Why would you think that?"

"If she's working with you, she's working with him. Does that make you nervous?"

"Why should it? Mitchell is a grown man; if he wants to take her to breakfast, that's up to him," Star said defensively.

"He took her to breakfast?"

"She said he did. I don't care." Star blew on her nails again.

"Uh-huh," Vee said. "You never really told me what she looks like."

"Casper," Star said, laughing.

"Girl . . ." Vee's laughter joined hers.

"I'm serious," Star said. "She's the whitest white woman I've ever seen. Her hair is white, her skin is white, even her eyes are white!" She laughed.

"White eyes?" Vee's deep laughter poured from the phone.

"They're not really white, but they're so pale blue, they might as well be. The only thing that saves her face is all the lipstick she piles on that big mouth."

"She's got a big mouth?"

"Yeah, like Carly Simon, which is really too bad, because I *like* Carly Simon. She's got this wide grin, all teeth, and she piles on the bright red lipstick. She looks like a sock with lips painted on it."

Vee's laughter flowed, making Star laugh with her. "Girl, you know you crazy, a stone fool!" Vee drew a deep, giggly breath. "You just ought to stop!"

Star held the phone between her neck and shoulder, smiling, listening to her friend laugh. "I may be a fool, but at least I know my job," Star said.

"Well, she must know hers, too. She's got to be sharp, or the NYPD wouldn't have sent her in."

"I'm sure she's good at what she does, handling kids,"

Star said. "She's a juvie officer, she's got no chops for Homicide."

"Seems to me that Juvenile is tough these days," Vee said. "She must deal with some funky stuff, what with the gangs and all that. How can you say she can't handle Homicide?"

"When she saw the little John Doe that was found on Christmas, she had to run out and lose her breakfast."

"So? As I recall, you were very upset by that baby. I didn't even see it, and I had nightmares just from what you told me. Anybody with a heart *would* respond to something that terrible."

"Yeah," Star said, grudgingly. "Still, I didn't run out of the room puking."

"So, she's got a weak stomach. That doesn't mean she's soft."

"Who are you, her mama?" Star snapped.

"Whoa!" Vee said. "Don't start none, and won't be none. Don't start wolfin' at me, 'cause you don't like her."

"I'm sorry," Star said, sincerely. "She just makes me very uneasy, like I couldn't depend on her to have my back. I think in a tough situation, she would freak out, and that could get us hurt or killed." She blew on her nails again. "Has Paresi said anything about her?"

"Nothing," Vee said. "Maybe *I* should be nervous, huh?"

"No. She threw it at him, but he didn't take it."

"That's good. What about Mitch?"

Star clicked her tongue disgustedly.

"Oh honey, she's done everything but wave her drawers in his face! He doesn't seem to be into it, but you never know with men." She tightened the cap on the bottle of nail polish. "If he wants to feed it, and jump it, hey!"

Vee chuckled. "Don't matter to you, right?"

"Right!"

"Now *your* nose is growing!" Vee said. "You talk a good game, but I know how you feel about him."

"He's my friend."

"He's more than that. You need to stop trying to fool yourself, stop trying to be so tough, and accept what you feel. He's crazy about you. The man is there for you. He's proven that. Besides, I saw that liplock on New Year's Eve."

"Everybody was kissing everybody."

"Um-hmmm, but everybody else came up for air."

CHAPTER FOURTEEN

Carlyle Biggs arranged rib-eye steaks on a Styrofoam tray. In spite of the cold in the cutting room, beads of sweat stood out on his forehead. Why couldn't the cops just leave him alone? Didn't they realize how he was hurting, how sorry he was, what a struggle he went through every day?

He pulled a sheet of plastic wrap from the gigantic roll over the cutting table. Carlyle wrapped the clingy sheet around the package of steaks and weighed it. The scale spit out a self-adhesive label containing the weight, safety precautions, use-by date, and price of the meat. He pulled it off the machine and slapped it on top of the package, near the right corner of the plastic wrap. He put the tray into a bin with other packets of wrapped steaks.

He looked up at the clock. Break time. Carlyle washed his hands, grabbed his jacket, and headed for the back of the store.

Outside, in the employee parking lot, he breathed deeply of the cold, lung-piercing air. He paced. It wasn't right. He'd paid for his sins, more than they would ever know. He should be left alone.

"Hey, Carlyle."

He turned at the sound of the voice. Kevin Lim stood in the rear doorway.

"Yes, Mr. Lim?" He walked toward his boss.

Kevin Lim dropped the cigarette he had been smoking on the wet ground and stamped it out. He shoved the pack into his coat pocket. "I just wanted to tell you that the incident yesterday means nothing, just in case you're worried."

Carlyle hung his head. "Thank you. I thought maybe I'd be looking for a new job soon."

"No." Kevin Lim blew his breath into his cupped hands. "I like you, Carlyle. You're a good worker. As long as you keep your hands clean and don't mess up, you've got a job here at Brookport Farms."

"Thank you, sir." Carlyle smiled. "I appreciate it."

"Yeah." Kevin Lim nodded. "Whew, it's cold enough out here to make me give up cigarettes. I'm going back upstairs. Don't stay out too long, we don't want you calling in sick."

"Yes, sir." Carlyle nodded. "Thanks again."

Kevin Lim went back into the store, letting the heavy steel door slam shut behind him.

Carlyle stood for a moment, his head bowed. Then he reached inside his jacket and butcher's smock. He unbuttoned the top three buttons on his shirt. His fingers caressed the small, red silk bag, suspended on a leather strip around his neck.

"Thank you, Desmond," he whispered. "Thank you."

Back in the squad room, Star sat at her desk. Her eyes gazed vacantly into space.

"Lieutenant Duvall." Lisel's voice jarred her.

"What?"

Lisel sat down at Paresi's desk, facing her. "I'd like to ask you something."

Star stared at her, silent.

Lisel stared back. Finally, she spoke. "Again, this morning, we were supposed to have a meeting. Where were you and Sergeant Paresi?"

"Tied up," Star said.

"How intriguing." Lisel leaned back in Paresi's chair, and swiveled slowly from side to side. "I know you don't like me. Do you want to tell me why?"

"Sergeant Werner, I don't dislike you. I don't know you."

"And you don't want to."

Star said nothing.

Lisel looked around the squad room. "Why do you sit out here in this fishbowl?" She leaned forward on Paresi's desk and folded her arms. "Your rank guarantees you an office."

Star stared at her blankly, still silent.

"Is it because you enjoy ruling the roost? Being queen of the hill?"

"I sit out here because I like it," Star said, looking her in the eye. "I get to feel what my squad is going through, be part of what they're doing. Behind closed doors, you're isolated, all your information is secondhand."

"Oh, I thought it was because you like being the only woman in this room, or at least, the only one on the same level as the men."

Star leaned closer to Lisel. "Above the men," she said. "Above, *Sergeant*. It's *my* squad. I'm the boss."

Lisel leaned back in the chair, a sly grin on her face. "Tell me, does Mitchell Grant like dominant women?"

"Ask him."

"I think he likes women like me, women who respect him and recognize his power."

"How did this get to be about Mitchell Grant?" Star said.

Lisel swung her hair back from her shoulder. "It's not. It's about dominant women." She tilted her head. "You just said you're the boss, right?"

Star sat back in her chair, her face blank.

"I just wondered if that attitude extended to other parts of your life . . . your relationships, for instance."

"My relationships are none of your business."

"Ladies." Paresi stood over them.

"Hello, Dominic." Lisel stood. "I guess you want your seat back."

Paresi moved around her and sat down. "It's nice and warm, thanks."

"Any time." She tossed her head, shaking her blond hair back over her shoulder. "Let's talk again soon," she said to Star.

"Let's not," Star replied.

Lisel headed for her desk across the room.

"Meow." Paresi smirked.

"Don't even," Star said.

Paresi raised his hands. "Hey, I'm just an innocent by-stander. You two have got to work out whatever it is." He opened his desk. "But it would probably go better if you stopped being such a brat and cut her some slack."

"Brat?" Star's eyes widened. "You think I'm being a brat?"

"What do you think?" Paresi countered. "She's not like you, Star."

"What the hell is that supposed to mean?" Star said angrily.

"Nothing," Paresi said. "Skip it."

They sat in silence for a few minutes, neither one looking at the other.

Finally Star spoke. "You know what I'm thinking?"

"That you'd like to kick me till I'm dead?" Paresi said, not looking at her.

"That's an idea." She laughed. "No. Carlyle Biggs."

He looked up at her. "We're probably thinking the same thing."

Star leaned toward him. "I'm thinking this whole thing is too pat. I mean, why would he go back to killing? Especially someone like St. John? Since we talked to him, I have a different take on Carlyle. I think you might have something. His feelings for St. John were way deeper than a friend's."

"So that means that maybe Carlyle and Desmond were . . ." Paresi wiggled his eyebrows.

"I'm not ready to go that far," Star said. "Desmond was all man, and then some. Carlyle seemed to have more of a hero-worship thing going."

"Don't forget we found Desmond with a rubber dick up his ass."

"Paresi!"

"What? It's the truth."

"I know, but I don't think it meant anything. Desmond had lots of women. Like Mitchell said, it was a toy. Maybe he and his lady friend were into some heavy role-playing."

"You play like that?" Paresi said, a smile in his eyes.

"No. Do you?"

"Maybe." He enjoyed the look on her face. "I don't go that far, but I like a little variety."

"I think you're taking me somewhere I don't want to

go," she said. "Is there something I should be telling Vee?"

"She knows."

Star's mouth dropped open.

Paresi laughed. "Hey, I'm not kinky, I just believe there's nothing wrong with a little exploring."

"Let's talk about that some other time, right now I want to concentrate on Carlyle. He grew up in Desmond's church, and I think he might have looked at Desmond as a role model."

"A voodoo priest, a role model?" Paresi said. "So that means Carlyle wants to get his own feathers and mojo juice?"

"No, not that . . ." Star looked frustrated. "I just think he respected Desmond too much to kill him. I think he really worshipped the guy." She looked across the room. "As much as I hate to agree with Kabuki Girl, Carlyle seems like a really good kid."

"Okay, so now what?"

Star shrugged her shoulders. "Desmond died in the saddle, obviously. Maybe we *should* be looking for a woman."

"The squad tracked down all of the women in his book, and every eligible one in his church. The reports say not one of them could have killed him. They were all grief-stricken, just like Carlyle," Paresi said.

The phone rang. She picked it up. Her face was impassive, but Paresi saw her hand shake. She picked up her pad and began writing.

"Okay, we're on it." She hung up.

"What?"

"Another cross shooting."

"Where?"

"Stanfield Street. 316."

"Isn't that Desmond's shop?" Paresi asked.

"No, it's the church."

"One of his people?"

"François Dulac."

Paresi stood up and grabbed his coat. "We taking our guest?"

Star looked across the room. "No choice. You tell her."

CHAPTER FIFTEEN

The smell of incense in the hallway outside the office in back of Desmond St. John's church was overpowering. Star reached in her pocket, searching for her Vicks inhaler. She didn't have it. The scent twisted its way through her nose and into her brain. The headache was instant and stabbing. She closed her eyes.

"Here." Her partner shoved his inhaler into her hand.

"Thanks." She took two deep breaths and handed it back. Paresi inhaled from the white plastic tube. He put the cover back on and slipped it into his pocket.

There were several uniformed police officers and members of BCI in the room. Star wove her way through the group.

On the sofa, near the back wall, she could see François Dulac.

His puny body lay naked, faceup, his dead eyes staring at the ceiling. One hand was laid across his slightly protruding belly. The other rested by his side. The corpse seemed curiously dignified, even in this humiliating tableau. One foot was on the floor, the other on the cushion of the blood-soaked beige sofa.

"Good grief." Star pulled on a pair of latex gloves and leaned down, close to the corpse. "Look at his nails."

The fingernails of the dead man were painted a brilliant, deep red.

She looked around for one of the BCI team. "Paulie," she called, pointing at the body. "Is he touchable?"

Paul DeLucca shook his head. "Not yet, Lieutenant, they got snaps, but I gotta get some video."

"Okay," Star said. She leaned closer to the body. "The nail polish looks dry, but I have to touch it to be sure."

"A perfect cross." Paresi looked over her shoulder. "Six shots all laid out in straight lines. Damn! Whoever this jimoke is, he's some shooter."

"Hey, baby." Star heard a booming voice from behind her. She straightened up and turned.

"Hey, Loman."

Loman Rayford, the head of the Bureau of Criminal Identification, stood behind her. He was an imposing figure, six foot five and one-half inches and nearly three hundred pounds. He had been on the verge of a pro football career when fate intervened and sent him into police work. Except for the knee injury that sidelined him, he still looked like he could take down Emmitt Smith and snap Deion Sanders in two without breaking a sweat.

"What are you doing here, big man?" she said. "I thought you'd be in the Bahamas by now."

"Me too. But Regina couldn't get the time off from her job, so I'm still here, freezing like the rest of the poor SOBs." He grinned at her. "But I got to say, looking at you, I'm warming up fast."

Star laughed and moved aside, making a space for him at the sofa. "Check this out." She pointed to François's hands. "What do you think?"

Loman peered down at the small, grayish body. "I

think them hoodoo charms don't work worth a shit. These suckers is dropping like flies."

"I mean about the polish." She laughed.

"Nice color for him," Loman said, grinning.

"I think he was shot while he was standing." Lisel Werner spoke from behind her.

"She's right," Loman said. He extended his hand. "Hello, I'm . . ."

"Loman Rayford." Lisel beamed. "I'm Sergeant Lisel Werner, NYPD."

Loman shook her hand. "Happy to meet you."

"It's my pleasure. You are very well known to the NYPD."

Loman smiled like a little boy being patted on the head by a favorite teacher.

Star bit her lower lip and stooped down, checking the blood-soaked couch for evidence.

"Well, well." Mitch's voice came from over her head. "Detective Rayford, still mesmerizing the ladies, I see."

Lisel turned to smile at him. His eyes were on Star.

Star stood up. "Hi, Mitchell." She moved back, giving him space at the couch.

His arm brushed her body, as he stood next to her.

"Lieutenant." He turned to Loman. "How's it look to you?"

Loman pointed to the blood on the wall behind the couch. "The consensus is he was standing when he was hit, but there's no bullet holes."

Mitch pulled a pair of latex gloves from his pocket. "Can I roll him yet?"

Loman moved back. "Not yet. Not till we get the video, and you get a closer look, here." Loman pointed to François's small, dead hand. "Peep that."

Mitch looked at the red fingernails. "Curiouser and curiouser," he said. "I can't begin to figure this out."

"Let's let Paul get in here," Loman said.

Everyone moved away from the couch. Paul DeLucca pointed his video camera and recorded François Dulac's final indignity.

"Two new touches," Mitch said. "The nail polish and, if you're right, the shots fired while he was standing. And if that's so, since there's no bullet holes visible in the wall, the bullets have to be in him, or the couch."

"With the amount of blood on the couch, he had to have been shot again when he fell," Star said, moving next to Loman. "How long do you think he's been officially deceased?"

Loman pointed to Mitch. "That's the doc's call."

"If the nail polish is totally dry, it could help establish a time, too. Right?" Lisel asked.

"Maybe," Star said. "But you can't base TOD on that. Some polishes dry in minutes, some take longer." She pointed to the body. "If he's wearing a base, two coats, and a sealer, then we're looking at at least a half hour to forty-five minutes."

"Done." DeLucca stepped back and turned to Star. "He's all yours, Lieutenant."

"Thanks, Paulie," Star said. She leaned over and lifted François's dead hand from his belly, holding it in hers. She gently rubbed her thumb over his index fingernail.

"Dry," she said, moving to the next finger. "Dry. The polish is totally dry, it's hard to the touch." She straightened up. "And, unless Mr. Dulac was used to having his nails painted, I'd have to say that the polish was applied after his death."

"Why?" Mitch asked.

"Because it's clean. No smudges. It was applied to a still hand."

"He could have been unconscious," Mitch said.

"Possible . . ." Star agreed.

Mitch slipped on his latex gloves and leaned over the body, manipulating François's thin arms and legs.

"Very flexible," he said, straightening up.

"So, what . . . about one or two hours?" Star asked.

"That's a good guess," Mitch said, "but we can be more accurate with a liver temp." He turned. "Jason."

"Yes, Dr. Grant?"

"Have you got a thermometer? I need a liver temp."

"There's one in the truck, I'll get it." The young man headed for the doorway. In a few minutes, he returned.

Star turned her back, as the long, metal probe was inserted into François Dulac's abdomen. She knew he was dead and couldn't feel it, but it was still too uncomfortable to watch.

Mitch leaned over Jason's shoulder, reading the temperature from the round, flat, glass-covered head. It was basically the same as a meat thermometer used in home kitchens, only bigger.

"Judging by his flexibility, Doc, I'd say he's dropping too fast," Jason said.

"Yeah." Mitch stepped back. "Must be all that extra ventilation."

The two men laughed.

Jason removed the metal spike from Dulac's body, and wiped the end with a disposable sterile wipe, which he then stuck into a small plastic bag. He put both the bag and the thermometer back into the black metal box by his side.

"Thanks, Jason." Mitch clapped him on the back.

"You're welcome, Doc. Can we move him now?"

"In a minute."

Mitch rolled François's small body on its side. "Here we go." He pointed a gloved finger to the two raised, bloody wounds in the center of the neck and back.

Loman, Star, and Lisel crowded around.

"It looks like we've got at least two rounds inside. Now if we can pull out something identifiable, maybe we can tie it up with Desmond," Mitch said.

"Yeah," Loman agreed. "The two-slug test. We only recovered two with Desmond, both of them from the bedding." He pointed at the wounds. "Except for the fact that the holes are small, those wounds almost look like dum-dums."

"With dum-dums, he'd be all over the couch," Star said.

"Right." Mitch pressed one of the wounds with his finger. "The bullet's definitely in there. Maybe the killer's experimenting with a different kind of ammo, giving us something new to worry about."

"What was that line around the bed?" Star asked. "We never heard back about that."

"Beats the hell out of me." Loman shrugged. "It was burned into the floor, I got that much out of it, but it was just a big circle around his bed. When the bed was moved, there was nothing underneath."

"Maybe it was for protection," Star said.

Loman laughed. "Guess they should have burned it a little deeper, and bought a pit bull."

Mitch signaled his crew to remove François Dulac's body from the couch. He turned to Star. "Any witnesses, anybody hear or see anything?"

"We just got here," she said. "But Paresi's in the office

next door, talking to Dulac's friend, Eric Stevens. He found the body."

"Can you see if Paresi's finished? I'd like to talk to Stevens," Mitch said, turning back to the couch.

Lisel moved alongside him, standing close.

Star signaled a uniformed officer. "Ellen, could you get Sergeant Paresi and Eric Stevens in here?"

The woman pointed. "Sergeant Paresi's over there, ma'am."

Star looked across the room. Paresi was in a corner, his back to them, talking on his cell phone.

"Oh, I didn't see him." She turned back to the officer. "Can you check next door, for Mr. Stevens?"

"Yes ma'am, he's the tall gentleman dressed in white, correct?"

"Yeah, that's him. If he's not in the office next door, check the chapel. He might be praying."

"Yes, Lieutenant." The officer headed out.

Star moved behind Mitch and laid her hand on his lower back. He turned. Her hand slid around his waist, and she kept it there, a point not lost on Lisel.

"Paresi's on the phone. My guess is he's trying to raise Sean Mallory at the D.A.'s office. After this one, we're going to bring Carlyle Biggs in," Star said.

"Sounds like a plan," Mitch said, his eyes never leaving hers.

"Hey, Doc." Loman stood at the foot of the couch.

"Yeah?" Mitch reluctantly turned.

"Think maybe I could get an early report on the autopsy for this one?"

"Sure, I'll make certain you get one right away," Mitch said.

"Thanks." Loman moved toward the hallway. "I'm going to have a look out here. Whoever did this didn't just materialize in the room." He winked at Star. "At least, I *hope* they didn't."

Star watched him walk toward the hallway, favoring his injured knee. She stood, still touching Mitch.

"If there's anything out there that will help, Loman will find it," she said.

Lisel swung her hair back from her face, and moved closer to Mitch on his opposite side.

"He's a good man." Mitch turned back to the scene and stepped back, allowing the gurney to be pushed past him. "I don't really understand this," he said. "Dulac wasn't involved in any way with the other cases, was he?"

"Not that I know of," Star said. "He's just the second guy in the church. He told me that he didn't even know Carlyle Biggs, and I believed him."

Two members of Mitch's team lifted the body from the blood-soaked couch, onto a plastic drape. They wrapped the plastic around François Dulac, and loaded the body onto the gurney.

"Look." Star pointed.

On the stained fabric of the couch, a long strip of red silk lay on top of a blood-soaked pile of dried herbs and leaves.

"Paul." Mitch waved the photographer over.

"I got it, Doc." The man aimed and took photos of the couch.

When he finished, Mitch reached down and picked up the piece of fabric with his gloved fingertips.

"Red silk," he said. He picked up a pinch of the herbs and leaves and looked carefully at it. "I can identify thyme and sage," he said. "In fact, I can smell the sage from here. I don't know what this other stuff is."

Star pulled two evidence bags from her purse. Lisel watched as the detective and the medical examiner worked in silent synchronization.

Star opened the bags and one by one, she held them up. Mitch dropped the strip of fabric into one bag, and a sampling of the herbs and leaves into the other.

Star sealed the bags. "This is beginning to creep me out," she said.

The policewoman walked back into the room, escorting a sobbing Eric Stevens.

"Thanks, Ellen," Star said.

"You're welcome, Lieutenant. I've got to get back out to the car; I saw some kids messing around out there, and my baton's in the front seat." She hurried away.

"Mr. Stevens." Star spoke softly. "I'm sorry to have to do this just now, but I have to talk to you, ask you some questions."

Eric Stevens looked toward the gurney. He put his head in his hands, and began wailing, "I found him, I found him."

Star put her arm around him. She turned and handed the evidence bags to Lisel. "Sergeant Werner, would you please give these to Detective Rayford?"

"Certainly." Lisel walked past the bowed and weeping Eric Stevens, and headed for the doorway.

Star turned back to the grieving man. He was looking at the plastic-shrouded corpse, his body trembling.

"I'm sorry, Mr. Stevens. I know he was your friend, but is there anything you can tell us, anything at all?" She looked into his wet, red eyes. "When was the last time you saw him?"

"This morning, around ten-thirty. We had coffee together. I left him to get prepared for our service this evening." He gulped air.

"The service . . ." He looked at Star, his face suddenly animated. "It must be canceled. I have to be with François to release the *loa*."

"Him too?" Star said.

"Yes." He looked again at the gurney. "He is not as powerful as Desmond, but he must also be freed. A *houngan* must never be buried without the release."

Star looked at Mitch.

"Same rules," he said.

"Very well, Doctor." Stevens wiped his eyes again, squared his shoulders, and pulled himself straight. "He is my friend, as well as our leader. I will honor him." He staggered briefly, and sat heavily in a straight-backed chair near the blood-soaked couch.

"Let me get you some water," Star said.

"Thank you." Eric Stevens's wet, reddened eyes closed as he settled into his grief.

Star patted his shoulder, and went across the room to the watercooler. She removed a paper cup from the stack on top of the bottle and filled it.

Paresi had moved to Dulac's desk, and was riffling through some papers there. "Well, well." He held up a handwritten note. "This is interesting."

Star walked to his side. "What is it?"

"A note to himself. Dulac didn't want to forget his meeting later this evening." Paresi looked at her. "With Carlyle Biggs."

When Carlyle arrived home from work, uniformed police officers were waiting. He made no attempt to escape.

He was handcuffed and put into the squad car without incident.

Now he sat in the pale green interrogation room. He was alone but he knew they were watching. Eyes had watched him all of his life, and even when he couldn't see them, he knew they were seeing him.

Star walked in.

"Hello, Carlyle."

"Ma'am." He stood. The steel cuffs binding his wrists made a soft, clinking sound.

Star reached into the pocket of her plum-colored trousers, and pulled out a tiny key. "Let's get rid of these."

She turned him around and removed the cuffs.

"Thank you, ma'am." He rubbed his wrists. "They were uncomfortable."

"I know." She indicated the chair he'd just vacated. "Sit."

Carlyle sat down.

"Do you want something to drink, some coffee, a soda or something?"

"No ma'am, I just want to go home."

"I know."

Star sat down facing him. Through the glass, Paresi and Lisel watched from the interrogation anteroom.

"She's got the wrong person," Lisel said.

"She's got our best suspect," Paresi countered.

Lisel looked at him. "Can't you see he's just a kid, he couldn't have done this."

Paresi stared at her. "He killed his whole family, Lisel, at fourteen. He's older now and he's experienced. We're doing what we have to do."

He turned the volume knob on the speaker near the glass. Star's voice filtered through.

"Carlyle, you're not under arrest, but I do want to ask you some questions and so I'm going to read you your rights. You have the right to remain silent—"

"They read them when they picked me up."

"That may be, but you're going to hear them again." Star started over.

"She's not going to get anything out of him," Lisel said to Paresi. "I want to talk to him."

Paresi held his hand up. "Just let Star do her thing right now."

Lisel sighed. "She doesn't know how to talk to him. I've worked with Carlyle, he'll tell me the truth."

Paresi looked at her. "He doesn't know you're here. I'd rather keep that fact between us for now."

Lisel stared straight at him. "I've spoken to him."

Paresi's face hardened. "When?"

"This morning." Her pale eyes looked angry. "When I found myself left out of this investigation again." She looked back at the glass. "I called him at work. I just wanted to see how he was doing."

"Did you tell him you were here?"

She looked sheepish. "I was annoyed."

"For crying out loud, Lisel, why would you do that?"

"You don't understand. I know this boy, I just didn't want to play this cat and mouse game with him. He's fragile."

The muscles in Paresi's jaw twitched. "Do you realize that your bleeding heart could fuck up this investigation?"

Lisel's eyes grew nearly transparent. She stared at Paresi. "You don't understand, Dominic." She pointed toward the glass. "I *know* him."

Paresi pushed a button. The red light on the wall behind Carlyle's head flashed. Star saw it.

"Hold it, Carlyle." She stood up. "I'll be back in a minute."

"Aren't you going to cuff me to the chair or something?"

"You're not running," Star said.

"No." Carlyle looked in the direction of the mirror. "I'm sure whoever's behind there would shoot me dead if I tried."

They stared at one another.

"I'll be right back," Star said.

"I'll be here."

"What's up?" Star walked into the anteroom.

"Carlyle knows Lisel's here," Paresi said.

"How?" Star looked incredulous.

"I told him," Lisel said. "I know him, Lieutenant. He's a good boy. I couldn't lie to him."

"Oh, that's just swell," Star said. "Just peachy." She turned to the glass.

Carlyle sat quietly, his head bowed, his lips moving silently.

"Looks like he's praying," Paresi said.

"He's very devout." Lisel stepped to the glass. "All he wants is a second chance."

"Well, since he's in on the whole thing, you may as well come talk to him," Star said.

Lisel nodded. "All right."

She and Star went back into the room.

Carlyle Biggs smiled when he saw Lisel Werner.

"Sergeant Werner!"

She walked to him and hugged him. "Hello, Carlyle."

"It's good to see you," he said. "I feel better now."

She held his hand and pulled up a chair next to him.

"Lieutenant Duvall here is just trying to get some information. There's been a murder at Desmond St. John's church," Lisel said.

"Who?" Carlyle looked surprised.

"François Dulac," Lisel said gently. "Do you know him?"

Carlyle shook his head. "No . . . no, I don't."

Star looked toward the mirror. Even though she couldn't see him, she knew Paresi was smiling. On the other side of the glass, he shot her a thumbs-up gesture.

"Liar, liar, pants on fire," Paresi whispered.

CHAPTER SIXTEEN

Lisel Werner called a taxi for Carlyle Biggs and gave him a twenty-dollar bill.

The two of them stood near the top of the stairs, just outside the double doors of the gray stone 17th precinct building. The white stone archway over the front protected them from the cold rain falling as they waited for the cab.

"I'm glad you were there, Sergeant Werner," Carlyle said.

Lisel pulled her black coat tighter around her slim body. A cold wind whipped up the stairs to their semi-sheltered place.

"I'm glad I could be here for you, Carlyle," she said. "I hope you know the officers are just doing their job. Nobody thinks you've done anything."

Carlyle smiled ruefully. "Then why did they pull me in?"

"It's just procedure," Lisel said. "Unfortunately your history and your affiliation with Desmond's church make you someone they'd want to talk with."

"They gave me my rights," he said softly.

"They were just going by the book." She put her hand

to his face, feeling his cold, soft skin. "You know I wouldn't let anything happen to you, don't you?"

"Yes, ma'am, you've always been good to me."

"I know you, Carlyle, I believe in you. I always have and I always will."

Lisel Werner leaned forward and kissed the young man gently on the lips.

From the marble lobby, near the door and out of view, Starletta Duvall watched.

The inside of Jessie Mae's restaurant was warm and filled with the soul-satisfying smells of barbecued chicken and ribs, collard greens, smoked ham hocks, fresh baked corn bread, and sweet potato pie.

Jessie only served one main course per evening, and tonight she offered barbecued ribs and chicken with collard greens. Star had been tasting Jessie's fiery sauce and smoky greens in her mind all day.

Steam from the hot pots misted the windows on the inside. Outside, a cold rain had turned into a fresh, powdery white snow. The place held a few late diners.

Star and Paresi sat facing one another in a shiny red leatherette booth in the back, near the counter and Jessie Mae's open kitchen.

"She kissed him, Paresi, I saw it," Star said, sprinkling crushed red pepper on a plate of steaming collard greens laden with great chunks of smoked meat.

"Maybe she wants him." Paresi blew on a forkful of the meat and greens mixture. He put it in his mouth. "Man, this is good."

Star broke a piece of corn bread from the large square on the bread plate next to her greens. "If she does, it's going to screw more than him, dig?"

"I hear you." Paresi sipped his Budweiser. "Think we ought to tell the cap'n that his hotshot New York cop might be a chicken hawk?"

"No, he wouldn't listen to that." Star tasted her greens. "Ooh." She sucked air around the food in her mouth. "This is hot."

"Here." Paresi passed her his beer. She sipped it and swallowed.

"Thanks." She wiped her mouth with a yellow paper napkin. "Besides, a chicken hawk is a *guy* who likes young boys, not a woman."

"Well, she's a chicken hawkess!"

They laughed as Jessie Mae came to the table.

She was a tall, coffee-and-cream-colored woman with a slow smile and long, sparkling silver hair. She made Star think of the screen sirens from the films of the forties.

Jessie wore her hair down to her shoulders, in a long page boy, secured by fancy hair nets whose colors changed daily to match her uniforms. She called them "snoods." With her bright colors and "sensible" shoes, Star always expected her to break out in a few choruses of "Boogie-Woogie Bugle Boy."

But Jessie loved the blues. Howlin' Wolf's "Smoke-stack Lightnin' " boomed from the authentic Wurlitzer in the corner. Jessie'd had the jukebox as long as she'd had her restaurant. Her only concession to the electronic age was that she'd had it refitted to play CDs.

"Y'all enjoying everything?"

Just looking at her made Star feel good. Her father had begun bringing her to the restaurant when she was a kid, after her mother died.

Jessie had opened her arms and heart to Star, and was a rock for her after the death of her father. She'd even catered Vee's wedding to Lorenzo. To them, she was family.

"Great, Jess, could I have another soda?" Star lifted her empty glass.

"Another Pepsi, heavy on the ice, comin' right up, baby." She raised a finger at Star. "Though you shouldn't be puttin' all that ice in a drink, not on a night as cold as this. It'll give you chills, later."

"Yes ma'am," Star said.

"That's okay. I know young folks knows everything." Jessie nodded sagely. "Just make sure you got something or *someone* to warm your feet on, when you go to bed tonight."

Star actually blushed. Jessie Mae looked at Paresi.

"How you doin', handsome, want another Bud?" She grinned at him, showing white teeth, with slightly pronounced canines on both sides of her mouth. "You *is* off duty, ain't you?"

"Never." Paresi smiled. "But I'll take another brew, thanks."

"You got it."

As she turned, a cold breeze, laced with a strong stench, shot up the aisle and through the restaurant. Jessie looked toward the door.

Standing just inside was what appeared to be a walking bag of dirty rags.

"Molly," Jessie called out. "Go 'round to the kitchen."

Star looked back over her shoulder. "German Molly." She looked at Jessie. "What is that crazy old fool doing here? Do you want me to call the wagon?"

"Naw, baby, she ain't no problem, she jus' lonely and hungry, that's all."

The filthy woman stood in the door. "Nigger," she said, loud and clear. "Nigger, nigger, nigger!"

Star put down her fork. "Hey, Jess, you don't have to take that. I'll lock her filthy ass up forever."

Jessie Mae patted Star's hand. "That's okay, baby, she just sad." She pointed toward the open door. "Molly, go out by the kitchen, Buster will give you some food. Go on, close that door!"

The ragged, muttering form turned, releasing a new onslaught of stench into the cold wind. She shuffled out of the door, letting it close behind her.

"Damn," Paresi said, fanning the air with his hand. "I thought I could take just about anything, but that's some serious funk!"

"I don't know why you feed that old cow," Star mumbled. "She's the most disgusting, racist bitch I've ever seen in my life!"

"Star calls her 'Frau Hitler.' " Paresi chuckled.

Jessie shook her head. "Now, baby, that ain't nice. Molly just old and lonely. She ain't got nobody. She just pitiful, that's all. Sad."

Star looked back at the door.

"Maybe, but she still thinks she's better than we are."

Jessie nodded. "That's just the lonely in her head, talking to her. She wasn't always what you see now. When she come here from Germany, during the war, she was a strong, strapping girl. She went to work as a maid for the Ludendorf family."

"You mean the real estate Ludendorfs?" Star said.

Jessie nodded. "The very ones. Old Miss Ludendorf was a invalid, and Molly and Mr. Ludendorf got very friendly. By the time his wife died, Molly had birthed him four children. He done right by her though, he married her and give them children his name. He didn't live too long after, neither."

"She probably killed him," Star said.

"Some folks think that." Jessie looked at her. "Old mister, he got that cancer. He was very sick. Some peoples say she pulled the plug on him. Anyway, she got all his money and property."

"So how did she end up a human dust bunny?" Star asked.

Jessie laughed, a deep-throated, rolling sound.

"Now, darlin', don't be like that. She didn't know how to handle what she had. She never had no real schooling. She could hardly read and write. Truth be told, she wasn't too smart. Peoples took advantage of her over the years.

"When her children growed up, they was shamed of her. Some even say they hated her. Imagine how hurtful that was. Her *own* babies. They took all the money she hadn't wasted, and scattered to the four winds. She started drinking, I guess, to live with the pain, and she ended up on the street."

"With you taking care of her, while she calls you names," Star said.

"Well, they even cussed the Lord Jesus, and I ain't nowhere near as fine a soul as he was. He give his life, the least I can do is give out some of the blessing he done give me. A little food ain't nothing."

The door opened again. Jessie looked up.

A short, toffee-colored man walked in. His round body was wrapped in a heavy brown tweed coat, dusted with snow. He was beaming and waving.

"Hey, Jess!" He began pulling off layers of clothing,

hanging them on the rack near the counter. "I come through a blizzard for them greens. Dish 'em up, gal!"

Jessie laughed. "Hey, Dookie. Sit your old butt down over there." She indicated Star and Paresi. "I got *paying* customers here."

The grinning man waved at them, and doffed his snow-dusted tweed cap, showing a thick crop of steel-gray hair.

"How y'all doing?"

The two cops waved back.

"I got to get to stepping." Jessie turned back toward the kitchen. "I'll bring y'all your drinks first." She looked toward the door. "Where's the other fine one, the doctor?"

Star shrugged. "I don't know. We got held up, so maybe he's dining somewhere else tonight."

Jessie Mae made a slight clicking sound with her tongue. "Well, tell him he missed a good meal."

"He'll just have to wait till next time," Star said.

"Maybe I'll just make up some and you can take them to him tomorrow. Greens is better when they sit overnight."

"Yes ma'am." Star nodded.

"That's just what I'll do," Jessie said. "I'll send him some sweet potato pie, too. He can't never get enough of that."

"He likes it," Star said.

" 'Sho he do. Anybody with a lick of sense loves my food." She went off.

Paresi watched her, laughing and joking with the man at the counter.

"Did you know she puts about a fifth of Jack Daniels in those sweet potato pies?"

"Get outta here," Star said. "So that's her secret ingredient. How'd you find out?"

"I asked her."

Star looked skeptical. "And she told you?"

Paresi winked. "No woman can resist me." He looked again toward the counter. "How old do you think Jessie is?"

"I don't know." She shrugged. "At least sixty, I guess, why?"

"Because next to you and Vee, she's got the best legs I've ever seen."

"You are such a hound."

"Bow-wow-wow!" Paresi grinned at her.

The next morning, Star, Paresi, and Lisel sat in Mitch's office while he went over the information on François Dulac.

"The weapon that killed François Dulac was a Smith & Wesson, regulation .38, six-shot revolver. An attempt to fashion the bullets into dum-dums was unsuccessful.

"They had been filed, but not deep enough to cause them to explode. I pulled two from the body, one intact, and one flattened. There was also one unexploded from the sofa. The other bullets are unaccounted for."

"Another cop gun, an oldie but a goodie," Paresi said.

"What?" Mitch asked.

"Cop guns," Paresi said. "All the murders, beginning with Carlyle's family, have all been committed with cop guns, including the ones last Thanksgiving in New York."

"I never thought of that," Mitch said. "Interesting. Are you following up on it?"

"As best we can. Anybody can buy these guns, but they are *all* cop guns," Paresi said.

Mitch closed the folder and passed it to Star. She opened it. Paresi and Lisel leaned in to look at the autopsy photos.

"Is the body here?" Lisel said to Mitch.

"It's downstairs, but it's being claimed this afternoon," Mitch said.

"Did they complete the ceremony?" Star asked.

Mitch nodded. "Last night." He leaned back in his chair. "I stayed here to be with Stevens. It didn't take as long as it did with Desmond. I guess this *loa* was anxious to come out."

"Did Stevens do it?" Star said.

"Yes. He was very distraught, but he managed."

"Alone?" Paresi asked.

"Yep, except for me," Mitch said. "Just the two of us."

"So that's why you missed dinner last night," Paresi said.

"Jessie's?" Mitch asked.

"Collards and barbecue," Star said.

Mitch sighed. "Oh well, it couldn't be helped."

"She sent you some greens and sweet potato pie," Star said. "No charge. I took it home."

"Are you going to give it to me?" Mitch smiled.

Star looked at him; a moment passed between them.

"Eventually," she said.

Lisel's throat went suddenly dry. She coughed twice and changed the subject.

"You must see some very bizarre things, Mitch," she managed.

"Yes, but this goes into a class by itself." He stood up and stretched. "It was a rough night. My back's killing me."

"I find it interesting that most tall men have back problems," Lisel said.

"It's caused by growing too fast," Mitch said, rubbing his lower back.

"Yes. My brothers are tall, and they suffered both bad backs and bad knees." She flexed her fingers. "I know some very good massage techniques, I've trained in shiatsu," Lisel said. "I'd be glad to help you."

Mitch looked at Star. "Thanks, but I'll be okay. I'm just tired."

Star stood. "Well, thanks for the report, I'm off."

"Where are *you* going?" Paresi asked.

"Personal." She nodded at him. "See you back at the squad."

Paresi looked shocked. "Without me?"

"I'll be back in a couple of hours. Mitchell, I'll call you. See you guys later."

She grabbed her coat, waved, and was out the door.

Carlyle Biggs felt the eyes on him. He looked up. Starletta Duvall was standing by the meat counter. He washed his hands and went out to her.

"Hello, Lieutenant." His voice was nervous.

"Carlyle."

"Something I can do for you?"

"Yes, I want a nice pork roast, something big enough for about eight. Can you help me?"

Star sat at Vee's kitchen table, barefoot, with her ankles curled around the legs of her chair.

Vee rooted around in the refrigerator, making room for the large pork roast Star had bought for her.

"So tell me again why I'm cooking dinner for y'all tomorrow?"

Star munched from an open bag of potato chips. "Because I had to buy something. I don't want him saying I'm harassing him."

"You are, aren't you?"

"Big time."

"So I'm cooking tomorrow because?" Vee closed the refrigerator door.

"Because I'm having leftovers with Mitchell tonight, and we'll be looking forward to the roast pork tomorrow."

"Is the sock woman coming too?" Vee leaned against the counter.

"Please, I want to enjoy this dinner, *and* keep it down. The Pale Rider is *not* invited." Star looked at Vee. "I saw something the other day that I can't believe."

"What?"

"I can't tell you, but let's just say it involved the Ice Queen, my suspect, lips, and maybe tongue."

"Get outta here!" Vee wiped her hands on a kitchen towel and sat down at the table. "You think she's involved with him? He's just twenty-one, he's a kid."

"That's something to give me nightmares," Star said. "Still, I saw what I saw."

"There could be a reason." Vee looked at Star. "You know you got a mind-set when it comes to her."

"Oh please, not you, too. You sound like Paresi. He says I'm acting like a brat."

"Who, you?" Vee said, wide-eyed. "Nah!"

The back door opened and Vee's fifteen-year-old son Cole came in, stamping snow off his workman's boots.

"Yo, five-oh in the house." He shut the door, grinning at Star. "How you doing, Auntie?" He looked at Vee. "Mama, what's for dinner?"

"Meat loaf," she said.

Cole made a face. "Not again."

"Cheer up." Vee looked at Star. "Thanks to your auntie harassing some poor soul, tomorrow night we're having roast pork and stuffing."

"Slamming," he said, hanging up his coat. "Way to go, Auntie. Get them bad guys, make 'em pay."

Star laughed.

Cole turned to Vee. "You'll be working tomorrow, should I come home early and get things started?"

"No, honey," Vee said. "Your auntie here is going to chop the celery and onions for me."

Cole looked at Star. "Sure you don't want *my* help?" he said to his mother.

"Get outta here, boy!" Star laughed and tossed the dishtowel at him. "I used to diaper your rusty butt!"

Cole went to her and wrapped both arms around her from behind, rocking her in the chair. "I'm just glad you didn't have to cook for me." He kissed Star loudly on the cheek. "I'm in my room, Mama."

He headed out of the kitchen and down the hallway. They could hear his laughter trailing behind him.

"Your kids don't respect me anymore," Star said, grinning.

"Hmmmph, they just know your cooking record." Vee got up, pulled a notepad and pen out of a counter drawer, and started writing.

"I've got to get some yellow cornmeal tomorrow, to make corn bread for the stuffing. And I'd better get a dozen eggs and some milk. These children put enough milk on cereal to float a couple of battleships. Then they leave the empty cartons in the refrigerator."

Star got up and went to the door. She pulled on her

boots. "You go, Martha Stewart. No Stove Top for you." She put on her coat and hugged her friend. "I've got to go back to the station and then hook up with Mitchell, so I can give him the greens Jessie Mae sent last night."

"What else are you going to give him?" Vee said impishly.

"A piece of sweet potato pie," Star said, with a wicked grin.

"I bet that'll beat a dish of vanilla ice cream." Vee laughed.

CHAPTER SEVENTEEN

Mitchell Grant and Star sat in the den on the sofa in front of the fireplace. Last summer, she'd made this room her main downstairs space, telling herself it was because the living room needed redecorating. Truth was, she barely set foot in there anymore.

They ate the last of the generous slices of Jessie Mae's sweet potato pie and sipped coffee out of Star's mother's fine china cups. Jake slept curled up in front of the fire. Paresi's gift of Motown music played on the stereo. The Temptations' "The Way You Do the Things You Do" gave way to Martha and the Vandellas' "Nowhere to Run."

"This pie is so good." Star put the last forkful into her mouth. "Paresi got Jessie to tell him her secret ingredient."

"Jack Daniels," Mitch said, "and lots of it."

Star looked surprised. "Am I the only one who didn't know that?"

"She told me because I cook," Mitch said. "I asked her for the recipe."

"Paresi says he charmed it out of her."

"I'm sure he did," Mitch said. "I don't think she'd buy him as a cook, although . . ."

"He's *Italian*!" they said together, laughing.

Mitch set the dessert plate and fork on the coffee table.

"This was a good dinner," Star said. "The greens were great, even for the second night in a row, and the chicken just hit the spot." She raised her cup toward Mitch.

"The Colonel thanks you," he said, returning the toast. He leaned back against the cushioned sofa arm, cradling his cup in his hands. "Can I talk to you about something?"

Star knew the tone. "Is this going to be about Lisel?"

"Am I that transparent?" Mitch said.

"No, it's just that the consensus is I'm behaving like a brat and treating her very badly."

Mitch put his cup on the coffee table. "I don't know what the bad blood is about, Star, but you should ease up."

"You sound like Paresi." Star poured herself more coffee and added a generous helping of cream. "I can't explain it," she said. "And it may seem irrational, but I just don't like her. I want to finish this thing up, and behave professionally about it. Then she can drag her tired self back to New York. I don't have time for mind games and she insists on pushing my buttons."

"I don't think she's doing it intentionally," Mitch said.

Star faced him. "She tries to undermine me. She doesn't respect my rank. She's always in my face, and when I blow, she's the innocent, and I'm the heavy. It's like she wants to make me look bad."

"I don't think she's got an agenda," Mitch said. "She's just a juvie cop who got involved in a sensational murder case, and now she's knee-deep in another one."

"Maybe," Star said.

"You don't sound convinced."

"Men just don't get it." Star sighed.

"Are you being sexist, Lieutenant?" he said, amused.

"No. I'm just saying there are some women who go

out of their way to mess up other women, and she's one of them."

"Why don't you just give her a chance? Ease up."

"Why does it mean so much to you?"

"It doesn't. I just don't like seeing you tied up in knots."

Star faced him. "Did you know she told Carlyle she was working with us?"

"I didn't know that."

"Yeah, before *I* gave her permission. And after we questioned him the other night, she called a cab for him, waited with him, and *kissed* him."

"Really?" Mitch looked surprised. "What kind of kiss?"

"What difference does that make?"

"She's known him for a long time. It could have been innocent."

"On the lips?"

"I've kissed you on the lips." Mischief sparkled in his deep green eyes. "It's always been innocent."

Star blushed. "We're not talking about you and me, we're talking about a police officer and a suspect. I don't care if she delivered him, she had no business kissing him, especially at the station."

"In full view of everybody?"

"No. They were outside, under the arch, waiting for a cab that *she* paid for."

"How did you see all this?"

Star looked down at her hands. "I sort of followed them downstairs. They didn't know I was there."

"Spying?"

"Yeah, so?" she said defensively. "It's my job to keep an eye on the suspect."

Mitch leaned back on the couch. "You're a dangerous woman, Lieutenant Duvall."

She laughed. "What? Why? I'm not doing anything you wouldn't do in my place."

"If I were in your shoes, I'd give her the benefit of the doubt."

"That's because you're not in my shoes and you never have been," Star said forcefully. "You don't have a clue what it's like for me."

Mitch's eyes grew serious. "That's where you're wrong, Star. I know what you've been through and I know how it's been for you on the job. But it doesn't give you the right to bulldoze somebody working with you."

In front of the fireplace, Jake woke with a start. He stretched, yawned, turned his backside to the fire, and was instantly asleep again.

"I'm not bulldozing her. I'm her superior officer. She reports to me. My other officers do what I ask, why can't she?"

Mitch took the cup out of her hand and set it on the table.

"Come here." He pulled her into his arms and laid down, taking her with him. "I can feel all that tension here . . ." He softly stroked her back. "And here . . ." His touch moved to her neck, gently massaging.

Star closed her eyes and relaxed, resting her head on his chest.

"The key to all this," he said, in a low, soothing voice, "is to let go. If you're right, and she's out to get you, she'll slip up and show herself. You've worked too hard for your position, for the respect. You can't let yourself be led into a confrontation. It's not professional, and it won't benefit you." His hand moved hypnotically up and down her spine. "On the other hand, if she turns out to be on the level, then you've savaged a fellow cop . . . not a good move."

In his arms, enjoying the feel of his body under hers, Star was unable to hold on to her righteous indignation. They breathed in unison. The sound of his heartbeat had the same calming effect on her as a newborn listening to its mother.

She tightened her arms around him, and snuggled deeper into his body. Mitch kissed her on top of the head, and squeezed her gently.

Suddenly Jake jumped up on the sofa, surprising them, making them both laugh loudly.

"Talk about a mood-breaker," Mitch said.

The curious cat blinked at him.

He tightened his grip on Star.

"May I suggest, Lieutenant, that your next pet be a goldfish?"

CHAPTER EIGHTEEN

The sun was out for the first time in weeks and the city felt the anticipation of a thaw. Star, Paresi, and Lisel Werner took their time walking up the stairs and into the county medical examiner's building.

After listening to Mitch's very persuasive argument, Star decided to lighten up on Lisel, even though her gut feeling was the same. She stopped at the door, and smiled at the woman.

"After you." She stepped back, allowing Sergeant Werner to enter the building first.

"Where's the bucket of water?" Paresi whispered behind her.

When they walked into Mitch's office, Star introduced Lisel to Lorraine Shelby, Mitch's secretary and former conquest. For once, she saw Lorraine's withering gaze aimed at someone else; she kept a straight face for as long as she could.

"How was your vacation?" Star said, all smiles.

"Just fine, Detective, just fine," Lorraine drawled in her deep southern accent. "I had a fine time." She pushed the intercom button, her eyes locked on Lisel, as the officer pulled off her black fedora and shook out her pale blond hair.

Mitch appeared in the doorway, dressed in a muted gray Cerrutti suit, with faint, dark blue pinstripes.

"C'mon in, folks." He stepped back into his office.

"Looking good, Doc," Star said, passing him.

"Thanks. Court this morning." He closed the door and sat down at his desk. Star noted his oval-shaped sapphire cuff links, encased in gold settings.

"Anyone for coffee . . . pastries?" he asked.

"No, not me," Star said. The others shook their heads.

"Okay, well let's get right to it." Mitch opened the file on his desk.

"Beginning with what we know, François Dulac was shot with a .38 Smith & Wesson, containing an attempt at homemade dum-dum bullets. There were traces of filing on the slugs, but it wasn't deep enough to get the desired effect, and as previously noted by Sergeant Paresi, the gun is a regulation police officer's weapon. Two bullets were removed from the body, and one from the sofa. No others were found at the scene."

He turned the page. "And the latest. In addition to the red nail polish, the body also bore traces of an oil on the soles of the feet and the palms of his hands."

"Lavender?" Star asked.

"Yep." He nodded.

"That gives us the tie to the baby, right?" Paresi said.

"That and the red silk fabric found on the couch. The herbs, thyme and sage, were also part of the contents in the baby's body cavity."

"Are we talking another sacrifice?" Star said.

Mitch shrugged. "That's a big jump but I think that church and its office should be gone over. It might be tricky, but with this information, I don't think you'll have too much trouble showing probable cause to get a search warrant."

"I think with this added stuff, we can get one for Carlyle Biggs, too," Star said. "Toss his place as well."

"Don't forget his locker at work," Paresi said.

"Right." Star nodded.

Lisel sat quietly, her eyes focused on Mitch.

Mitch looked at his Rolex watch. "I've got to go." He closed the file and slid it across to Star. "Here's your copy, Lieutenant. I'll probably be in court for most of the day, but I'll be coming back here afterwards, so if you have any questions . . ."

"I'll call," she said.

As he stood the intercom on his desk buzzed. He pushed a button. "Yes, Lorraine?"

"You have twenty minutes to get to the courthouse, Doctor." Her voice filled the room.

"On the way. Thanks."

Mitch got his overcoat from the closet. Star noted that it was another beautiful cashmere. Gray, and a perfect blend with his suit. He pulled it on, and wrapped a dark blue silk scarf around his neck. His style was effortless. She wondered if he even realized his own elegance.

"Sorry kids, got to travel." He opened the door. "If you need to look at anything, Lorraine will help you."

He walked out to the outer office. His secretary handed him a dark blue Mark Cross leather briefcase.

"The Michaelson file," she said.

"Is everything in here?"

"Yes, Doctor, the pictures, police reports, and all of the lab results as well."

"Thanks." He was out the door.

Star stood up. "Let's go back to the office. I need to meet with Captain Lewis before we move on this."

Paresi buttoned his coat. "You go ahead, I think I'll take a run over to the church, have a talk with Stevens." He turned to Lisel. "You want to ride with me?"

She looked at Star.

"It's fine, Lisel," Star said, picking up her coat. "I'll be with the captain. We can all hook up this afternoon."

Lisel's eyes searched Star's face, looking for some telltale sign that Star was going to trip her up. She saw none. "Fine. I'll go with Dominic, *Star*," she said with emphasis.

"Good." Star walked into the outer office.

"Lorraine, would you call the precinct and ask them if they have an available car that they can send for me?" She turned to Paresi. "I'll hitch a ride with the uniforms."

Paresi fished the car keys out of his pocket. "Ciao." He nodded toward Lisel. She preceded him out of the office, without a glance at the secretary.

Star sat on the couch, waiting for her ride, trying her best not to laugh at the sick look on Lorraine's face.

CHAPTER NINETEEN

"I don't know what this city is coming to." Captain Lewis leaned back in his chair, his arms folded over his chest. "Voodoo gods, sacrifices . . . This world is on the way out."

"Could be, Captain," Star said. "But before we all go up in smoke, we need to find out who's behind this stuff."

Lewis sat forward. "Has Lisel been any help at all?"

Star looked at the framed photograph of the chief on the wall behind Lewis's head. "Yes and no, sir."

"Explain," Lewis said, his blue eyes piercing.

Star sighed. "She's given us a lot of information on Biggs, but she's not very professional, sir."

The captain ran his hand over his chin. "I've been hearing rumbling, Lieutenant."

"Rumbling, sir?"

"The word is that you hate her guts and you've done everything you can to make her life hell."

Star shook her head. "That's not true, Captain."

Lewis leaned forward on his elbows. "Is it true that you and Paresi have dumped her on more than one occasion when she was supposed to be part of an investigation?"

"I wouldn't say dumped, sir."

"Just what would you say, Lieutenant?"

Mitch's voice floated in her head. She had to be careful,

"Sometimes it's been better not to have Sergeant Werner with us. Her methods are different than ours . . ." She hesitated. "And she's way too chummy with Carlyle Biggs."

"Explain."

Star took a deep breath. "She told him she was here, working with us, before I gave permission for her to do so. I called him in for questioning on the Dulac murder and she'd already spoken to him. She eventually came into interrogation and talked to him with me."

"Did she get anywhere?"

The image of Lisel kissing Carlyle Biggs flashed in Star's mind. Mitch's voice was back in her head. Be careful.

"No, sir." She looked down at her hands. "Neither one of us came up with too much."

"Get back on it," Lewis said. "And see that she's included. She's here to help."

"And if she doesn't?" Star's voice trailed off.

"Then she's on the next flight out. We're paying a fortune to keep her quartered at the Weybourne Hotel."

Lewis waved his hand in dismissal. "Bring me something. Yesterday."

Star stood. "Yes, sir."

"And tell your partner I expect more cooperation from him as well."

"Yes, Captain."

"Where is he, by the way?"

"At the church. In fact, he asked Sergeant Werner to go with him. They went over to talk to Eric Stevens."

"Why aren't you there?"

"I wanted to try and get a search warrant for the property, and for Carlyle Biggs's locker at work, and his house."

Lewis leaned back in his chair. "You've got good probable cause. Let me talk to the D.A., see what I can do."

"Thank you, sir." She headed for the door.

"Lieutenant?"

"Yes, sir?" She turned and looked at him.

"Be careful."

"I will."

Back at her desk, Star dialed Paresi's cellular number.

He picked up on the third ring.

"Hi," she said. "It's me."

"What's up?"

"I just had a meeting with Lewis. How soon will you be back in the office?"

"About thirty, forty minutes," Paresi said.

In the background Star could hear Lisel's voice.

"What's going on?"

"I can't talk here, I'll see you when I get in," Paresi said.

"Good news or bad?"

"A little of both. See you later."

He hung up.

Star sat holding the receiver. From what she could hear, Sergeant Werner was using a time-tested method of women to get information from men. Though it was muted, the sound of Lisel's voice was definitely that of a woman flirting heavily to get what she wanted.

Star hung up the phone. Listen to what Mitchell said, don't jump to conclusions, she told herself. Give her the benefit of the doubt.

CHAPTER TWENTY

Paresi and Lisel walked in just as Star returned from the ladies' room. Paresi was carrying an ornate, beaded bottle. He put it down on Star's desk.

"What's that?"

Paresi took off his coat and sat down. Lisel stood over them.

"It's a little gift from Eric Stevens," Lisel said, taking off her coat.

Star picked it up. "What's it for?"

"It's a libation bottle," Lisel said. "It's used to give offerings to the *loas*."

Star ran her fingers over the elaborately beaded bottle. A slow smile spread across her face. "Is there fabric under here?"

"Yep." Paresi grinned.

Star picked at the beads, a few came off. "Well, well, well . . . Red silk, imagine that."

She picked up the phone and punched in Loman's extension. "Can I come see you, Big Man?"

"Come on up, baby, you know my door is always open to you."

"I don't trust myself alone with you," she said. "I'm bringing company."

"Bring 'em on, I like a crowd. You and me can show 'em how it's done."

"On the way." Star hung up and picked up the bottle. "Shall we go see the wizard?"

The three of them headed for BCI.

Loman Rayford, wielding a pair of tweezers under a bright magnifying light, carefully picked the multi-colored beads from the neck of the bottle. When he'd cleared a sizable patch of red silk, he used a razor blade to cut the fabric away from the brown glass bottle. When he'd gotten a patch, he used the tweezers to gently pull it away from the bottle and transfer it into an evidence bag.

"I'll run it against the fabric taken from the Dulac scene," he said.

"What about the material taken from the baby?" Star asked.

"It didn't match. It was the same grade of silk, but the color was off. It didn't come from the same dye lot."

"Would that be enough to say it didn't come from the same bolt?" Star asked.

"Yeah." Loman looked at her. "When a bolt is dyed, the color intensity is the same. But when they dye another bolt, the color will change, even if the same mill does it. Sometimes the change is slight, but it's there."

"But if it's the same grade of silk . . ." Lisel said.

"Doesn't matter. Lots of mills could use that grade." Loman sealed the evidence bag. "The ID is in the dye."

Lisel turned to Star. "So if we prove the silk from the bottle and the silk from Dulac's murder scene are the same, do you think we can get a warrant to search for more than just fabric?"

"I don't know." Star shrugged. "Captain Lewis is talking to the D.A., but it's still thin ice. I mean so what if the fabric on the bottle matches, they could just say that since Dulac was killed in that office, the killer just used material he found."

"Right," Paresi said. "It doesn't prove anything."

"Let's not get too gloomy, children," Loman said. "Don't forget, I'm on this now." He looked at Star. "You are going for a warrant on Biggs as well, right?"

"Yeah, his locker at work, and his house." She shook her head. "If we go down, we're going down on the whole enchilada, not just a piece of it."

"Good girl," Loman said. "This might help." He opened his bottom file drawer and pulled out a folder marked 15-1225-20-ST. JOHN, DESMOND. Inside, pictures of Desmond's murder scene were filed according to bedroom, morgue, and autopsy photos.

Star looked over Loman's shoulder as he went through them. He pulled out a color photo of Desmond's bedroom. In the background was the altar that was positioned near one of the windows.

Loman laid the picture on his desk. He went back into the file and pulled out another shot. This time, the focus was on the altar, in close-up.

"Well, well, well," Star said.

Loman looked at her. "You get right to the point."

"What?" Paresi looked over her shoulder.

Star pointed at the picture. "Remember this?"

In the foreground, on the altar, stood the bottle they had joked about at the scene. The one with the scissors and mirrors.

They all leaned in, studying the photo. The material adorning the bottle was silk. Three panels, one white, one black, and one red, sewn together with coarse, black thread.

"Oh yeah." Paresi grinned. "Tell me we have this bottle."

"Follow me." Loman led them to the elevator. They rode to the basement and got off in front of the property room.

"Hey, Earl." Loman spoke to the uniformed officer who sat reading a *Sports Illustrated* magazine at a desk behind the chicken-wire-covered window.

"Yo, Loman, what it be?" Earl Collins came to the window and opened it. He was a wiry, butterscotch-colored veteran of nearly fourteen years in the department. Two years ago, he'd been shot in the stomach during a routine domestic disturbance. Earl, riding solo, was first on the scene. A drunken lunatic, who'd beaten his wife to a paste, fired on him as he got out of the car.

Though critically wounded, Earl returned fire and killed him. His courage earned him a Commendation for Bravery, and a soft inside job until he retired.

"Hi, folks, how's everybody?" He smiled at Star, Paresi, and Lisel.

"We're cool, Earl," Star said. "We just hope you can help us."

"I'll do my best, Lieutenant."

Loman showed him the picture. "Number 15-1225-16DSJ, the Desmond St. John case," Loman said.

The officer nodded. "Back in a minute."

"I can't believe we might be able to link something here," Star said, her voice excited.

Earl came back to the window, carrying a large, brown paper bag. He set it on the counter and pulled out a pad of forms and a pen. "Sign for it here, my brother, and it's all yours for as long as you need it." He slid the paperwork and the pen across the counter to Loman. "Press hard, you're going through four copies."

Loman signed, and Earl tore off the last page and handed it to him.

"Keep this for your records."

Star held the bag in her hands. "It's heavy." She opened it. They all looked inside.

"Wow." She turned to Loman. "I hate to admit it, but this thing is very spooky."

"Should be." Earl laughed. "It's a *wanga*."

"A what?" Star's eyes widened.

"A *wanga*," Earl said. "A sorcerer's bottle."

"How do you know this stuff, Earl?" Paresi asked.

"My sister-in-law, Hattie." Earl leaned on the counter. "She's from Port-au-Prince, makes the best damn peas and rice you ever tasted." He shook his head. " 'Course I can't eat 'em no more, but even the memory tastes good!"

"I'll bet," Star said. "Tell me, Earl, does she know anything about voodoo?"

The officer raised his hands. "Hey, I don't ask. That stuff scares me, but I do know that I don't mess wit' her. I keeps on her good side." He laughed. "She used to go to Desmond St. John's church, and there was a time when she spent a lot of money at the Hoodoo Man shop. In fact, Corrine, my wife, said she worked some roots for me when I was in the hospital. I try not to think about that, though."

"Think she'd talk to us?" Star asked.

"Don't know, Lieutenant, but I s'pose so. She's a changed gal, been away from that stuff for a while. She's a Baptist now."

"Tell her it would help us in our investigation," Star said.

"I'll see what I can do," Earl said. "She's at work over at Mercy Hospital."

"What does she do?" Paresi asked.

"She's a nurse in pediatrics. Her name's Hattie Jeannot."

"Is she working now?" Star asked.

Earl looked at his watch. "She's on till midnight. Want me to call her and tell her you want to talk to her?"

"Yeah," Star said. "Tell her we're coming over."

"Yes, ma'am." Earl reached for the phone.

CHAPTER TWENTY-ONE

Star liked Hattie Jeannot the minute she saw her. She was a small, plump woman with a big open smile, and skin the color of black grapes.

She wore her hair in its natural, kinky state, cut so close to her scalp it was nearly shaven. What was left she'd dyed a golden blond. In each ear she wore a tiny golden cross. On her left hand she wore two rings, a large ruby stone on her index finger and a thin gold wedding band on her middle finger. Though hospital rules had changed and nurses now wore colorful uniforms, Hattie wore white. A spotless, starched white uniform that rustled with every step she took toward the detectives. Her white nurse's shoes were immaculate.

When she spoke, her eyes lit up, and her voice had the same singsong rhythms as François Dulac's.

"I'm so pleased to meet you," she said to Star, extending her hand. "Earl called to tell me you were coming."

"Thank you for seeing us," Star said. She turned and introduced Paresi and Lisel Werner.

Hattie's eyes darkened for a second when she looked at Lisel. She beamed at Paresi, but her gaze kept wandering back to the pale woman standing next to Star.

"Come, I am on my dinner break, let us talk in the cafeteria. It is practically empty during this time."

They entered the elevator and rode up to the dining room. Two orderlies played a game of cards at one table, while a young nurse spooned blueberry yogurt into her mouth, without taking her eyes off the latest Anne Rice.

Hattie led them to a large round table in the center of the room. "Would you like something?" she asked, in her musical voice.

"Not for me, thank you," Star said. The others also demurred.

"I will only have a piece of fruit and some tea," Hattie said. "I am not fond of the meals they serve here." She slid her dark hands over her stomach and hips. "The good thing about that is, it helps me try and cut the pounds. I'll be right back."

They made themselves comfortable. She came back to the table carrying a tray. On it was an empty salad plate, a large apple, a foil-wrapped chunk of cheddar cheese, two packets of saltine crackers, and a cup of steaming black tea.

Paresi rose and pulled the chair out for her.

"Thank you, it is rare to see a gentleman these days, and such a handsome one too." She winked at him.

"Thank you," he said.

"Do you mind if I eat while we talk?"

"Not at all," Star said. "Go right ahead." She opened the folder in front of her and pulled out a Polaroid of the bottle Loman had removed from Property earlier. "Do you know what this is?"

Hattie put the apple on the pale green salad plate and cut it in half, and then into quarters. "Oh, indeed." She wiped her fingers on her napkin. "That is a *wanga*, a sorcerer's bottle," she said.

"Earl told us you used to belong to Desmond St. John's church," Star said.

Hattie nodded, and opened her cheese and crackers.

"Yes, I did. We grew up in the same area. Desmond had a large following even before he came to America." She cut a piece of fruit and put it in her mouth. She followed that with a bite of the cheese and the crumbly crackers.

"He became very successful here," Star said.

Hattie nodded, and swallowed. She took a sip of her tea. "Oh, indeed. He was most revered by the people in our area. When he came here we all heard of his great success. No one was surprised, Desmond was a most powerful *loa*."

"So you believe he was the incarnation of Legba," Star said.

"Oh my, yes. He had power we had never seen. I myself saw him perform miracles."

"What kind of miracles?" Paresi asked.

"He could cure all sicknesses and there was talk that Desmond could raise the dead."

The detectives looked at one another.

Hattie cut another slice of her apple. "I myself never saw him do it, but the word was he could do anything. He had the ears of all the *loas*, and they, like us, loved Desmond. He was a favored child."

"Why did you leave the church?" Lisel asked.

Hattie stared at her for a moment as if hypnotized. "Your hair is so white," she said. "Like Ezili Doba."

"Who is Ezili Doba?" Star said.

"The Great Mother," Lisel said.

Everyone at the table looked surprised.

"I saw a statue in Mr. Dulac's office," she said, the color rising in her face, her cheeks flushed. "It was written on the base."

Hattie flashed that smile. "You are right. She *is* the Great Mother. The Virgin, white and pure." She stared again at Lisel. "Your hair must be very fine, like baby hair. Hard to fix, yes?"

Lisel flushed again. "It's very fine, but I manage."

Hattie smiled. "Yes, I can see that you take great pride in the way you look."

Star looked at Paresi. He turned the corners of his mouth down, as if puzzling over this turn of events.

Hattie touched Lisel's hair. "Very fine, like corn silk."

Lisel put her hand over Hattie's. The contrast of their skin colors was startling. "Yes, it's very soft and fine," she said.

The women stared at one another for what seemed like a full minute.

Hattie blinked, as if waking up. "I'm sorry, I did not mean to wander like that." She sipped her tea. "Since you know I left the church, Earl told you that I am no longer part of the *Voudon*, yes?"

"Yes," Star said. "He told us."

Hattie settled back in her chair, smiling. "I am Baptist now. I was dunked in the water even, at New Bethel Church on the East side." She looked at Lisel. "The old ways are seeing a new birth, though. For some of us who have gone, it is hard to stay away."

Paresi leaned in. "Can you tell us something about the bottle?"

"Oh, yes." Hattie picked up the picture. "A sorcerer's

bottle is very powerful magic. The colors are from the rite of *Petwo*."

"*Petwo?*" Star asked. "What is that?"

"It is about us. Our nation within the nation of Haiti. We use *Petwo* to evoke the spirits. There is an offering. We crack the whip, light gunpowder, and pour cane liquor for the *loas*."

"Then what?" Paresi said. "Party time?"

Hattie laughed. "I cannot tell you. I can only say that the bottle is very powerful. It encompasses all that we are, and it is ever changing."

"What are the mirrors for?" Star asked.

"To show our views of the afterlife. Water, the passage between life and death, death itself, which is new life. The bottle speaks many things, too many to go into here."

"We found this bottle," Star said as she pointed at the picture, "in Desmond's bedroom. Do you have any idea why he would have had it?"

Hattie smiled again. "Because he could harness the forces of the bottle. He could move among the *loas* without fear. He was one of them. They loved him."

"I see." Star nodded.

Hattie looked at her watch. "Oh, I'm sorry, I must go back on the floor. My dinner break is over." She stood. "I hope I have been of some help. If you need me again, please call me."

"Thank you." Star stood alongside her. "I know we're going to want to talk to you again. Is it all right if we come back here, to the hospital?"

Hattie reached into her pocket and removed a notepad and a small gold-plated pen. She wrote something and handed it to Star.

"Here is my direct line in Peeds, and my home telephone number and address. Anytime you need me, please call. I'll be glad to help in any way I can." She smiled up at Star. "Excuse me, but I must go."

She picked up her tray, and hurried to the cleaning station. They watched her put her dishes in the receptacle provided, and head for the door. She turned and waved, just before she disappeared.

"That was wild," Paresi said. "But I like that whip thing." He leered at Star.

"You would." She picked up her coat.

"Are we going back to the station?" Lisel asked.

"I don't know." Paresi aimed a wicked smile her way. "Maybe a sacred virgin shouldn't be riding with a guy like me."

Everyone laughed, including Star. "He never stops," she said to Lisel. She buttoned her coat. "I'm going in for a minute, I want to look at that bottle again."

"I'll go with you," Paresi said. "Lisel?"

"Uh, no . . . if it's all right with you two." She looked at her watch. "I've got a dinner engagement."

"Go ahead," Star said. "We'll see you in the morning."

Lisel smiled. "Thank you." She put on her hat. "I'll give your regards to Dr. Grant."

"Pardon?" Star said.

"Mitch." Lisel grinned. "He's my dinner date."

Back in the squad room, Paresi watched Star writing a note to Loman regarding the bottle. When they arrived back at the station, he had already left, and the bottle was locked in his desk.

"So, aren't you going to say something? You didn't say a word on the way back in," Paresi said.

"About what?"

"Lisel, having dinner with Mitch."

She looked at him. "Why should I care? He's a grown man. He can have dinner with the devil, if he wants. It's none of my business."

Paresi shrugged. "You looked surprised, when she said it."

"Did I?"

"Not so she would notice, but I saw it."

Star put the note in an envelope. "Could you drop this off in Loman's box? I'm tired, I'm going home."

Paresi took the note. "Sure, but don't go home. Let's do something."

"Vee's got classes tonight."

"I know, I meant you and me. Let's hit Floogie's. My treat. We haven't been in for a while."

"Paresi, I don't want to do a cop bar tonight. I'm going home."

Paresi pulled on his coat. "Then I'm going with you."

She managed a smile. "I don't remember inviting you."

"Yeah, you did. You told me you would teach me the Hitchhike, so tonight's the night, and I feel like dancing."

She shook her head. "I'm not getting rid of you, right?"

"Now you're catching on."

"Okay, okay. We'll get some takeout and tonight I teach you the Hitchhike, Jerk, Monkey, Swim, Pony, Mashed Potato, *and* the Roach."

"Sounds very retro, but tiring. I need Vee for that kind of workout. I've got a better idea," he said.

"What?"

"How about takeout and an Al Pacino film festival?"

"*Scarface*?" she said.

"Yep, along with another one. Your choice."

"*Frankie and Johnny*."

"Okay," Paresi said. "But if you get a love story, then I get a hot one, deal?"

She nodded.

"*Sea of Love*," they said together.

After stopping at Paresi's apartment, so that he could change into jeans and a black T-shirt, they hit the video store. Then they picked up two bottles of Chianti and a large sausage, pepperoni, and mushroom pizza with extra cheese from Paresi's uncle Angelo's restaurant.

Tall, broad-shouldered, and azure-eyed like his nephew, silver-haired Angelo Paresi caught Star up in a bear hug, kissed her on both cheeks, and told her she was too skinny. His bosomy wife Rosa agreed, and added another bottle of wine, antipasto, and cannolis for dessert to their order.

After spirited talk, mostly in Italian, over Angelo refusing money for the food and wine, Paresi kissed his uncle and aunt good-bye.

Now they sat, shoulder to shoulder, leaning against one another on the sofa in Star's den. Remnants of the feast on the coffee table lay in front of them.

"We ate it all," she said, sighing heavily.

"It's a curse." Paresi rubbed his flat stomach. "The Paresi family motto is, 'Food left on a plate comes back to haunt you.' " He touched the fingertips of his right hand together, imitating his uncle. "You gotta eat every bite, it make you strong, eh?"

"Your family's great," Star said. "And we're the same

way. Eat till you drop, party till you puke. That's the motto."

"You forgot fuck till you faint," Paresi said, turning his head to look at her. "It's called living life, and you haven't been doing that since last summer."

"Don't start." She pointed to the television. "Look at Al, he's about to snort the desk!"

They watched their favorite scene in *Scarface*.

"Agghhh!" Paresi grimaced, as Al Pacino snorted his way through a mountain of cocaine on the screen. "I *love* this."

They applauded.

"I wonder if that's real coke," Paresi said.

"They couldn't use real coke, it's illegal." Star slid further down on the sofa. Her blue-jeaned knee rested against Paresi's. "Besides, Pacino would have died if he'd done that much coke."

Paresi shook his head. "Al's tough, he could handle it. He's Italian."

They looked at one another and burst out laughing.

On the floor, under the coffee table, Jake opened his emerald eyes, yawned, and rolled over.

They watched the screen in silence.

"So," Paresi said softly. "Wanna talk?"

"What do you think?" She stared resolutely ahead.

"I think you should."

Star kept her eyes on the screen.

"You ever take a life, Dominic?" she asked, not looking at him.

"Yeah. My second year on the job."

Star turned to him.

"I didn't know that."

"I know." Paresi reached for the Chianti bottle. He

poured two glasses, emptying the bottle. He silently blessed his aunt Rosa, then opened their third bottle of wine for the night and topped off his drink. Star put her hand over her glass.

"No, thanks."

Paresi leaned back on the sofa, his glass in his hand. "It's in my jacket, but I guess the brass didn't inform anybody when I went to Homicide, except Lewis."

"When I asked for you as my partner, he never said anything," she said.

Paresi looked at her. "Would it have made a difference?"

"No." She shook her head. "What happened?"

"I was on patrol one night, and we got a call about a fight, over at that Puerto Rican dance club that used to be on 73rd Street."

"I remember that place," she said. "They were always in trouble for one thing or another. Lots of players used to hang out there. It finally shut down."

"Yeah, the two scumbags who owned it neglected to file the proper papers. They stayed in business mainly by paying off a few bad cops, and some suits in the license bureau."

"I remember." Star nodded. "They skipped town after the place was shut down." She looked at Paresi. "It was a big scandal."

"Yeah."

"So tell me what happened."

He took a deep breath. "We got there just a couple of minutes after the call went out. Some young, shit-faced Rican was mouthing off at the squad that beat us there."

"Is he the one you killed?"

Paresi shook his head. "No. It was his brother." He

closed his eyes. "The dude came out of the club, fucked up. He was so wasted, he didn't even have eyes. Just little pinholes in his face. He started shouting in Spanish. We couldn't understand him, but Reese Nichols was try-ing to calm him down."

"I remember Reese. He left the job."

"Yeah, mostly because of this, I think." Paresi took an-other drink of his wine, and set the glass on the low table. He leaned forward, his arms resting on his thighs. "Any-way, this guy is going off on Reese and his partner, and before anybody could blink, he had Reese's gun."

Paresi's eyes were seeing something visible only to him.

"I drew my weapon and told him to drop it." He looked at Star. "He turned and pointed the gun at me . . . I shot him."

She took his hand. "Dominic."

"I shot him. And I kept shooting, till my gun was empty." His grip on her hand tightened. "Turns out my first shot hit him in the neck and broke it. He dropped like a stone, but I couldn't stop shooting."

Star put her arms around him.

"I still see it," Paresi said. "It's been over seven years, and I still see it. The way he looked. The surprise on his face when the first bullet hit him."

He closed his eyes. She hugged him.

"It all happened in seconds. The other guys didn't even have time to react, but it was like slow motion to me. Afterward, they took my gun, called a sergeant, and sat me in back of the squad car. I went before the committee. Turns out the Rican was dusted. He was so full of PCP, he was ten floors higher than the moon. All the testimony said I had no choice. The killing was judged justifiable, and I was cleared."

He looked at her. His blue eyes were dark. "After seeing the department shrink, and doing everything by the book, I still think about it. I know it was him or me, but I still took a life."

She didn't say anything. She just held him. Paresi put his arms around her. Star laid her head on his shoulder.

After a few minutes, she spoke. "Does it ever go away?"

"No," he said. "At first, you think about it every minute of every day. You don't sleep, because you can't close your eyes without seeing it. Finally, you talk about it, you get it out, and then it starts to hurt less and less. You stop being mad at yourself and everybody else. You start living again, but it never, ever goes away."

She looked up at him, tears in her eyes.

"I know." Paresi rocked her gently. "I know, baby."

Outside, Mitchell Grant parked his midnight blue Porsche Carrera in front of Star's house, and got out.

As he walked up the path, he saw Paresi's black Dodge Viper parked in the driveway, close behind Star's burgundy Honda. He looked to his left. The curtains and blinds of the den were open.

A blue-gray light from the television screen illuminated the darkened room, and the two figures on the sofa. Star was curled up in Paresi's arms like a child, her head rested on his shoulder.

Mitch stood on the walkway, watching them. A sudden and sharp ache kicked at his gut, and he forgot how to breathe. When Paresi gently kissed Star on the forehead, the pain in Mitch's stomach raced to his chest and kicked him squarely in the heart.

He turned, and without a sound, went back to his car.

CHAPTER TWENTY-TWO

Lisel Werner was twenty minutes late for work. She arrived at the squad room just as Star got off the elevator from BCI. The two women practically collided at the double doors.

"Good morning, Star," Lisel said, opening a door.

"Sergeant." Star walked past to her desk.

"I'm sorry I'm late," Lisel said, following her.

Paresi looked up.

"I got in so late last night that I overslept." Lisel took off her long black coat and her fedora. "I'm afraid Mitch and I were together a lot longer than we'd planned. We just lost track of time." She smiled at Star. "You're not upset are you?"

"Why should I be?" Star said, without turning around.

"It's just that I know you're a punctual person and I'm *so* late."

Star could *hear* her smile.

"It's fine," Star said. "You wanna get some gloves and pull up a chair? I'll brief both you and Sergeant Paresi at the same time."

"Just a sec." Lisel hurried to her desk, got a pair of latex gloves and her chair. She rolled it up alongside Star and Paresi's desks, and sat down.

"To begin with," Star said, pulling on her gloves, "the bottle's been dusted and treated, but you can't be too careful, so glove up." She removed the bottle from the evidence bag and set it atop her desk.

Both Lisel and Paresi pulled on latex gloves.

Star pointed to the bottle. "When I lifted this yesterday, it felt heavy. Loman opened it for me this morning and it's got about three inches of sticky sediment inside. Be careful with the cap," she said, handing the bottle to Paresi. "Those scissors are sharp."

He cautiously opened the top and sniffed. "Lavender," he said.

"Uh-huh."

Paresi passed the bottle to Lisel. She sniffed it.

"It's lavender all right."

"Lavender oil, to be exact," Star said. "Loman took a sample. It's all over the inside of the bottle, as well as encrusted around the neck."

"Meaning it's been poured out over a period of time," Lisel said, and handed it back to Star.

"Exactly." Star took it and pulled tightly on the silk cloth. Under the white section of the fabric, the words "Barbancourt Rum" became visible.

"Barbancourt Rum is a Haitian rum. The factory that makes it is headquartered in Port-au-Prince."

"It's also what Dulac and Stevens used in the ceremony involving Desmond's body," Paresi said.

"The releasing of the *loa*?" Lisel asked.

The two detectives looked at her.

"I've been doing some research," she said. "I like to be on top of everything." She looked pointedly at Star. "Including my work."

"Do I see daylight at the end of this tunnel?" Paresi said, drawing Star's eyes back to him.

"Maybe." Star put the bottle back on her desk. "I'm waiting for a call from Sean. Things look good for getting warrants to search the church and Carlyle's home and locker at work."

"Are these warrants going be extensive?" Paresi asked.

"In a perfect world," Star said. "We're asking for interiors, exteriors within a three block radius, as well as clothing and furnishings. Plain sight of course is understood, as long as nobody gets a case of Superman eyes."

"Superman eyes?" Lisel asked.

"X-ray vision," Paresi said. "No opening anything that isn't covered in the warrant . . . you know, drawers, cabinets, closets, like that."

"Oh," Lisel said.

"We're looking for anything containing red silk fabric, herbs, notably sage and thyme, and lavender oil, et cetera," Star said. "I think—"

The ringing of the phone interrupted her.

"Excuse me." She picked it up. "Homicide, Lieutenant Duvall." She glanced briefly at Lisel. "Hello, Dr. Grant, what can I do for you?"

Lisel sat up in her chair. "Is that for me?"

Star shook her head without looking at Lisel. "No." She sat up straight. "No, Doctor, not you, I was talking to Sergeant Werner."

She listened intently, and then glanced at Lisel. "Yes, uh-huh, I see, sure . . . when?"

A look of surprise crossed Star's face. "Dr. Grant?" Mitchell Grant had hung up.

Star looked at her watch, and tried to cover. "We'll be there. Fine. Good-bye." She hung up the phone.

Lisel was perched on the edge of her seat, a slight smile on her face. Star's ruse hadn't fooled her.

"That was certainly abrupt. Is everything all right?" she said.

"Everything's swell," Star said. "Eric Stevens was brought in this morning."

Both Lisel and Paresi looked shocked.

"He wrapped his car around a tree."

"That church is going to run out of hoodoo men soon," Paresi said.

"Do we have to deal with that? It's not a homicide, is it?"

Star looked at Lisel. "Stevens wrapped his car around a tree, because, it appears, he lost consciousness at the wheel."

"So?" Lisel shrugged.

Star faced her. "Dr. Grant says a photograph of Stevens was nailed to the tree."

"And?" Lisel's eyes were wide.

"And, it was painted with a border of red nail polish. Tests show it was the same polish used on François Dulac. The picture had nine nail holes in it, but only one nail. The one that stuck it to the tree."

"And that means . . . what?" Lisel asked.

"It means he might have been murdered," Star said.

Paresi absentmindedly stroked his chest, feeling the raised comfort of the golden cross beneath the fabric of his shirt.

"By the power of voodoo," he murmured.

CHAPTER TWENTY-THREE

Mitchell Grant was in a prep room near the crypt, looking at the body of Eric Stevens, when the detectives arrived.

The corpse lay naked on a steel table. The bloody white plastic drape that had covered it hung down from the sides. Its light brown skin had a pale, ashen look. There were several large pieces of glass embedded on the left side of the face and cuts on the left hand. A dark, purplish bruise marked the left hip and outer upper thigh. A brown paper bag, holding Eric Stevens's clothing and possessions, was wedged between his ankles. The body had not yet been washed. It was a gruesome sight. Star glanced at Lisel. Her eyes were on Mitch.

The doctor looked up. "Detectives." He nodded at them.

"Looks like a regular smash and mash." Paresi sounded relieved.

Mitch didn't look at him. "Not this time." He stepped back from the corpse, allowing an aide to attach a toe tag.

"I'm just taking a fast once-over, but I can tell you right now, he didn't die from the crash." He peeled off his latex gloves, and looked at the detectives. His gaze made Star uneasy.

"There are no broken bones. I expect the X rays to confirm that. But it's odd." His cold eyes moved to Paresi. "As you know, no breaks is almost impossible in a car crash as severe as the one he was in."

"You mean he wasn't braced," Star said.

"Right." Mitch nodded, not looking at her.

Star looked back at the body on the table. "That means he was either drunk or unconscious when he hit."

"Right again, Lieutenant," Mitch said. "But he wasn't drunk. There's no smell of alcohol on the body, and there was no sign of alcohol in the car or in the vicinity of the crash."

"So what do you think?" Paresi said. "Was he epileptic? Could he have had a seizure of some kind?"

"No sign of seizure either," Mitch said, turning his back. "His mouth is clear, no foam or excess saliva . . . It's as if he just died for no reason."

"You're scaring me, Doc," Paresi said.

"I'm scaring myself," Mitch said, without turning around. "I'll do this one, and I'm going to be extra thorough, so it'll take awhile." He turned, facing the detectives. "You want to watch?"

"No, not me." Star turned to Paresi. "You can stay if you want. I've got to go check on something."

"What?" Paresi asked.

"I'll tell you later," she said.

Mitch turned to Lisel, and smiled for the first time since they had entered the room. "How about you, Sergeant Werner, are you staying for the post?"

"I'd love to watch you work," Lisel said.

"Good, I'd like your company," Mitch said.

Star turned angrily and slammed through the aluminum double doors. They clattered and swung from the force of her exit.

Paresi looked at the doors, and back at Mitch. He saw a look in the doctor's green eyes that totally unnerved him. If he hadn't known better, he would have thought that Mitchell Grant wanted to punch his lights out.

After visiting Loman in BCI, Star sat at her desk, telephone receiver to her ear, waiting for Hattie Jeannot to answer her phone. After six rings, a sleepy voice with a singsong accent picked up.

"Hello."

"Hi, Ms. Jeannot," Star said. "This is Lieutenant Duvall. I'm sorry to wake you but I've got an emergency. If it won't disturb you, or your family, may I come by your house for a few minutes? I really need to talk to you."

"Sure, Lieutenant," Hattie said around a yawn. "You won't be disturbing nobody. My old man been at work for hours, and we got no little ones, so come right down. I'll be looking out for you."

"About twenty minutes?" Star said.

"Yes, I'll just jump into the shower so that I will be awake enough to talk. I'll see you soon."

Star arrived at Hattie Jeannot's door with a pale blue box stamped on top with a Collette's Bakery logo, and two tall cappuccinos in matching, insulated, disposable cups. Hattie opened the door at her first knock.

"Hi." Star smiled. "I'm so sorry to wake you but something happened early this morning and I need your help."

"Come in, Lieutenant." Hattie's dark face was clean and makeup-free, but her eyes were still slightly reddened from too little sleep. Her plump little body was wrapped in a pink and white chenille bathrobe. Her feet were bare. Star noticed her polished red toenails.

"I brought breakfast," Star said, presenting Hattie with the blue bakery box.

"Oh, that was kind." Hattie pointed toward the kitchen. "We can talk in there."

"I know you're watching your diet, but being awakened this early demands something yummy." Star pointed at the box. "I hope you like chocolate croissants."

"I've never had them but they sound delicious. I am a slave to the cocoa bean."

"I heard that!" Star put the cardboard tray holding the coffees on the table. She made herself comfortable, while Hattie bustled around the kitchen, getting plates, glasses, and a half-gallon carton of Tropicana orange juice from the refrigerator. She took a silver cake cutter from a drawer, and finally sat down.

Star opened the cappuccinos. "Good, the foam held."

"Oh, you gon' spoil me, Lieutenant." Hattie, using the broad cake cutter, daintily scooped up a croissant and put it on a plate, which she placed in front of Star. She picked up a second pastry for herself. "This is turning into a party," she said. "I like waking up this way."

The two women giggled like girls.

They ate the warm, flaky, chocolate-laced rolls and sipped their coffees.

"Me too," Star said. "It's the least I can do. You've worked all night, and here I am, interrupting your sleep. I appreciate your seeing me, Ms. Jeannot."

"Oh please, girl, I am entertaining you in my robe, call me Hattie. It's not every day I have a real celebrity at my breakfast table."

"Me?" Star said.

"Sure. I read all about you in the papers last summer. I said to myself, she is a very brave girl. Then, just recently I saw you on the news right after Desmond was killed."

"Oh, that." Star licked warm, melting chocolate off her fingers. "It was Christmas, and some jerk was trying to get me to act stupid in front of the cameras."

"I saw." Hattie poured them each a glass of orange juice. "I thought to myself that you handled him very good. You made me proud, Lieutenant Duvall."

"Thank you." Star sipped her coffee. "But please, call me Star. When somebody wakes you up and bogards themselves into your kitchen, I think you should be friends."

"I would very much like that." Hattie smiled. She took another bite of the croissant. "Oh my, this is true heaven. Now I must have them every day . . . My diet, it is over."

They both laughed.

"Duvall." Hattie looked at Star. "Are your people from the islands?"

"No, my father's side is from New Orleans and my mother's folks are from Chicago."

"Oh, that's interesting. I remember reading that your father was a policeman. I'll bet he would be very proud of you. Is your mother still alive?"

"No." Star shook her head. "She died when I was twelve. My dad raised me."

"Only child?"

"Yes."

Hattie reached over and touched Star's hand. "I can see your daddy's pride in your face. He is still with you, you know. Both of them are."

"Thank you." Star sipped her coffee. "I'm having a fine time, Hattie, but I guess I should get to the reason I woke you up. I'd like to ask you about something."

"What do you need?"

Star reached across to the chair next to her and picked up the file folder she'd brought. She opened it and pulled out two evidence bags. One held the red-bordered, punctured photograph of Eric Stevens and the other, the three-inch nail that had been driven into the tree.

"Have you ever seen this man before?"

Hattie's hand flew to her mouth. "Oh my, that is Eric Stevens."

"You know him?"

"When I was in the church, he was very active with Desmond and the others."

She fingered the photograph through the plastic. "Nine holes." Hattie looked at Star. "He must be dead."

"Yes," Star said. "How did you know?"

Hattie picked up the bag containing the nail.

"How did he die?"

"A car crash."

"Did he hit another car?"

"No, a tree."

Hattie laid the two packets holding the picture and nail on the bright, red-and-white tablecloth. "This picture was found on the tree, correct?"

Star nodded. "Yes."

"This nail color on the picture." Hattie pressed her finger to the plastic.

"I wondered about that," Star said.

"Red. It is the color of Legba. Each *loa* has its own color, food, drink, all that." Hattie looked at her. "He was murdered, Star. This is a death charm."

"What?"

"To kill, you must take a picture of the intended, and paint the color of the *loa*, who you honor, on it. Then you must drive a nail into the picture every day. On the ninth day, you drive the final nail, and the person dies."

"Are you serious?" Star said. "Nobody really believes that, do they?"

Hattie leaned forward. "Eric Stevens believed, and he is dead." She took Star's hand. "Do not misjudge the power of *vodou*, Star. It is the way of our people, our African ancestors, yours and mine."

Star shook her head. "I just can't swallow that. I know some people believe, but I don't."

Hattie's grip on Star's hand tightened. "Listen to me. You must search Eric's house, and the church. Places he frequented. Find a board. In the board you will find eight nail holes. The ninth was driven at the place of his death. Find that board and you will find your killer."

The woman's words sent a chill through Star's body.

"Hattie . . ."

"Ssshhhh." Hattie put a finger to her full lips. "I know you don't believe, but hear me. I left the church because of the bad magic they do. I cannot put my soul in the hands of devils. You find that board . . . and you find your killer."

CHAPTER TWENTY-FOUR

When Star got back to the precinct, Paresi was reading Loman's report on the bottle, and Lisel was in talking with Captain Lewis. She took off her coat and sat down.

Paresi looked at her. "So what was the big emergency?"

Star looked over her shoulder, at Lewis's glass-enclosed office. "How long's she been in with the captain?"

"A few minutes, why?"

"I don't want to tell her about this."

"Why?"

"Trust me. You and I need to talk."

"Okay." Paresi leaned forward. "So . . . ?"

"I went to see Hattie Jeannot."

"Earl's sister-in-law?"

"Yeah." Star looked over her shoulder again. "I don't want to talk in here, let's go upstairs."

"Okay."

She and Paresi headed for the double doors. Lisel's voice rang out from behind them.

"Are you two dumping me again?"

Star turned, looked at the woman standing a few feet from them, and lied. "No. Sergeant Paresi is just going upstairs for a drink, and I feel the need for a double

210

chocolate-chip muffin and a cup of tea. Would you like to join us?"

"No, thanks." Lisel folded her arms, and flashed a smile that never reached her eyes. "I ate so much last night, I haven't had an appetite all day."

"We'll be back in a minute." Star turned to Paresi, and hissed through gritted teeth. "Bitch!"

"That's my girl." Paresi grinned and opened the door for her.

Upstairs in the lunchroom, Star sat facing the door with a cup of milky tea in front of her. Elvis had put it on the table the minute she sat down. After having eaten two chocolate croissants, she declined his offer of a free muffin.

"So what's up?"

"What was all that at the door?" she said. "I thought you were on Morticia's side."

"Why?" Paresi stirred sugar into his coffee.

"You told me I was too hard on her."

"You were." He sipped his coffee. "But you lightened up. Now she seems to think she's got some kind of thing going with Mitch, and she should rub your face in it." He put the spoon down. "Bust her slats."

Star laughed. Elvis looked up at the sound.

"I'm glad you're on my side, and speaking of Mitchell, did he seem strange to you today?"

Paresi shrugged. "A little . . . He seemed sort of pissed off about something. But hey, weirdness goes with his job."

"I agree," Star said. "But he's never weirded out before."

"Everybody has bad days," Paresi said.

"You're right." She leaned in close to her partner. "Thanks for last night."

"My pleasure." He looked at her. His eyes were tired. "But the next time I decide to drink three bottles of wine and sack out on your couch, remind me of the realities of morning, okay?"

"Deal." She touched his hand. "I'm grateful . . ."

"I know."

"What about the post?" She sipped her tea.

"I wasn't there. I came back here, but Vampira stayed."

Star swallowed a smile at Paresi's description of Lisel.

"She says it was nothing that Mitch could see." He stirred his coffee. "He's going to send over the reports later."

"Hattie says it was voodoo."

"Get outta here." Paresi rocked back on the legs of his chair.

"No." Star beckoned him. He leaned close and she whispered. "Hattie said the picture with the nail holes is a death sign. She said the killer nailed eight holes into the picture and the ninth nail is what caused Stevens to die."

"You believe that?"

Star shrugged. "I don't know what I believe."

Paresi ran a hand through his hair. "Listen, if you can kill somebody by knocking holes in a picture, get me a camera, a hammer, and a keg of nails; then tell Lewis to say cheese!"

They both laughed.

"Will you be serious?" Star smiled. "Hattie said the final nail was driven into the tree where Stevens crashed, and she was right. I mean, how would she know?"

"Maybe she killed him," Paresi said.

Star pointed at his cup. "Have some more coffee, why

don't you? Seriously, Paresi, Hattie said we should search for a board with eight nail holes. She said when we find the board, we'll find the killer."

"So now we're going to ask for a search warrant for a board?" Paresi said. "I hope they don't put us out on traffic until the weather gets warm."

"Oh ye of little faith," Star said.

When they returned to the squad room, Star found a message from Impound on her desk. She dialed the number.

"Impound, Lucatis."

"Hi, Stevie, this is Lieutenant Duvall."

"Hey, Lieutenant. I got some news for you."

"Go."

"That car that got cracked up this morning . . ."

"Yeah?"

"When we got it in and started working on it, we found something really strange under the accelerator."

"What?"

"Can you come down? You gotta see this."

"We're on the way."

Steve Lucatis lead the three officers back to Eric Stevens's totaled red Dodge Spirit sedan. He opened the passenger door and handed Star a flashlight. "I didn't take it. I thought you guys might want to have the honor."

Star took a paper cover, and placed it on the seat. She leaned in on one knee, aiming the flashlight at the floor.

"So, you're a new face." She heard Steve Lucatis chatting up Lisel.

"I'm NYPD," Lisel said.

The pain-in-the-ass squad, Star thought to herself. She

rooted around with her latex-gloved fingers. She smelled it before she saw it.

"Paresi, I need a bag."

"Here you go." He handed her a plastic evidence bag.

"Hold this." She gave him the flashlight.

Paresi leaned into the car over her, balancing himself on the dash with one hand, and pointing the light at the floor with the other.

Star tugged on the item with both hands. It came loose.

She fell against Paresi. He caught her, and the two of them backed out of the car.

It was then that he saw what she held.

"Holy shit," Paresi said.

Star couldn't speak.

They gaped at the item.

In her gloved hand, Star held a doll in the shape of a man. It was crudely made of black cloth with human African-American hair protruding from the top. The entire effigy had been soaked in lavender oil. Pinned to the doll was a strip of parchment paper, with something written on it.

Star looked closely at the oil-soaked paper. She recognized the liquid that had been used as ink. Though the words were smeared, she was still able to make them out.

It was a name.

Eric Stevens.

Written in blood.

CHAPTER TWENTY-FIVE

Star and Paresi dropped a shaken Lisel back at the Weybourne Residential Hotel, where she was staying. During the ride, she had been silent and paler than Star had ever seen her. When she got out of the car, her good-bye was so soft, neither one of them was sure they'd heard it.

"She's really shook," Paresi said, pulling away from the curb.

"I still think she's a cow," Star said. "But I have to admit, this stuff is beginning to get to me."

"Want to stop at St. Timothy's and light a few candles?" Paresi said, half jokingly.

Star pulled her coat tightly around herself. "After what I just saw, a bonfire would be more like it."

"I could use some comforting myself," Paresi said.

She turned to him. "Like?"

"Think you can handle a little dinner?" he asked.

Star looked at him. "It's Wednesday, right?"

"Yeah."

"Gumbo at Jessie Mae's."

"With dirty rice." Paresi licked his lips.

"Drive!" she said. "Duh-rive!"

* * *

215

When Star and Paresi arrived the next morning, Captain Lewis called them into his office and handed them a search warrant for Carlyle Biggs's locker at work and his home.

"One down and one to go," he said. "The church is going to be a problem. It *is* a house of worship."

"Well, at least Carlyle isn't off-limits," Star said. "Thanks, Captain."

They went back to the squad room. Lisel arrived a few minutes later.

"I'm sorry I'm late."

"Another big evening?" Paresi said.

"No, I was very shaken by what happened yesterday and I took a drink." She looked at him, her face drawn. "Just to calm my nerves. I don't tolerate alcohol very well. And so I slept much too much. I awoke with a terrible headache this morning." She smiled wanly.

"It's called a hangover," Star muttered, reaching for her coat.

"Are we going out?" Lisel asked.

Star waved the papers at her. "Search warrant. We're paying Carlyle a little visit."

Lisel's face grew whiter. "I'll go with you."

Carlyle Biggs stood quietly, watching the officers search through the contents of his locker.

"It'll be fine, Carlyle." Lisel spoke softly to him. "It's just procedure."

"Yeah?" Carlyle looked at her, his eyes dead. "I'm fair game, right? I mean I *am* a convicted murderer."

Lisel patted him gently on the back. "Everything will be all right, I promise."

The locker held nothing out of the ordinary.

"Well, Biggs, looks like the road show travels to your house," Paresi said.

Carlyle didn't speak. He put on his coat and turned to Kevin Lim, who had stood by during the search.

"I'm sorry," he said.

"It's fine, Carlyle," Lim whispered. "I believe in you."

Carlyle kept his studio apartment very tidy. He sat expressionless and silent in an overstuffed brown easy chair, while the detectives and uniformed officers rummaged through his belongings.

Lisel stood beside him, casting pained looks his way.

Paresi opened a tall, whitewashed, wooden cabinet that stood behind a chair in Carlyle's kitchen area. "Hello!"

Instead of dishes or food, Paresi found a small table shoved inside. It was laden with bottles, statues of saints, candles, and pictures. "Lieutenant," he called out to Star.

Prominently displayed on the secret altar was a bottle, identical to the one found at Desmond's home. A sorcerer's bottle.

Paresi carefully opened it and sniffed. He passed it to Star.

"Lavender oil," she said.

Paresi put the cap back on the bottle.

Star picked up one of several glass apothecary jars filled with dried green matter. She opened the jar. "Sage," she said to Paresi.

Paresi picked up one of the photographs. "Biggs, who is this?" He turned the picture so that Carlyle could see.

"My mother," Carlyle said softly.

"I didn't recognize her," Paresi said to Star. "She looks a lot different without the hole in her head."

Another photo sat near the back of the table covered with a square of red silk cloth. Star picked it up and uncovered it. "Well, well." She turned the picture toward Paresi.

"Desmond," he said.

"Yep." Star shook her head and turned to the quiet young man. "Carlyle, you're coming down to the station with us."

She turned to Paresi. "Give him his rights."

Biggs looked at Lisel. A tear slid down his cheek.

"Don't worry," she said. "We'll get you an attorney, nothing is going to happen to you."

Star and Paresi looked at one another.

Inside the interrogation room, Carlyle Biggs was as still and silent as a statue. He hadn't moved for almost two hours. He'd been Mirandized again, just after his arrival. He still refused to speak without an attorney present. Now he sat waiting for his court-appointed lawyer to arrive.

Lisel sat with him, stroking his hand, touching his face tenderly. Star and Paresi stood in the anteroom behind the one-way glass.

"You know, she knows we're watching her," Paresi said. "Is she nuts or is it that she doesn't give a damn?"

"Who cares?" Star said. "Her attachment to this kid is way over the top."

Paresi looked at his watch. "It's almost time for the late crew, so where's this jimoke?"

"On the way, I guess." She sighed. "Lord knows he needs a lawyer."

"Now don't you start."

"No, listen," Star said. "I've been doing this a long

time, and you get a feel for people. I don't think this kid is the killer."

Paresi stepped closer to the glass. "Let's not forget that Junior ventilated his whole family at fourteen, and he had all the stuff that's been turning up in this case. *All* of it."

"No. He kept regular voodoo supplies, if there is such a thing. It's like you having olive oil and Parmesan cheese in your house."

Paresi turned to Star. "Whoa, is that some kinda slam?" he said mockingly. "You calling me a spaghetti-bender?"

She smiled. "Well, Pete, if the mustache fits."

They laughed.

"No, seriously," she said. "He had the things they use in their rituals."

Paresi put his hands in his pockets and leaned against the wall. "Loman's got that piece of red silk that was over Desmond's picture. He's testing it to see if it connects in any way to the other pieces."

"I don't think it will," Star said.

Darcy poked his head into the room. "Hey, Star, me and Rescovich are going on a call. Everybody else is out, the squad's empty."

"You think you'll be back before the shift change?" she asked.

Darcy shrugged. "I don't think so. We're headed over to the projects."

"Another gang call?" Star asked.

"Don't know. They just said two people are down in an apartment. The uniforms are there now."

"Okay. Watch yourselves. I'll see you when I see you."

"Right." He closed the door then instantly opened it again. "I almost forgot—Mitch Grant is on line three."

"Thanks." She picked up the phone. "Lieutenant Duvall."

"It's about time," Mitch said. "I've been waiting here for a while. I was just about to hang up."

"Darcy just told me you were on the line. What can I do for you, Doctor?" she said, curtly.

Mitch's coldness matched hers. "I just wanted to let you know that I've got the results on Eric Stevens."

"And?"

"He was poisoned."

"What?"

"There was an abundance of fluid in the pericardium. Tests show that the natural serous fluid was inundated with a drug called Veronal."

"Veronal? What's that?"

"It's a barbiturate, a downer. The uptown name for it is Barbital. It's used mainly in gas form as an anesthetic, but it's also available as a liquid."

"How was it administered?"

She could hear the rustling of papers.

"My guess is the initial dose was given with a saturated cloth, which knocked him unconscious. And a larger, lethal dose was then injected directly into his heart. There was a needle stick in the left upper chest, and in the sac. I also found traces of red silk fibers in the windpipe, which means he breathed them in."

Paresi leaned close to her. "What's he saying?"

She put her hand over the receiver. "Eric was murdered," she whispered.

"Tell me this isn't happening," Paresi said. "Tell me voodoo does not exist."

"Star, are you talking to me, or to him?"

"I'm talking to you. I was just telling Paresi that Stevens is a homicide."

"Can't he back off long enough for me to fill you in? This is important information."

The hostility in Mitch's voice stunned her.

"Geez, I'm sorry. Go ahead, Doctor." She looked at Paresi.

"Thank you," Mitch said, sarcastically. "I think the drug was administered while he was in the car. There were traces of the fabric from the headrest on his neck and in his hair. So the killer caught him from behind, put the saturated cloth over his nose and mouth, and knocked him out."

"Uh-huh," Star said. "Then he was hit with the needle."

"That's my take. After that, the car was set in motion."

"And the tree jumped in the way," she said.

Mitch didn't respond.

Star looked at Paresi. "That's some scenario, Doctor. I guess someone put the doll in the car before any of this stuff happened."

"Doll?" Mitch said. "What doll?"

"I forgot, I didn't tell you," Star said.

"No, you didn't. What about the doll?"

"A voodoo doll. It was found wedged under the accelerator of Steven's car, with a note attached. BCI has it and Loman says the hair on the doll and the blood used to write the name on the note are definitely Stevens's."

"This is the creepiest thing I've ever come across," Mitch said. "But Eric Stevens was not voodooed to death. He was drugged and murdered."

"At least that's what we want to think," she said.

"What's he saying?" Paresi asked.

"Lieutenant, can you tell your partner to hold on?"

"He just wants to know what you're saying," Star said.

"Tell him to put it back in his pants, okay? You've got a job to do."

Star's mouth dropped open. She spun her chair away from Paresi. Color rose in her face, her voice croaked out in a raspy whisper.

"What the hell is wrong with you? I'm not the one pulling everything that walks by. Besides, you got nothing to say about me or Paresi, after spending last night with Morticia Addams!"

"That's enough!" Mitch said, and hung up.

Star slammed the phone down. "That man makes me so damned mad!"

"What's going on?" Paresi said. "I've never heard the doc raise his voice before, and I could hear him from here!"

"I think he thinks we're screwing around with each other."

"Get out!" Paresi looked amused. "Did he miss the part where we've been together five years, and that I date your best friend?"

Star looked in the direction of the interrogation room. "I think he's been listening to a lying blond buzzard!"

"He wouldn't pay any attention to anything she has to say," Paresi said.

"Well somebody's pulling his coat, but I can't deal with that right now." She sat down. "Paresi, Carlyle isn't our killer."

"How do you know?"

She took a deep breath and told him how Eric Stevens died.

"Carlyle couldn't have done that. He wouldn't be

smart enough to know what kind of drug to use, or to set up that whole crash thing."

"Maybe they use those kinds of drugs in their rituals," Paresi said. "He could know a lot more about drugs than we think. Don't they smoke peyote and do mushrooms and stuff?"

"That's the Indians, Paresi, Native Americans, not the Haitians."

"Hey, I thought it was the hippies. Same difference. Besides, don't forget, a doll was in the car. Biggs grew up with witch doctors, he could have whacked Stevens."

Out of the corner of her eye, Star saw the door to the interrogation room open. A tall, handsome, dark-skinned black man walked in. Star noted his well-tailored navy blue suit and gray overcoat. "Who's that?" She went to the glass.

Paresi walked up behind her. "I think his name is Willis, Mark Willis. He's new in the sucker pool, I know that."

"When did he come aboard?"

Paresi shrugged. "He joined the public defender's office a few weeks ago, I think. I'm not sure. But I know he moved here from Hartford. He's one of those 'they can all be rehabilitated' guys."

"He'll learn," Star said. She turned up the volume on the speaker. Lisel was talking to the attorney.

"I'm one of three working on this case," she said. "The others will be in shortly."

Mark Willis nodded, and turned to Carlyle.

"I just got your case, Carlyle, so it's going to take me a little while to get up to speed." He had a deeper voice than Star expected. To her he sounded like the actor Avery Brooks.

"It's okay," Carlyle said softly.

"You'd better get in there," Star said to Paresi.

"Where are you going?"

"To get some aspirin. I've got a headache. I'll be there in a minute."

"Okay."

They went out into the hall and Paresi walked into the interrogation room. Star went back to her desk and rummaged around in all the drawers. She found their shared aspirin bottle. Empty.

She looked around the squad room.

Lisel, she said to herself. Somebody that pale had to have a drug stash.

She went to Lisel's desk, opening drawers, looking for aspirin. She found nothing. As she closed the bottom drawer, Lisel's purse, which had been on the desk, fell over the side. The latch opened and her belongings scattered on the floor.

Star stooped down to pick them up. She put them back into the purse and set the purse on Lisel's chair. As she turned to go upstairs to buy aspirin, her eye caught something shining on the floor.

She reached down and picked up a golden filigree lipstick case.

"Bozo Red, no doubt," she muttered.

Star turned the case in her hand. It was unusual. She looked on the bottom, where the color and manufacturer's label usually are located. There was nothing.

She opened the lipstick. "I was right." She twisted the tube bottom and the bright red stick of color rose in the case. "Yech!" She twisted the bottom again, pulling the lipstick back into the tube. She put the cover on and turned to put it in Lisel's purse.

The filigree case felt strange in her hand. She looked at it again. The raised design caught her eye. At first she thought the case was covered with some kind of vine design. She looked closer.

It wasn't vines. The golden raised figures were snakes, entwined and facing away from one another.

She stood there. *Don't freak,* she thought. A lot of designers use snakes in their ads, and a lot of women wear red lipstick. Besides, it's bright red. The other reds have been deeper, darker.

She tossed the lipstick back in Lisel's bag and headed for the door to go upstairs to the vending machine. As she passed her desk, she saw the photo album that had been confiscated from Carlyle's apartment.

"This should be in interrogation." She picked up the book. It slipped from her hands and hit the floor. She stooped to retrieve it.

As she stood, a six-by-nine-inch brown envelope fell from between the pages.

Star put the book on her desk and looked at the envelope.

"I thought we went through everything," she said. "Where did this come from?" She opened the envelope.

Her heart began beating fast. She couldn't believe what she was holding in her hand.

A photograph. A five-by-seven of Carlyle and his family. It appeared to have been taken on a beach. Carlyle looked to be around ten or eleven. He stood in front of his parents with his two brothers, all of the boys mugging for the camera. A nice family picture, with one addition. Standing with her arm linked through the arm of Carlyle Biggs Sr., and grinning with big, red lips directly into the lens, was Lisel Werner.

"She said she knew Carlyle's father, so she was a family friend," Star muttered.

She got ready to put the picture back in the envelope when Lisel's earrings caught her eye. Star looked closely. She opened her middle desk drawer and pulled out the magnifying glass.

Her startled gasp echoed in the empty squad room.

Dangling from Lisel's visible ear were two long, entwined, twisting snakes. Their flat heads were embedded in Lisel's earlobe and faced away from one another, just like the ones on the lipstick tube.

A light went on in Star's brain. She had seen them before, the same twisted, entwined serpents. She closed her eyes, trying to remember. She squeezed her eyelids together, trying to bring the shadows in her mind into focus. Nothing.

She went to the anteroom and pushed the button, causing the red light mounted high on the molding to flash. Paresi saw it.

"Excuse me," he said to the others. "I'll be right back."

"What's up?" He closed the door to the anteroom.

"I've got to go out."

Paresi pointed at the glass. "You're supposed to be in there."

"You handle it, I've got something I've got to take care of. I'll be back as soon as possible."

He looked hard into her eyes. "I don't like this."

"Don't worry, Dad," she said, trying to smile. "I'll be all right. I'll also get back sooner if you don't question me and let me go now."

"Fine," he said, his jaw set. "The next shift is due in about an hour. If you're not back by then, I'll have somebody else sit in, so call me, okay? Let me know where you are."

"Deal." She pointed at the glass. "Take care of that. Keep your eye on her."

"Why? What do you know?"

"Nothing . . . yet. Just make sure she doesn't stifle Carlyle. Let him talk."

"Right." Paresi pointed toward the door. "Go. Get out of here."

Star hurried out to the squad room and grabbed her coat. She put the envelope and photograph into her purse. Paresi watched her disappear through the double doors before he went back into interrogation.

"Isn't Lieutenant Duvall joining us?" Lisel said.

"She's not feeling well." Paresi sat down. "She'll join us as soon as she can."

CHAPTER TWENTY-SIX

At the manager's desk, in the Weybourne Residential Hotel, Star flashed her badge and a smile.

"Hi," she said to the freckle-faced, red-haired man on duty. "I'm Lieutenant Duvall, Brookport PD."

He smiled. He looked like a grown-up Norman Rockwell poster boy. "What can I do you for, Lieutenant?"

"Well, your name would be nice."

"Oh." He giggled. "Yeah, I'm Robbie McGuiness. I'm the night manager." He extended his hand.

"Hello, Mr. McGuiness." Star shook it.

"Call me Robbie, that's my name."

"Great . . . Robbie."

She leaned on the desk. "You have a detective from New York staying here."

"Oh yes, ma'am. Ms. Werner."

"Yes, Ms. Werner," Star said.

"She's not in right now." Robbie reached for a pad. "You wanna leave a message?"

"No, Robbie. I know she's not in. In fact, I just left her at the precinct. We're working on a case together and she left some very important material in her room. She asked me to come and pick it up."

"Oh, sure." He reached behind him and pulled down a key.

"Room 325, third floor, about the fourth door down. The elevator is right over there." He pointed toward an old-world, birdcage-style glass and filigree iron elevator.

"Well, thank you, Robbie." Star took the key. "I might be up there for a few minutes, so if you don't see me come back down, don't worry. She wasn't sure where she left it."

"It's a small suite, ma'am, you won't have to look too hard." He grinned.

"Thanks."

Star headed for the elevator. She got in and pushed the button for the third floor, then smiled at Robbie, who was leaning out from the desk, still grinning at her.

"This is almost too easy," she muttered to herself as the door closed.

Lisel's suite consisted of a living room with a small dining area, a kitchenette, and a bedroom. Everything was neat and spotless.

Star pulled a pair of latex gloves from her pocket and put them on. She went into the bedroom, opened the closet, and turned on the overhead light.

All of Lisel's wardrobe hung in orderly fashion. Skirts together, tops together, dresses, etc. Her shoes and many colored pairs of leather and suede boots were arranged neatly across the floor of the walk-in closet, heels turned out and toes pointing to the wall. The boots even had wooden, vertical shoehorns inserted, so they stood straight.

"Not too anal, are we?" Star said.

She stepped back, looking at the clothes displayed on the hangers. The blond detective had planned for a long stay in Brookport. In addition to winter clothing, she had packed three lightweight jackets, and a lined London Fog raincoat was hanging near the back of the closet. Star looked overhead. She counted a dozen sweaters, neatly folded and resting in stacks of four on the top shelf.

She closed the closet door and went to Lisel's dresser. There were several bottles of cologne displayed on the left side of the dresser top. She opened one and sniffed at it. A deep floral fragrance wafted from the bottle. She looked at it. White Shoulders. She snorted derisively and put it back in place.

Star stood in the center of the room, her hands on her hips. Everything was neat and orderly. She wondered how much of it was the maid service and how much was Lisel.

She walked into the bathroom and turned on the light. Again, spotless. She looked in the wastebasket. Empty. She opened the medicine chest. Nothing out of the ordinary. A tube of antifungal cream was the most exotic thing she could find among the bottles and packets of aspirin, Midol, Benadryl, and Theragram vitamins.

Star closed the medicine chest and opened the drawer in the cabinet just beneath the sink. A tortoiseshell comb and brush rested inside along with a portable hair dryer. Star picked up the comb and then the brush.

"No hair in either of these," she said out loud. "Everybody has hair in their combs and brushes."

In her mind she heard her great-grandmother Queen Esther's voice: "Don't nevah leave no hair nor nails 'roun, chile, 'cause hoodoos can get aholt of 'em, and *kill* you!"

Star dropped the comb. "Stop it," she admonished herself. "You're freaking out for nothing." She picked it up and put it back in the drawer.

Under the big mirror and over the sink, a small chest ran the length of the mirror. Star opened it. Inside she found a tube of Rembrandt whitening toothpaste, two plastic packs of unwaxed dental floss, a bottle of eye drops for contact lens users, two boxes of disposable contact lenses, and a bottle of alpha hydrox skin lotion. Star read the label on the bottle. "Prevents wrinkles." She laughed out loud. "Glad I don't have to worry about that." She put the bottle down. "Black don't crack."

She closed the chest and opened the larger cabinet beneath the sink. There, she found several rolls of toilet paper, and a large, opened box of hospital-sized sanitary napkins.

Star chuckled. "Well, this is something." She peeked into the box. Half of it was empty. "Talk about your heavy periods!" She pushed the box back to where she found it. "No wonder girlfriend looks like Dracula's daughter."

She closed the cabinet and headed back out to the bedroom. Star looked at the nightstand by the bed. A Seth Thomas alarm clock, a hardback edition of *Jane Eyre* marked with a long, blue grosgrain ribbon bookmark, and a two-pound box of Godiva chocolates rested on the table.

Star ran a finger along the top of the candy box.

"NYPD certainly must get a fatter check than we do." An unwelcome thought entered her mind. "Unless Mitchell gave her this." She looked at the bed. "Wonder if he's ever been up here?" she said aloud.

Dismissing the thought, she opened the gold-covered

box. Inside, each of the costly chocolates nestled in splendor. She noted that only three of them were missing. For a moment she thought about helping herself but decided against it.

She looked in the wastebasket between the bed and the chest. There were no wrappers or anything else. Star sat down on the side of the bed and opened the bottom drawer of the nightstand. Inside there were two other hardback classics, Voltaire's *Candide* and Charles Dickens's *Nicholas Nickleby*.

"Snooping on a fellow officer," she said aloud. "I *should* feel bad about this, shouldn't I? . . . Nah!" She pulled the drawer out to the farthest extension and moved the books aside. There was a small white box near the back of the drawer. She opened it.

"Peach stationery, trimmed in white, how dainty." She removed the top sheet of paper. The blood rose in her face.

There, beneath the first sheet, was a second peach-colored page. On it, Lisel had begun writing an unfinished note.

Star swallowed the anger rising in her, and read it.

Dearest Mitch, it read. *Last night was the most amazing night of my life. I can't think of it, without wanting . . .*

"What?" Star said. "Wanting what? To jump him again?" She was shaking. "And he has the balls to come at me about Paresi!"

She bit her lip, breathing hard, as she sat still, eyes closed, collecting herself. When she could think again, she started to put the paper back.

It was then she noticed the M in Mitch's name. It was written with a slight flourish. The same as the capital M on the note that Paresi had found on François Dulac's desk, the reminder of his meeting with Carlyle Biggs.

She stared into space, seeing the piece of paper in Paresi's hand.

"No . . ." Star stood and folded the note. "Still, it wouldn't hurt to check." She put it in her pocket. She put the box of stationery back, closed the drawer, and smoothed the bedspread, erasing any sign of its having been sat on.

She walked back into the living room, and across the floor into the small kitchen. It held a little stove with four burners, a small refrigerator, and a cabinet over the sink with two shelves.

Star opened the cabinet doors. There was nothing on the shelves except for two plates, two glasses, and two coffee mugs, all with the hotel logo.

She turned to the refrigerator and opened it. Empty, except for a bottle of water from a Swiss mountain stream, or so the label said.

She was about to leave when she noticed that Lisel's small, round dining table had a drawer in it. She pulled one of the two chairs aside and opened it. Inside there were two sets of silverware; knives, forks, and spoons. She pulled the drawer out as far as it would go.

"Well, well."

At the back of the drawer, she saw a square-shaped object wrapped in red silk. Embroidered on the silk fabric were two entwined snakes facing away from one another. Above their heads, sewn in golden thread, she read the words *Damballah* and *Ayida Wèdo*.

Star pulled the whole thing out.

"Holy God." Her knees gave way. She sank heavily into one of the chairs.

She remembered where she had seen the entwined snakes. On a wall hanging in the office of Desmond's church, the first time she and Paresi had called on François Dulac. The flag bearing the snakes hung over his head, as he sat behind the desk.

Beneath the soft material, Star could feel the object in her gloved hand. It was rough and hard. Holding her breath, she unwrapped it.

Her heart thundered in her chest. Her throat went dry, and sweat broke out between her breasts. She felt moisture on her forehead and upper lip. Tiny specks of water appeared on the backs of her hands, under the latex of the gloves.

"Sweet Jesus of Nazareth," she whispered.

In her hand, Star held a piece of white pinewood.

In the wooden square she counted eight nail holes.

CHAPTER TWENTY-SEVEN

When Star arrived back at the squad room, the questioning of Carlyle Biggs was finishing up. She didn't even bother to remove her coat—she went directly into the interrogation room. Paresi took one look at her and knew something had happened.

Mark Willis was packing up his briefcase as she walked in.

"Lieutenant Duvall?"

"Yes." She crossed the room and shook his hand.

"Sorry I missed this," she said. "I had to go out for a little while."

"How are you feeling?" Paresi said. "I told them you weren't well."

Star picked up on him. "Yes, I went to the drugstore, and I was lucky enough to find what I needed."

"Glad you're feeling better," Mark Willis said, not looking at her. "I understand you're the officer in charge, correct?"

"Yes, I am."

"Then it's my duty to tell you what I've told your colleagues. You don't have a case."

Star nodded. "Yes, well, you might be right." She

235

turned to Paresi. "Sergeant, I would appreciate your briefing me on this meeting."

"Be glad to," Paresi said.

Mark Willis picked up his gray overcoat and slung it over his arm. "You *do* know you can't hold him."

"If you say so," Star said. "But I need to talk to my people first."

"Very well, do what you want. I've got an urgent matter that came up, so I can't stay, but he walks. Tonight. I'm going to see to it." He opened the door. "Carlyle, I'm going downstairs to take care of the paperwork. They'll call when it's done. I'll see you tomorrow."

"Thank you," Carlyle said, softly.

The public defender looked at Star, and walked out of the room.

"Can I really go?" Carlyle turned to Lisel.

"I'm sure." She patted his shoulder. "After the paperwork is processed, but I'd like you to wait for me. I have to talk to Lieutenant Duvall. Afterwards, we can have a coffee and talk."

Carlyle nodded.

"Oh, Lisel," Star said, "before we talk, can you give me a moment with Sergeant Paresi? It's not about the case. It's personal."

Lisel smiled. "Yes, I'll wait here." She turned to Carlyle and took his hand. "I'll keep my friend company."

"Thanks." Star nodded toward the door and walked out. Paresi followed her.

"What's going on?"

She pulled him into the anteroom. "I need to keep an eye on her."

"Why? Where did you go?"

Star opened her purse and pulled out a plastic evidence bag containing the peach-colored paper.

"What's this?"

She smoothed out the paper in the bag, and held it.

"Read it."

Paresi read the unfinished note. "Guess Mitch rocked her world. I thought he'd changed, but it looks like the legend lives."

"I don't mean that," Star said, an edge to her voice. "Look at the handwriting. Doesn't it look the same as the note you found on Dulac's desk . . . the note about meeting with Carlyle?"

Paresi looked closer. "I can't swear to it, but I do remember thinking that Dulac's handwriting was a little flowery, for a guy."

"That's not all."

She pulled out another plastic evidence bag. This one contained the fabric-wrapped wooden square.

"What's this?"

"Open it."

Paresi opened the bag and carefully unwrapped the material. He looked at Star. "Is this the . . . ?"

"Yes. The block of wood that Hattie said would give us the killer." She pointed at the square. "See, there are the eight nail holes."

"Where did you get this?"

Star indicated the glass. "From her hotel suite. It was in her dining room table, in a drawer, pushed to the back."

Paresi looked at her. "Star, you didn't have a warrant. This stuff would be inadmissible."

"I don't care," she said, her voice cold.

"Are you saying . . ."

"That she's the killer?" Star's eyes searched Paresi's. "What do you think? I found a picture of her in Carlyle's family album, and I've got a note with familiar-looking writing, and the block that Hattie told me about."

"The block and the note are certainly suspicious," Paresi said. "But it's all circumstantial, until we can at least compare the handwriting, and as far as the picture with Carlyle's family . . . she knew his father."

He looked down at the evidence bags in his hand. "Besides, you scooped this without a warrant, it won't matter."

"I'll put it back," she said, her eyes blazing. "I'll swear it was all lying out in plain sight. I'll say I went up to visit her, and found the door open. I went in to check her out, to make sure she was safe."

"Knock it off," Paresi said. "Get a grip, you're scaring me."

Star was breathing hard. "You think I'm being paranoid? I knew all along she wasn't right, but everybody kept saying I was jealous, or I was acting like a brat!"

"Calm down," Paresi said. "I'm on *your* side, remember?"

She pulled the photo out of her large shoulder bag. "Look at this!"

She handed it to him. "The family was on an outing, and she was with Carlyle Senior and his wife. Look."

"So?" Paresi studied the picture. "It was taken when Carlyle was a kid." He looked at Star. "That's why she's so protective of him. She knew him back then. It doesn't make sense she would try to set him up."

"Right, but dig the way she's holding on to Carlyle Senior."

"Yeah, she's clinging, but so what?"

"Check what she's wearing on her ears."

Paresi looked closely. "They look like snakes."

"Bingo! Give this man a bottle of Haitian rum. The snakes are the same snakes I saw on the cloth hanging in the office in Desmond St. John's church. They're gods. Voodoo gods. Damballah and his mate, two entwined snakes."

"Star, you're getting way out there."

"I know, I know. But that's not the end of it. When I was searching her place, after I found the note and the wood, I got ready to leave. Then I realized I hadn't looked in the closet by the door."

"Yeah?"

"I looked. I had to."

"What did you find?"

"This." She pulled a smaller bag out of her purse and handed it to Paresi.

He held the plastic bag by the corner, staring at the bottle of deep, brilliant red nail polish inside.

Star looked back at the glass. "It's exactly the same color that was on Dulac's nails, and on the picture of Stevens."

"Are you sure?"

"Positive. It's an unusual shade of red. Believe me, I know. I went through a time where I wore nothing but different shades of red nail polish."

"I remember," Paresi said.

Star looked at the glass. Behind it, Lisel had her arm around Carlyle, her face close, talking quietly to him.

"I think she's doing something to Mitchell, too," Star said.

"No shit," Paresi said, derisively.

"No." Star turned to him. "Not that . . . For some reason, I don't think he's doing her."

"You don't?" Paresi said. "Then what's she talking about in the note?"

"If he did it, last night was the first and only time," Star said. "I don't think he would touch her, but if I'm wrong, it's only been one time."

"Maybe," Paresi said.

"I think she's messing with him, making him think crazy things. Maybe that's why he's acting so strangely."

Paresi looked over Star's head at the two people in the interrogation room. "I don't know. Could be. I've never heard him lose it like he did tonight."

"She's putting something on him. She wants him. Granma Queen used to say a witch woman could make a man do anything. You heard him, he was practically raving at me over the phone."

Paresi looked at her. "Maybe he knows we were together last night."

"So what? We've been together lots of nights. He's never gone off like that." She pointed at Lisel. "I'll bet she put some kind of suggestion in his mind, made him think you and I are sleeping together."

Paresi shook his head. "This is getting way weird."

"I'm telling you, she knows this stuff, but she slipped up. Remember what she said, when Hattie said she looked like that white goddess . . . Ezeal, Ellie Mae, or whoever."

"Ezili Doba," Paresi said. "The Sacred Virgin."

"Right." Star nodded emphatically. "She knew what it was. She said she read it off the base of the statue, but she knew all along. She also knew about the ceremony to release the *loa*."

Paresi looked at the woman through the glass.

"But what I can't figure," Star said, "is why she got Stevens to give up that spirit bottle. Didn't she know that would help us?"

Paresi shrugged. "If she's what you think she is, she was yanking our chain, having a laugh, watching us run all over . . . She never counted on anybody knowing exactly what that bottle was." He looked back at the glass. "She fucked up."

"Yeah . . . maybe," Star muttered.

Paresi turned to Star. "What do we do?"

"Get her out, away from Carlyle."

"Done."

He gave her back the evidence bags. She stuffed them into her purse. They went back into the interrogation room.

"Lisel," Star said. "We need to talk to you in the squad room. Carlyle can stay here, he'll be okay."

Lisel stood. She leaned down and patted Carlyle's cheek. "I'll be right back."

Carlyle nodded, his eyes sad.

As they walked out into the squad room, Lisel, walking behind Star, closed the door. It was then that she saw, visible in Star's large, open purse, the plastic bag. She saw the patch of red silk fabric with gold threads inside.

Lisel moved so fast, neither detective was prepared. In an instant her Glock .17 was drawn. Her arm was around Star's throat, yanking her backward and pressing painfully against her windpipe. The barrel of the gun bit into the flesh at Star's temple.

"Don't move," she said.

Paresi reached for his gun.

Lisel cocked her weapon. Her arm around Star's throat pressed harder, cutting off more of her air. Star's eyes went wide as she was dragged across the floor.

"I said, *Don't move*."

Paresi raised his hands and backed up two steps, moving slightly to her left.

"Throw down your weapon, Dominic," Lisel said.

"No." Paresi shook his head.

"No?" Lisel tugged on Star's throat, and laughed. "Did you say no?"

She pressed her cheek against Star's. It felt dry and hot.

"I was wrong," she cooed. "He's not in love with you, he's gonna get you killed."

She yanked on Star's throat again, pulling tighter.

Star gagged, and a sharp pain stabbed behind her eyes. Her head began to pound.

"Don't do this, Lisel," Star croaked, her hands stiffly up and out in front of her, trying to keep her balance, as Lisel jerked on her, painfully choking off her air and bending her body backward.

"Don't do what?" Lisel's voice was cold. "Why did *you* do this? Why did you go to my hotel?"

"What are you talking about?" Star's voice rasped. "I haven't been to your hotel," she lied.

Lisel's eyes blazed with hatred. She pressed her arm harder against Star's throat. Star gasped, trying to gulp air and force it past her constricted windpipe.

"I can see the cloth," Lisel said viciously.

Paresi kept moving, his hands up, inching closer.

Lisel pressed the gun against Star's head.

"One more step, Dominic, and she's dead."

"Stop," Star croaked. "Stop."

"Listen to her," Lisel hissed. "She's the *boss*!"

In her grip, Star went limp, letting herself become dead weight.

Lisel struggled to hold on. The barrel of the gun slipped and momentarily pointed up toward the ceiling.

Star got a breath, and the leverage she needed. She grabbed the arm around her throat with both hands, and rammed her hip into Lisel's pelvis, knocking the woman off balance. Star pivoted, bent sharply from the waist, and flipped the blond woman over her shoulder.

Lisel hit the floor, and the gun flew from her hand. It fired as it banked off Rescovich's desk. The bullet shattered his favorite, fourteen-year-old, "lucky" coffee-stained mug and lodged in a corner of the wall.

Carlyle Biggs rushed in from the interrogation room.

The detectives were scrambling on the floor, trying to keep Lisel away from the weapon.

Carlyle ran from the squad room. A group of blue-shirted officers were already running up the stairs. He stood at the top, shouting for help.

Paresi threw himself on Lisel, pinning her to the floor, his forearm across her throat.

Star scrambled for the Glock.

Lisel screamed, flailing wildly, her hair flying. She spit at Paresi and sank her teeth into his flesh.

"Fuck!"

He slapped her with an open palm. She pushed him off her. He fell back, blood soaking his blue denim shirtsleeve.

Lisel went after Star.

Paresi grabbed her. She slid out of his grip and tackled Star, knocking her to the ground.

Star went down hard. The wood floor smacked her abdomen and breasts. She cried out. The gun she was holding slipped from her grasp.

She rolled over on her back. Lisel attempted to stomp her. Star grabbed the woman's booted foot and tossed her off balance. Lisel went down.

Star struggled for the gun.

Lisel tore at her, shrieking and screaming.

Paresi got to his feet and grabbed her, pulling her off Star.

With an angry shout, he shouldered the screaming woman and rammed her body against a file cabinet.

Lisel's screech died in her throat. She slumped against the gray metal cabinet. Paresi stood hunched in front of her, both of them gasping for breath.

Lisel shook her head and blinked. In less than a second, and before Paresi could get out of her way, she kicked him hard in the testicles.

His breath left him. Pain rocketed through his body. Nausea raced into his throat. He saw stars.

"Son of a bitch!"

Paresi swung at her, and smashed his fist into her face. There was the solid sound of flesh connecting with flesh.

Lisel fell back, stunned. Blood poured from her mouth. All of the air in her body came out in a loud whoosh. She dropped to the floor.

Star grabbed the gun and got to her feet. She looked back at her partner writhing on the floor in pain.

"Paresi!"

She shoved the weapon into her pocket and ran to him.

"Oh Jesus!" Star said. "Oh Jesus!"

The room filled with blue uniforms, Carlyle Biggs behind them, tears rolling down his face.

Several officers ran to Paresi.

Star put her arms around him, getting blood on the sleeves of her coat.

"I've got him." She held Paresi in her arms, his face against her, shielding him. She forgot her own aching and bruised body. She didn't want the others to see his pain.

"See about her." She indicated Lisel, who was lying on the floor, her back against the file cabinet. "And get the paramedics up here, on the double."

Paresi groaned. She pressed her face against his.

"Oh, honey . . . oh, Dominic. Everything will be all right, okay? The E.A.'s on the way. You'll be fine. You'll be fine."

Paresi was doubled up, his hands between his thighs. "I'm gonna puke," he whispered.

Star reached over and grabbed Richardson's wastebasket. She got it to him just in time.

Lisel came to and saw the men around her. She shook her head, spit out what looked like a tooth, and scurried backward on the dirty floor, like a cornered animal.

"No!" she shrieked, as the officers scuffled with her. Sergeant O.W. Greene got her on her stomach and put his knee in the center of her back. He slapped the handcuffs roughly on her wrists.

"Get away from me!" She continued kicking wildly.

Sergeant Greene pulled her to her feet. She didn't even

look human. Her hair flew in all directions, blood-flecked spittle flew from her mouth.

"It's not over!" she yelled. "It's not over. *I am Ezili Doba, and I will kill all of you.* I'll make *him* do it." Her wild eyes locked on Carlyle. She screamed at him in French.

The officers didn't know what she was saying, but Carlyle looked as if he'd been stricken by a heavy hand. He fell to his knees, pure terror on his face.

"Get her out of here!" Star shouted, and then leaned down, whispering to Paresi.

"I've got to see Carlyle, okay?"

Paresi nodded. His eyes closed. "Go ahead . . . go ahead."

She raised her head. "Did anyone call the paramedics?"

"Yes, ma'am." A uniformed officer came to her side. "Is the sarge okay?"

Star again covered Paresi's pain-wracked face with her body.

"He'll be fine . . . just check on the medics. Get them up here."

"Yes, ma'am." The officer headed for a phone.

She turned back to her partner, whispering in his ear. "They'll be here in a minute, okay?"

Paresi's breath was harsh and rapid. He lay with his eyes closed. He reached for Star.

"Did you get her?"

Star laid her cheek against his. "She's in custody." She squeezed his hand. "I've got to see Carlyle, okay?"

"Go, go on," Paresi said.

"I'll be right back."

She got up and crossed the room.

Carlyle was kneeling, sobbing.

"Carlyle, are you all right?"

He grabbed her, squeezing her tightly, pulling her down.

"Save me. Save me." He looked at Star. "She'll kill me, she'll kill me. She *is* the Ezili Doba. She *will* kill me!"

The uniformed officers dragged Lisel, still screaming, from the room.

Star stood and helped the nearly hysterical boy to his feet. She walked him to a chair. "Sit here, wait. Let me look at my partner. I'll get some help for you. Just stay here."

Carlyle put his head in his hands, and wept as if he were being torn in two.

Star went back to Paresi. He had gotten to his knees, his face pale and sweaty. She helped him to his feet, then looked at his blood-soaked shirtsleeve.

"Oh my God. She took a chunk out of you. I've got to get you to the hospital."

"I'm okay," Paresi said. "How's Carlyle?"

"Don't be brave," Star said. "You need a doctor."

He leaned heavily on her.

She helped him to his desk. Carlyle's moans echoed in the room.

"I'm not gonna die." Paresi looked up, his face lined with pain. "But I can't say the same for Carlyle. Go on, go back to him, I'm all right."

"You sure?" Star could feel the pain in Paresi's eyes.

"Yeah."

She helped him lean on the desk and went back to Carlyle.

"Can I go ... can I go with her?" he said, his eyes blank. "Maybe she will forgive me, talk to me."

"Forgive you for what, Carlyle? You've done nothing."

Carlyle started to cry again. "She'll kill me. She'll kill me. She has the power."

Sergeant Greene came back into the room. He went to Star. "You all right, Lieutenant?"

"I'm fine, O.W., where's the E.A.? Sergeant Paresi has to go to the hospital."

The wiry, dark-skinned man headed across the room toward Paresi. Something caught his eye and he picked it up from the floor.

"What's that?" Paresi asked.

Sergeant Greene held the small, white, blood-covered object in his hand. "Looks like a tooth. Guess it's the lady's. We should pack it in ice and send it to the hospital so they can put it back in."

"Give it to me," Paresi said.

Greene handed the tooth to the injured detective.

Paresi took it and dropped it into the empty Seven-Up can on his desk. He tossed the can to the floor, stomped it flat, and pitched it into the trash.

Sergeant Greene went to him and patted him on the shoulder. "The paramedics are on the way, Dom," he said.

Paresi didn't speak. He leaned against the desk, sweat pouring down his face.

Star went back to him. She looked at his bloody arm, and then gently rolled the soaked fabric away from the wound.

"Jesus, Dominic." She tenderly touched his face. "It's going to be all right, the E.A. is on the way."

Paresi rocked back and forth in pain. "I hurt like

hell." He looked at Star. "Do you think she's poison or something?"

"Yes!" Carlyle was on his feet. "She can kill you, she can kill all of us. She has the power."

Star tried to hold him back.

"No." Carlyle pulled away from her. "She learned. She learned from Desmond. She will kill all of us."

Paresi and Star looked at one another.

The paramedics came through the doors.

At the hospital, Paresi was given a shot for the pain, and his wound was cleaned and dressed. Star stayed with him, only leaving the room as ice was applied to his testicles. She knew he was going to be all right, when he invited her to stay and hold the ice bag.

After he was given a tetanus shot, medication, and blood had been drawn for an HIV test, Paresi was released.

Star draped his coat over his shoulders and put her arm around him.

"I didn't want to say anything until you were taken care of," she said. "But O.W. told me how you disposed of Sergeant Werner's tooth."

Paresi shrugged. "She bit the hell out of me and used my nuts for soccer practice. She damn near wiped out the next generation of Paresis. I was a little upset!"

The two of them laughed.

"Think I can get Vee to kiss 'em and make 'em better?" he said.

"You are a sick man." Star grinned. "But in spite of what Lisel did, you cold-cocked her, and knocked her tooth out. That means a report."

Paresi shrugged. "Is it going to go in with the one about how you searched her place without a warrant?"

"Touché."

"Besides, I was distraught," he said. "But hey, now I got some dynamite drugs, I feel better." He shook the vial of pills. "You took a couple of good hits, wanna share?"

"I've got my own," she said. "While you were being iced, they took a look at my chest."

"I coulda done that." He leered.

Star laughed. "You are crazy, you know that, don't you?"

"Baby girl, after tonight, crazy takes on a whole new dimension," he said, putting his good arm around her shoulder. "Now let's discuss reports."

"What reports?" she said.

Paresi kissed her forehead, and they walked out into the emergency room lobby.

The young doctor who had examined Carlyle was standing near the desk. His name tag read Dr. Joel Rivers. He was new; Star had never seen him before.

"I'm admitting Mr. Biggs for observation," he said.

"Is he hurt?" Star asked.

"No." The light-brown, sad-eyed young man shook his head. "But he's in shock. He went catatonic when I was examining him. I gave him something to help him sleep. I'd like to keep him at least forty-eight hours for observation, unless he's under arrest."

"No, he's not under arrest," Star said, "but I'd appreciate a call before he's released."

"Done, Lieutenant." The doctor wrote instructions on Carlyle's chart.

"Was Sergeant Werner admitted?" Star asked.

"She's in the psych ward," Dr. Rivers said. "I'll take you."

CHAPTER TWENTY-EIGHT

The two detectives stood outside the door of Lisel Werner's room, watching her through the glass window. Star noted with a silent, grim satisfaction that without makeup, she had no face.

Lisel lay against the pillows, her wrists in restraints, her eyes dead. She saw them. Her head snapped up. She started to laugh. A vacant space was visible between two teeth on the left side of her mouth.

Star turned to Dr. Rivers. "Can we talk to her?"

The doctor shrugged. "Might as well, she's not reacting to any of the drugs we've given her."

Star pushed the door open. She and Paresi walked in.

"Hello," Lisel said. Her bruised mouth formed an evil smile. The gap in her teeth made it even more sinister.

"We need to talk to you," Star said.

"Really?" She looked at Paresi's sling, and bandaged arm. "What's the matter, baby, got a boo-boo?" She laughed, and ran her pink tongue over her lips.

It made Star shudder.

"You taste very good, Dominic," Lisel said. Her missing tooth gave her speech a soft, sibilant sound. She licked her lips again, and closed her eyes. "Mmmmmm . . . very sweet."

Her eyes snapped open. She gazed malevolently at Paresi. "Pity you're such a stupid bastard. We could have had some fun."

Paresi looked at her. Star could feel his rage.

"That's what I get for being a gentleman," he said. "Pulling my punch. I should have broken your fucking jaw . . . closed up that filthy, raggedity mouth for a while."

"The only thing you ever pulled was your dick!" Lisel said. "You don't have the balls to play rough, asshole."

Paresi looked at Star. His head tilted slightly. His eyes grew dark. She stepped in front of him, and put her hand on his chest. His heart was racing.

"This won't take long," she said, moving him back with her body.

Lisel didn't seem to realize that Star had just kept her from being punched. She strained at the leather straps around her wrists. "Hey." She stuck her tongue through the hole in her smile and waggled it at Paresi. "Did you find my tooth?"

Star felt Paresi's body push against her. She stood firm, one hand on his chest, the other holding his free hand.

"Don't . . ." she whispered. "Please, Dom, don't . . ." She touched his face, making him look at her. "Think of the paperwork," she said.

The blue color came back to his eyes. Paresi stepped back. "You win."

"Hey! You deaf?" Lisel called. "Where's my tooth?"

"I threw it away." Paresi said.

Lisel laughed wildly. "It's okay, I can grow another one."

"How many sets of fangs do snakes have?" Paresi said to Star.

She turned to Lisel. "I would advise you to shut up."

Lisel's eyes narrowed to slits. "Remember who and *what* I am." She aimed another dark glare at Paresi. "Come see me in a week, and I'll show you my perfect smile."

Paresi turned away.

Star pulled a mini tape recorder out of her purse and turned it on. She stated her name, the date and time, and the people present in the room into the microphone.

"My, this looks official. What would you like to know?"

Lisel's eyes roamed to Paresi. "Aren't you going to sit down? Come, sit on my bed, near me, so we can be close to each other." She laughed again.

Paresi positioned himself near the door, his eyes on Lisel.

"He's so cute," she said.

"I want you to tell us about Desmond," Star said. "But first, I'm going to give you your rights."

"I know my rights," Lisel said coldly.

Star ignored her, pulled up a chair, and began. "You have the right to remain silent . . ." She rattled through the speech, her eyes on Lisel.

"Do you understand what I've just told you?"

"Yes. You told me that you're going to send me to jail forever."

"Do you understand?" Star said again. Her gaze leveled on Lisel's pale face.

"Yes. I understand."

"Do you want an attorney present?"

Lisel smiled, and stayed silent.

"Do you want an attorney?" Star repeated.

Lisel shook her head.

Star indicated the tape machine. "Say it."

"No," Lisel said.

"No what?"

"I do not wish to have an attorney present."

"Thank you," Star said. "Now, tell us about Desmond."

Lisel looked at the machine in Star's hand. "He was mine," she said. "Do you need to know anything else?"

"I want to know it all."

Lisel rolled her head on the pillow. "I loved him, but he loved Carlyle more than me."

"Carlyle?" Star said. "Are you saying . . ."

"They were lovers, Detective. They made love to each other. They penetrated one another's bodies. They licked and sucked—"

"We get it," Paresi said, interrupting her. He sat down on a chair near the door.

"Look at him. Isn't he something? He can't take it."

Star sighed. "Sergeant Werner . . ."

Lisel sneered at Paresi. "What's the matter, Nicky, you got a secret? Got a taste for cock? You sure have got the mouth for it, darlin'."

"So when does your head start spinning around?" Paresi said.

Lisel laughed. "Men are so stupid, aren't they, Starletta? Take Mitch." She looked at Star for a reaction. She got none.

"Did you read my note? Be sure and give it to him. Tell him I'm sorry I didn't get to finish, but just thinking about him . . . well." She licked her lips. "He's fabulous, you know. But he's really easy. He thinks you're fucking your partner. I told him you were, and he believed it!" She winked at Paresi. "Maybe I should have told him the truth. That you really prefer *him*, huh?"

Paresi stared at her.

"I don't blame you, baby," she said to him. "He's really beautiful. Ever see him naked?"

Star bit her lip. The machine in her hand trembled.

Lisel saw it, and tuned into Star's anger. She turned on that jack-o'-lantern grin. "He went to your house last night, after we were together. Did you know that? I knew he would. I made him do it."

She glared at Paresi. "I knew you'd be with the wop, and I wanted him to see you. I *made* him see you together."

She cackled.

The sound ripped through Star. Her entire body clenched. She gripped the tape recorder so hard that her hand froze in an agonizing, screeching cramp.

"Save it." Star transferred the machine to her other hand and flexed her fingers. "I don't believe that voodoo crap. I just want to know what you did."

"What I did?" Lisel rolled her pale eyes skyward. "Well, last night I fucked your boyfriend!"

She stopped, staring at Star. A low chuckle rumbled from her throat. "Oh, you mean like further back, a few years ago, when I fucked Carlyle's father."

Star's face remained impassive.

"He fell in love with me." She tilted her head, like a child. "Why are black men so crazy for white women, Starletta?"

Star said nothing.

Lisel shrugged her shoulders. "Guess I shouldn't ask

you, your taste is for white meat, right? Long, tall, blond, and I'm sure you know, amazingly hung!"

Star's heart pounded. Her temples ached. Still, she remained impassive.

"But we're talking about my passionate past with Carlyle Senior? Right?"

Star was quiet.

"His dumb, pickaninny wife never figured it out. When Desmond came along, Carl let me go. He gave Desmond whatever he wanted, including me *and* his son."

Lisel nodded her head, as if talking to someone they couldn't see. "That's right. He wanted the boy, so at the age of eleven, Carlyle was given to Desmond.

"The bastard claimed they never made love until Carlyle was old enough, and wanted it, but little by little, that boy took Desmond's love from me."

"You and Desmond were lovers," Star said.

"You don't listen, Lieutenant. Roll back your tape. I just told you that niggers love white flesh. Carlyle never suspected, but I guess he figured it out tonight."

"Desmond took me into his church, and paraded me right in front of his congregation. He told them I was the Ezili Doba. I was always masked, and heavily veiled, so no one ever saw my face."

She shook her head. "Stupid black bastards, they believed him. They believed anything he said. I was his sacred, white virgin . . ." She arched her eyebrow. "We stretched the last part. Truth is, I was the white woman he wanted. He hatched all that Ezili Doba shit to keep the sisters from skinning his black ass!"

Her laughter filled the room.

"Last year, Reverend Tilton and Judge Addison got

anonymous letters regarding my relationship with Desmond. I guess one of the sisters in the church finally put two and two together. So, I had to pay them both a visit. They threatened to go public with what they *thought* they knew. It would have cost me everything."

"So you killed them," Star said.

"And made it look like Carlyle had gone around the bend," Paresi said.

Lisel turned her head to look at him. "It would have worked, too, but Carlyle was back in the lockup by the time I did it. I thought he was staying over with Reverend Tilton and his wife. That way, he would have been free when the killings happened. I didn't find out that he was locked up until it was too late. They just chalked it up to a copycat."

"The cop guns?" Paresi said.

"Mine," she said. "All of them. I have quite a collection. I was hoping to add yours to it." She smiled at him.

Paresi lowered his head, and put his good hand over his mouth.

"I think I'm making your partner sick," Lisel whispered conspiratorially to Star. "Got an upset tummy, baby?" she cooed at Paresi.

"Get on with the story," Star said.

"Oh yes." She pulled against the straps on her wrists. "My face itches, up by my nose. Would you scratch it for me?" she said to Star.

"No."

"Then I can't concentrate." Lisel closed her eyes.

Star reached past her and pulled a plastic straw out of the nearly empty water cup near her bed. She shook the water from it, and put the dry end to Lisel's face, moving it up and down against her skin.

"To the left and up." Lisel sighed. "Yes, that's the spot." Star continued scratching.

"Thank you."

Star tossed the straw into the wastebasket near the bed. "Go on."

"Let's see, I sent those two good Samaritans packing and went back to Desmond. When I got pregnant, I took a leave of absence from the job. Desmond moved me here, into his house."

"Clarendon Square?" Star said.

"Yes. I had the baby on Christmas Eve, in that house. I was attended by women from the church. They were curious about me, but much more afraid of Desmond. He swore everyone involved to secrecy. No one talked."

"That explains the hospital-sized sanitary napkins," Star said.

"You are thorough, aren't you?" Lisel said. "So admirable."

"The baby that was found on the highway?" Star asked.

Lisel closed her eyes. "He was mine."

"You sacrificed your own child?" Star said, incredulous.

"Jesus." Paresi stood up, a sick look on his face.

"The baby was weak, Lieutenant. He would not have lived. I needed help from Damballah. I needed strength, so I gave him my child. Desmond was making love to that boy, while I tore my body, pushing out his son."

"How could you look at that baby in the morgue?" Paresi moved to the foot of her bed, his blue eyes deep and stormy. "How could you do that, knowing he was yours."

Lisel shrugged. "I buried him, didn't I?"

"What was all that running from the room?" Paresi was livid. "Acting like it made you sick."

Lisel looked at him as if he were a slow puppy. "I *was* his mother. Wasn't I?"

"Star . . ." Paresi looked like he was going to rip Lisel's skin off.

"It's almost over," Star said, ignoring the smile on the woman's face.

The fingers on Paresi's hand in the sling twitched. "I don't know how much more of this I can take," he said.

"Interrupting tape, call of nature break," Star said, and noted the time. She turned off the tape recorder and looked up at him. "It's not worth it to beat the shit out of her, Dominic. She's just a poor, crazy bitch. Why don't you go get a coffee, I'll be finished soon."

"I'm not gonna leave you alone with this bitch. She's the fucking Antichrist. This is *The Exorcist*, for real!"

Star took his free hand. "It's nearly over," she said. "Let's just finish."

Paresi looked at Lisel. "All right." He squeezed Star's hand and went back to his chair.

Lisel's eyes glowed with suppressed laughter. "Is the big man through threatening the poor little woman?" she said in a silly tone.

"I just saved your life," Star said.

Lisel started to say something. But the look on Paresi's face across the room changed her mind.

Star turned the recorder back on. "Resuming tape," she said, and again noted the time.

"How long was Carlyle in the house, before you had your baby?" Star asked.

"He stayed mostly weekends. He had the job at the market, and his own little place. In fact, Desmond stayed there some nights."

"And when Carlyle was in the house, you two never ran into one another?"

"It's a big house, Lieutenant. Besides, I was immensely pregnant. I preferred to stay in my suite." Lisel shifted her weight on the bed. "I knew they were fucking, but when I heard them while I was having Desmond's baby, I couldn't stand it."

"So you killed the child," Star said.

"No." She dropped her head back, shaking the hair from her face. "The baby died at my breast. He was sickly. He only lived a few hours or so." She tried to sit up. "These restraints are so painful, please take them off."

"No," Star said. She looked at the tape indicator. "Where did Dulac and Stevens fit into this?"

Lisel sighed. "I'm getting tired."

"Do you want to stop?"

"No. I'll be gone by tomorrow."

"Taking a trip?" Paresi said.

"Making plans for you." Lisel nodded at him.

"Go on," Star said.

"A few years ago, Desmond introduced both François and Eric to me. He told me if I ever needed anything, they could be trusted."

"Were they involved in this?" Star asked.

"François came when I called. He took the baby and discarded him for me."

"Christ," Paresi said.

Star remembered the small man's reaction and protestations when she showed him the picture of the brutalized infant. He'd taken that child out on the highway, and he'd been in the house, *after* Desmond was killed. The thought that he'd faked them out made her sick.

"After Desmond was buried, they came to me for money to keep quiet."

"So you killed them?"

"Yes."

"The red nail polish?"

"I gave them as a gift to Legba. I left his colors on them."

"What about Carlyle's family?" Star asked.

Lisel lay back on the pillows. "That's ancient history. Carlyle did that." She sighed. "But only because I made him. Carl had second thoughts about me being with Desmond. He got drunk one night, and raped me. So, I decided it was time for him to go, and take his sorry family with him."

"How did you make Carlyle do it?" Star said.

Lisel stretched, pulling at the restraints. "He's a very impressionable boy. The night I killed Desmond, when Carlyle came to and found the body, he thought *he'd* done it. He screamed and screamed."

She smiled at the recollection. "I got on the intercom and said I was Ezili Doba. I told him that he'd sinned in my eyes, that he had to leave and tell no one what he'd seen and done."

She shrugged her shoulders, and looked up at the ceiling. "He ran out of that house so fast, he beat his breath to the sidewalk!"

"He believed you," Star said.

"Why not? I *am* Ezili Doba." She turned her face to

Star. "You may think you've intimidated me, but I'm just resting. My magic is very powerful." She looked at Paresi. "As the both of you will surely learn."

CHAPTER TWENTY-NINE

Mitchell Grant put on his gold-rimmed, aviator-style glasses and looked at the clock on the mantel. It was 3:15 in the morning, and still he couldn't sleep. Whenever he closed his eyes, images of Starletta Duvall in Dominic Paresi's arms danced in his mind. After tossing and turning for hours, he had gotten out of bed and come downstairs, where he made himself a pitcher of very potent vodka martinis.

He lay stretched out on the dark green leather sofa, in front of the fireplace. It had been especially made to accommodate his height. His martini glass was balanced on his chest.

He'd always found James Taylor's voice soothing, and so the singer's live double album played from his Bose system. He massaged his temple with one hand, and tried not to think about how depressed he was.

The thought to call one of his many female friends entered his mind. He knew several that would come, even at this late hour. But a fill-in woman for a night was the last thing he wanted. He had spent a perfectly dreadful evening with Lisel Werner twenty-four hours ago, before getting the shock of his life, so other women were definitely not worth it.

He decided to keep drinking. Besides, there was only one woman he wanted to see, and when he closed his eyes, she appeared . . . in his friend's arms.

He was near the end of his fourth cocktail when the doorbell rang. He turned his head and looked at the clock again. Had he really heard it, or was he as close to being toasted as he felt?

The sound of the melodic chime filled the room again.

It *was* the doorbell. The night man in the lobby hadn't called to announce anyone, and he wasn't expecting any visitors.

He picked up the glass and took another sip from his martini, a neat trick when you're lying flat on your back.

Maybe it was Robin, but she was back at the university, and she had a key.

The chimes rang out again, insistently this time.

Mitch sat up, glass in hand. The room spun for a few seconds. He slowly stood and steadied himself on the arm of the sofa. His bare feet were suddenly cold. He pulled his midnight blue silk robe around his lean body, and went to the door. He looked through the glass peephole.

"I'm hallucinating," he said out loud, and opened the door.

Starletta Duvall stood there, looking more than a little tired and lost.

"I heard the music, but I thought maybe you were asleep. I was about to go."

Mitch stepped back. "C'mon in."

She walked past him, catching the faint scent of Givenchy's Xeryus cologne. She noted that he even smelled good when he was by himself. The thought that he just might not be alone came to her mind, but she fought it down. After the night she'd had, she couldn't handle any more surprises.

"I was just getting pleasantly hammered," Mitch said. "Can I interest you in a martini?" He held up his nearly empty glass. "This one happens to be vodka, but I've got gin, too, your choice."

"Neither," she said. "Thanks."

"Okay." He nodded. "How about some wine?"

"That would be nice." She pulled off her coat. Mitch took it, and tossed it on the bench near the door.

Star went into the living room. She put her purse on the coffee table, next to his martini pitcher, and sat down on the sofa he'd vacated.

From her seat, she could see the second floor. She knew that upstairs, in addition to the bedrooms, there was a gym, complete with state-of-the-art equipment, a sauna, and a hot tub. Mitch had offered his facilities to Paresi and to her when her partner complained about the condition of the equipment in the police gym.

The loft area was her favorite spot in Mitch's two-story, ten-room penthouse apartment. Though the lights were low, she could see the doctor's very impressive library. Floor-to-ceiling bookcases stood beneath recessed lighting, filled with every kind of book imaginable. Mitch was an avid reader, with a keen appreciation of practically every type of literature: classics, sci-fi, history, biographies, scientific and medical studies, everything up to and including the latest Walter Mosley and John Grisham. Two comfortable Eames chairs, each with its own reading lamp and footstool, rounded out the space.

Now she looked at him intently. His habitually well-combed blond hair fell in a thick wave across his forehead, and he was wearing glasses, which he rarely did. He seemed vulnerable all of a sudden.

Star smiled inwardly. He was also nearly three sheets to the wind, but on him, even that was appealing.

"You're wearing your glasses," she said, a little smile tugged at her lips.

"The better to see you with, my dear." He nodded at her. "Besides, I'm too drunk to put in contacts, especially at this hour."

She loved that his eyes were deeply green behind the gold-framed glasses—no colored contact lenses for this man.

He walked barefoot into the open kitchen, and set his martini glass down on the counter. From her spot on the sofa, she could see him in the semi-darkened room as he opened an under-the-counter wine keep.

"Don't tap a bottle just for me. Whatever you have open will be fine," she called out.

He appeared at the counter. "You sure?"

"Yes, as a matter of fact, forget the wine," she said, her tone harsher than she intended. "I'm sorry. Could I just have a glass of water, with ice?"

"Whatever you say."

Mitch closed the wine keep and opened a cabinet above the counter. He pulled out a large Baccarat crystal drinking glass. He went to the double-doored refrigerator and put the glass under the crushed ice dispenser. When it was filled, he opened the refrigerator and poured a glass of imported mountain spring water for her. Star noted that it was the same brand she'd found in Lisel's refrigerator.

He came back to the living room, carrying both drinks, and handed her the glass of water. For the first time, Star realized he was naked beneath his silk robe. Lisel's taunts rang in her mind. She pushed them away.

She'd never seen so much of him before. She took in his long legs. They were strong and well-shaped. Golden hair glinted on his calves. Thick blond hair glistened on his chest, disappearing down his body into the long silken wrap of the robe as it crossed and tied at his waist. Even his feet were beautiful. Long and gracefully arched, with no signs of corns or calluses. His toenails were clean and neatly and evenly trimmed.

He sat down opposite her, and took off his glasses. His emerald eyes were slightly red from a lack of sleep and an abundance of martinis.

"Any particular reason you're here?" he said, his voice seeming suddenly cold.

"I like shocking your doorman. I showed him my badge. I'll bet he thinks you're going to be led out in handcuffs."

Mitch didn't say anything.

"I guess you don't want me here," she said.

"I didn't say that."

Star reached for a coaster from the dark wood container on the coffee table, and set her glass down.

"I'm sorry we've been fighting," she said. "What you're thinking is all wrong."

"What am I thinking?" Mitch rubbed his eyes.

Silence stretched between them, filled by "Carolina in My Mind."

She turned, so that her body was facing him.

"That I'm sleeping with my partner."

The pain that he had been so persistently drowning in liquor came roaring back.

"I never said that."

"No. But you feel it. You were practically ranting at me the last time we spoke."

Mitch put his glasses back on. "I never rant, Lieutenant."

"You were yelling at me so loudly, Paresi could hear you through the phone."

"Sorry." He reached for the pitcher, and poured himself the last of the liquor. "I didn't mean to upset your partner."

Star took a deep breath, as he sat, sipping the cocktail, his eyes cold.

"There is nothing between Paresi and me. You know that. We've been partners for five years, for Christ's sake."

"And the point of that is . . .?"

Star counted to ten in her mind.

"The point, is that Paresi and I have been together a long time. If nothing happened during five whole years, does it make any sense that we would start climbing one another now, especially when he's dating Vee?"

Mitch was silent.

"Think about it," Star said. "Why would I do something like that? Why would he? Paresi is my partner, and my friend. We've been through wars together. We love each other, but it's not *that* kind of love. We're not sleeping together!"

"Technically, Lieutenant, sleeping is absent, unless, of course, you're totally exhausted," he said, maddeningly.

"You should know."

"What?"

Star took another deep breath. She didn't want to fight, but the words tumbled out of her mouth anyway.

"At least I didn't spend last night climbing some homicidal maniac!"

"What?

"I know you slept with Lisel Werner."

Mitch looked at her for a moment and then burst out laughing.

"I'm glad you think this is funny," she said.

"Funny?" He roared. "God . . . funny doesn't cover it." He looked at her. "Do you honestly think I'd take Lisel Werner to bed?"

"You were with her last night."

"Yes," he nodded, "I was. And I spent the whole time wishing I was with you. She asked me to dinner, to talk about the case. I couldn't say no . . ."

He shook his head. "Lisel Werner . . . God . . . you ever look at her?"

"Yeah . . ."

"She looks too much like Carole Ann." He leaned forward, his robe falling further open.

"A woman who made nearly twenty-five years of my life a living hell . . . you think I could be attracted to a woman who's almost a dead ringer for my ex-wife?"

"She said . . ."

"And you believed her?" He looked disappointed. "Star, I don't want anybody else.

"Last night, all she talked about was you and Paresi, how close you were, how he's always there for you. She asked me if you two were sleeping together. I told her no, and she laughed.

"I don't know why, but even after I left her, that laughter was in my head. I went to your place.

"I saw you and Dominic through the window. I saw you in his arms, and I lost it.

"I know you're close, but lately, it seems like you two are inseparable. I felt it Christmas night, when we sat through that ceremony for St. John. I felt it at Vee's party.

I know it's irrational, and I know it's stupid, but so help me, I started to think maybe she was telling me the truth."

Star reached for his hand.

"Mitchell, Paresi and I are *not* having sex," she said, slowly. "It was a suggestion planted in your mind by Lisel Werner."

Mitch raised a skeptical eyebrow. "Are you saying I'm a puppet, Lieutenant?"

"No . . . she's . . . just listen." Star took a deep breath. "Paresi was injured tonight."

"Is he all right?" Mitch's concern was genuine.

"He is now." She looked at him. "He's with Vee."

A sob rose in her throat, but she forced it down. "He was bitten severely . . . nearly to the bone, by Lisel Werner."

"I don't follow you." Mitch put down his drink.

"We arrested Sergeant Werner tonight for the murders of Desmond St. John, Eric Stevens, François Dulac, and the infant John Doe, who, by the way, was *her* child." Tears rolled down her face.

Mitch looked stunned. "This isn't . . ." He couldn't find the words.

"It's like a horror movie, Mitchell," Star said, wiping her eyes. "She *made* you think those things. She's a practicing voodoo witch. She was Desmond St. John's lover. She had his baby. Then she . . . she sacrificed it." More tears rolled down her face.

Mitch reached for her.

Star lay in the king-sized bed. The smell of freshly brewed coffee woke her. She sat up, not realizing for a moment where she was. Then she remembered. She smiled and lay back, wrapping herself in the burgundy sheets. The smell of bacon joined the coffee. Breakfast. She was ravenous. She untangled herself and headed for the shower.

Mitch was slicing mushrooms when she came downstairs, barefoot and wrapped in one of his robes, a white terry cloth. Her face was clean of makeup, and drops of water still glistened in her short, close-cropped hair.

She walked into the kitchen. "Good morning," she said.

He looked at her. The sight of her made his heartbeat quicken. "Sure looks like one."

She stood close to him, her hand against his back. His skin felt warm beneath the indigo blue silk.

"Is there anything I can help you with?"

He leaned down and kissed her. "Cooking is not your strong point, Lieutenant." He kissed her again.

"I know when I'm in the way. Do you mind if I check on Paresi?"

"Not at all. Ask him if there's anything I can do for him."

"Will do." She went to the phone and called Vee.

She had dropped Paresi off at her friend's house before going to see Mitch. He had spent the night in Roland's room. Vee's son had gladly given up his bed for the injured detective. Vee said all the kids thought Paresi's "war wound" was "way cool."

Star laughed. "How's he doing?" she asked.

"He's still asleep," Vee said. "I think it's all the drugs they gave him. I'm staying home today to look after him."

"Po' chile," Star said. "When he wakes up, tell him I'll be around later to see him."

"I'll do that," Vee said. "Hey, where are you? I tried to call you after Dominic went to sleep."

"I'll see you later," Star said.

"Uh-huh," Vee said, knowingly. "Tell me, are you blind and bow-legged?"

Star smiled. "Maybe by this afternoon." She laughed. "Already my sight's growing dim, each step is an adventure, and neither of us is going to work."

"It's about time, and I wanna hear all the details," Vee said, laughing.

"You're about to hear the dial tone, Verenita." Star grinned. "Good-bye." She pressed the button, disconnecting them, and then called her office.

Captain Lewis sounded weary. She told him she was taking the day off.

"Take a couple," he said. "I've just finished going over the reports from last night. Both you and Paresi have earned some time."

"Captain," she said. "I'm sorry about Sergeant Werner."

"Me too," Lewis said. "She needs a lot of help. She's being transferred to the state mental hospital. It's gonna be a while before we can bring formal charges against her."

"I'm sorry, sir," Star said again.

"Yeah . . . Listen, Star, Darcy wants to talk to you. Enjoy your time off, try to get some rest, I'm gonna transfer now."

"Thank you, sir." She waited on the line. Darcy picked up.

"Hey, Leo, what's up?"

"Morning, Lieutenant," Darcy said. "I just wanted to make sure you're all right. It's all over the station what happened with Sergeant Werner last night. Did that NYPD chick really go apeshit and bite a plug outta Paresi?" The detective started to laugh.

Star smiled into the phone. "Yes, she did."

Leo burst out laughing. "Did they give *her* a rabies shot?"

She laughed with him.

"I'm gonna be off for a couple days, Leo. Take care of things for me, okay?"

"You got it, Star."

She hung up the phone and went back to the kitchen.

"How's Dominic?" Mitch asked.

"Sleeping," she said. "Vee says he's out cold."

"Good. He's going to be in pain when he wakes up. He needs all the rest he can get."

"Darcy thinks it's all pretty funny."

"That's because nothing can penetrate Darcy's hide. If Lisel had tried biting him, she would have lost *all* her teeth, instead of just one."

"Between you and me," Star said, "Paresi *punched* it out."

They looked at one another and laughed.

Mitch poured her a cup of tea. He set milk and sugar, buttered oat bread toast, raspberry jam, and a bacon, herbed cheddar cheese, and fresh mushroom omelet in front of her. He sat facing her across the table, drinking black coffee. He was barefoot. His robe was loosely tied. She stared at the thick hair on his chest, thinking how soft it was. He smelled of a clean, crisp, citrusy soap. He had showered, but he hadn't shaved. A golden glint of beard was visible.

She reached out and touched his face. "I like you like this," she said, stroking his skin.

"Like what?"

"Slightly scruffy," she said, caressing him. "In my mind you're always put together."

Mitch gazed at her. "Is that so . . . Well, in my mind, you're always . . ."

"What?" she said teasingly.

He took her hand. His eyes never left hers. He kissed her palm, and pointed at her plate. "Eat," he said.

"Yessir." She put a white linen napkin in her lap. "I'm famished." She looked up. "You must be hungry too. Aren't you having anything?"

Mitch grimaced and shook his head. "It took everything I had to face those eggs, to make *your* breakfast," he said.

"But you're a pathologist. You've got a cast-iron stomach," she said, amused.

"Not when it's filled with martinis."

"I didn't notice it slowing you down earlier," she said.

Mitch chuckled. "You just might have something there—a miracle hangover cure."

"If you need another shot of it . . ."

His eyes were warm. "I wouldn't want to take you away from your breakfast," he said. "And, there are your bruises. How are they this morning?"

"I think the 'kiss it and make it better' method you employed worked," she said.

"Did it now?" His eyes grew deep and full of mischief.

Star looked at him. "Got more eggs?"

"Plenty."

"Then you can duplicate all this." She indicated the food.

"In a heartbeat."

"Then let's go cure your hangover."

"And take another look at those bruises," he said.

"Definitely."

She held out her hand. He took it, and for the first time since he was about ten years old, Mitchell Grant blushed.

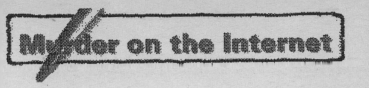

New York, Inside and Out

For lesbian private eye Lauren Laurano,
murder gets personal . . .

SANDRA SCOPPETTONE

The Lauren Laurano Mysteries

EVERYTHING YOU HAVE IS MINE

I'LL BE LEAVING YOU ALWAYS

MY SWEET UNTRACEABLE YOU

LET'S FACE THE MUSIC AND DIE

"Sandra Scoppettone's mysteries are a sparkling combination of detective story, lesbian comedy of manners, steamy New York atmosphere, and social critique."
—*San Francisco Chronicle*

Meet Liz Sullivan

A struggling freelance writer from Palo Alto, California, escapes an abusive relationship, survives by living in her VW bug, and manages to become entangled in murder.

The Liz Sullivan Mysteries
by LORA ROBERTS

MURDER IN A NICE NEIGHBORHOOD

MURDER IN THE MARKETPLACE

MURDER MILE HIGH

MURDER BONE BY BONE

And coming this September:

MURDER CROPS UP

"A refreshing and offbeat take on the female detective."
—*San Francisco Chronicle*

Charlotte, North Carolina, reporter Natalie Gold has always been crazy for horses. But she didn't know that love would bring her face-to-face with murder . . .

The Natalie Gold Mysteries
by
JODY JAFFE

HORSE OF A DIFFERENT KILLER

CHESTNUT MARE, BEWARE

And coming this May:

IN COLT BLOOD

". . . Sharp, thoroughly entertaining . . . Horse lovers will go for Jaffe's work especially, but she's so deft and funny that she also provides a good time for those of us whose habitual reaction to the arcana of horse training and showing is a quiet snooze."
—*Washington Post Book World*